For my Darlin'
Tricia Ann Underwood
who lived so much of this.

A Death In Our Family

[signature: L. S. Miller]

A Novel By

L. S. Miller

ISBN: 1469923793
ISBN 13: 9781469923796

Library of Congress Control Number: 2012900870
CreateSpace, North Charleston, SC

Chapter One

I just discovered I'm dying and not in the 'so what everybody is' sense but more immediately, with a finite and premature end date. My first reaction, as I sat on the examination table in my underwear staring back at the semi-sympathetic stranger who delivered the news was…relief. Now I could stop worrying that my life style might kill me. It actually had. Or would soon enough. And I can get off this damn diet, I thought, have a drink whenever I feel like it and start smoking again. Today.

After the 'how long' and 'what can I expect' question-and-answer session, while I was driving home, the reality began to sink in. My first thoughts were narcissistic. My second expanded the list of effected parties beyond the immediately imperiled to those who might be impacted to some degree. The names and faces of my associates after fifty years of existence quickly formed a family tree that I was sure would number in the thousands if I took the time to categorize them. I realized two things almost as quickly. The number of people who would be truly upset by my demise was easily quantifiable on the digits of my body and I probably shouldn't waste any of my remaining time worrying about half of them. Time suddenly was the resource of which I had a minimum and what I had of it had to be managed carefully, manipulated for maximum effect, hoarded like Scrooge's gold.

There had been so much death in our lives lately, mine and Amanda's, my significant other of six years. Both our fathers, the father of a friend, a smattering of relatives and neighbors and the teenage sons of two couples that we knew well. Too much death too close together, especially for someone as empathetic as Mandy, especially her father Jack who had been her business partner and best friend as well as her emotional and psychological well spring. She wasn't going to handle my bad news very well.

And my kids. I had finally been convinced by Amanda that my girls, Gloria and Jessica, needed their father even though they were fully grown and living on their own so I had begun a campaign of rapprochement with them that was easier to initiate than I had expected and going much better than I had anticipated. My initial rejection of the daughters I had always loved far more than their mother had everything to do with getting as far away from the evil bitch as possible once she left me and nothing to do with any lessening of my love for my girl. The girls, unfortunately, were again forced to interact with their mother on a daily basis as the relationship she had left me for had lasted an impressive sixteen months. Now she was back in the area and causing all kinds of problems for my children.

I have almost always chosen not to dwell on my past mistakes other than the occasional fleeting daydream about some lost love or career move that may have been unwise. But during my entire marriage to the Hell Bitch, I would ask myself how I had gotten into such an intractable fix and why I couldn't get out of it. The answer was always the same—I got in because of the girls. Gloria was part of the bargain from the beginning and Jessica the reason for the actual marriage and that's why I stayed. And it was easier to stay than to leave and face their mother's wrath.

Would I trade the girl's existence for a chance to live a different life, have back those squandered years of drug and alcohol abuse, of anger and strife, discord a daily regimen? Yesterday my answer would have been emphatically no. Today? I have to think about it.

Fortunately, Mandy was working so when I got home I had a few hours to plan. I wasn't ready to tell her the truth about my diagnostics or spin a convincing lie regarding the 'therapy session' that I had told her I was going to. Therapy, in the form of a counselor that we both had spent time with, made a believable cover for the testing and consultations that had led up to today's revelation.

I had entered into counseling with Mandy because I realized that a good relationship requires a good deal of work and after the disaster of my marriage, I wasn't going to let Mandy get away if there was anything I could do to keep her by my side. And to make her happy. Again. She hadn't been for months and months after her father's death and I wanted my joyous baby, my wacky, twisted, devil-eyed darling to come back from that internal haunted place that she had gone off to when Jack died.

And she was getting there. A *lot* of counseling for her, some happy pills and all the love and attention I was capable of giving her. And I was getting better too, at curbing my own self-indulgence. I'm not Saint Francis, never will be, and I especially wouldn't be now, but I'm not Hitler either and I had been moving in the right direction. I was scared for her, scared that my death would send her back to the haunted place that I'd been trying to pull her from. Scared that my death would be the end of her as well.

I had her covered financially. Not that she'd never have to work again, she's only 35 and I'm not rich, but we own a home together, I have a few bucks put away and she's my beneficiary.

Thinking about my financial situation brought another issue roaring into my mind. I wanted to quit my job, now, call the Senior VP and tell him he was a one-dimensional blowhard and I had worked my last day for him. But what could I tell Amanda short of the entire truth and I wasn't ready for that yet.

And I needed the money, at least until I could inventory my assets and determine how much I had and how long it would last. And however much I spent now would be that much less left for Amanda once I was gone. And I had an obligation to see Jessica through school. Shit. I could end up having to work till the day I died. That would take whatever minor advantage there was out of the foreknowledge of death.

Something else had been percolating inside my head. What is my legacy? What have I ever done? Who will remember me, and for what? Who will *care* kept coming back to me.

Amanda and my kids. And my mother, a hardheaded politician who had fought in the public school wars you thirty years. Patricia had mellowed with age but she remained the source of my emotional detachment, my alcoholism and my self-centeredness. And I loved her. She loved me unequivocally throughout my delinquent youth, through drunken car accidents and the lawsuits they spawned, despite the questionable moral fiber of the girls I brought home, through bad relationships and a worse marriage. She was my banker, an advocate and a friend. She would miss me. And she loved Mandy as much as I did, amazed, I think, that I had finally gotten it right.

Amanda's mother Clara wasn't going to be of any help to her. She liked me well enough and knew I was good for her daughter. I didn't take her shit but if I was self-centered then she was self-deluded about her self-obsession and as master a manipulator as the Hell Bitch. Only Clara's was manipulation by guilt, 'the Silent Treatment' a forte, Mandy especially vulnerable to it and Clara using it for any and all offense, the Eisenhower cold war doctrine of atomic deterrence applied to mother-daughter interaction.

What was now stopping me from telling Clara or anyone else exactly what I thought about them, how they acted, what they were doing wrong with their lives? Now that I was dying I was suddenly an authority on life, wasn't I? On life, its meaning and how to live it. Hell yes you are, the Bad Angel on my left shoulder screamed. The Good Angel got a chance eventually, informing me that I was no more wise now then I had been that morning only now I didn't give a damn what people thought of me and he cautioned me to *watch out!* He didn't get a chance to say what to watch out for because the Bad Angel intruded with a whole list of things to say to Clara. I didn't need the Good Angel to tell me to be careful, not to go off half-cocked, screaming into the night. I could spend my last months in a padded cell.

Another idea jumped in. If money was an issue, why not steal some? From a bank seemed obvious. Only people so dumb they end up on true-crime TV shows got caught robbing their *first* bank. Or people who were just unbelievably unlucky and despite my present predicament, I didn't think I fell into either category. Bank robbers were caught through dogged police work, the result of months, even years of investigation. They could catch me after I was dead maybe but more likely I could hit a couple, three banks, get away with enough money to make our last days pleasant and no one would ever know. It was something to think about. Along with about three million other things.

Righting wrongs came next in my bizarre thought parade. Same element of risk but no financial reward and, come to think of it, probably considerable monetary outlay required to do anything really serious like blowing up a Dow Chemical plant. Not that I have anything against Dow, it was just a very sixties kind of target which was probably the last time anything so radical had crossed my mind.

A Green Peace type statement would be more in line with my current politics, not that I'm philosophically aligned with any group that's that far from center and not that I'm politically active in any meaningful sense. I did vote for Clinton. Twice. Maybe I could blow him up. Revenge of the blue dress and all that. But I still liked the guy even if he was a randy, pussy-obsessed raconteur. At least he's demonstrably human.

But righting wrongs, doing good deeds, had a certain appeal. Instant legacy. A bold stroke by a desperate man. "Who but he, this champion of the people, could have brought about such profound change?" I imagined the screaming banner headline above the story. "DYING MAN…" does what? What do I feel that strongly about? What does anybody feel that strongly about? America. We love it, everybody else hates it. Blow up Saddam? Not likely. Saving endangered species? Not for me, I'm carnivorous. And I used to like to hunt a little although I never bagged a snail darter or a bog turtle. A couple snappers for soup but they're an awful lot of work. Drugs. All right–thinking people hate illegal drugs. Except we all used to do a little blow and hit a bong now and then. Just legalize it. How about urban sprawl? I could burn down a couple subdivisions near some obscure park and create what in their place? A loss for the insurance industry and a lot of new work for some contractors. Hopeless.

I began to realize just how apolitical I'd become. Pollution? Under control. Welfare reform? Leave it to the Republicans– nobody will get any. Social security? I'm never going to collect. Nuclear power? Dying of its own inefficiency. There had to be something. I needed to think more globally. World hunger. There certainly is plenty of that but what could any one individual do about it? Grow wheat instead of creeping red fescue in your front yard? Shoot a Somali guerilla? Aids. The way it looked, that was the cure for world hunger, at least in Africa. I didn't see anything I could do in the short run about that either. War. Start one or stop one? Both seemed equally unlikely.

Maybe the answer was not macro but micro, something small scale and close to home. What does everyone have that no one wants? Poverty? Somewhere in the community, usually. I'm sure even Princeton and Martha's Vineyard have at least a few poor people although I suspect they're needed to mow lawns or muck out septic tanks. Crime, traffic congestion, pollution again. This was getting me nowhere and maybe there was nowhere to go with it anyway. I was better off worrying about Amanda.

My poor baby. The death cycle had taken a terrible toll. Jack succumbed, literally in her arms, a year ago but my reckoning of the inception of the age of death was his first stroke, a mini, but a wake up call nonetheless. And he had heeded it, seeing the specialists, taking the tests, restricting his diet at least when Amanda was around. Followed by another mini and then another.

Chapter Two

If Jack's first stroke was the opening scene in the tragedies that were befalling us, then my father's death came at the end of act one. But at least he died after a long and colorful life, in his eighty-fifth year and with warning aplenty.

I was at work when my mother called, tracking me through my secretary in those prehistoric times before the cell phone. I'm in the construction business, a senior manager with a big commercial developer, a builder of such socially imperative structures as convenience stores and gas stations. Exactly what I'd like to be remembered for. If I had five years left instead of one, I couldn't begin to destroy all the crap I've built in my lifetime. Fortunately for future generations, most of the crap gets torn down within fifteen years or so anyway. Unfortunately, it's almost always replaced by something just as heinous.

Mom's message was that Tex–a nickname earned along with a BA from the University in Austin and bestowed upon him by his Pennsylvania friends amongst whom he had resided for forty years– had broken his hip. Falling off a ladder isn't that uncommon and neither is a broken hip in an older person. But falling off a ladder at eighty-two, while laying up limestone on your ranch house, is. And that injury on a sixty-year-old hip means surgery and a few months of PT. On Tex, it meant the beginning of the end and we all knew it, especially after seeing him in a wheel chair, then hobbling along behind a walker. He'd mortared his last rock.

The ranch, when they bought it, had been five hundred acres of stunning views of granite knobs and sandstone draws but not much else. No power, no water, no structures of any kind. It was just right, an unblemished mound of clay ready for Tex to mold and shape and kiln into the family home he had always wanted. We were a pretty big clan and spread out from Philadelphia to San Diego. This was to be the centering place, geographically right on the money and symbolically perfect, a return to the family's homesteading days on the Texas plains in the 1800's.

The first time I saw the land, Tex and I arriving in an International dump truck towing a Caterpillar front end loader older than I was, I knew it was going to take a lot of work and I asked him about his plans, what he was going to build, how, scheduling questions, priorities, all the things a big shot commercial builder might ask a prospective client. And his answer was essentially, I'll build what comes to me as I feel like it. There *was* no schedule. There *were* no priorities beyond a well and a power pole. This was so unlike my father, the on time, on budget, hard charging general contractor I'd grown up with that I was unsure how to deal with this new guy who was grinning like a cowboy at a whore house as we tramped across the land, him pointing vaguely at various features of the property saying the house will be up there, the garden down that way, the garage back yonder. Yonder? When did my Dad start saying yonder? When we crossed the Texas state line apparently.

I gave it another try. How long do you think it will take, I asked. He looked at me like I was suddenly someone else's offspring and then he said, 'the rest of my life, of course', politely leaving out the 'you dumb shit' that I knew he wanted to tack on the end.

That's when I finally began to get it. This wasn't a construction project that had some time line, liquidated damages the incentive to move your ass. This was a labor of love, the fulfillment of a lifelong dream, something he'd been thinking about for the whole forty years that he'd been gone, not a Pennsylvanian *ever*, always a Texan who had been forced to be away from the Promised Land for a while but who knew he'd be back. It was just a question of when.

It took me even longer, years, to realize that he didn't *ever* want it to be finished. He wanted to work on that house, on the ranch, in perpetuity. If he ever completed all the tasks that he imagined, what then? What would be left?

Chapter Three

W hen Mandy got home the evening of my diagnosis, I pretended everything was normal. The next morning I told her I felt like crap and was calling in sick. She left after her usual last minute whirlwind of preparation. I never minded the clutter. Her pre-work mess was a constant affirmation of her presence, picking up after a small price to pay.

I worked on our finances. If I lived a year without working and without extravagance, Mandy would inherit a house without obligation and my 401-K. But not much else. We would spend all our liquid assets and I'd have to cash the mutual funds just to survive. And if I quit my job, what was the point of sitting around doing nothing? What would I do if I *did* have money? What had I always wanted to do? Get off my ass and get in really awesome shape, lift weights till the veins popped on my biceps but what was that going to accomplish, make me look better at the viewing?

I have never had too much interest in seeing the world but I had a great time in my youth sporting around America in my Volkswagen. Mandy and I had always fantasized about a Big Road Trip both as a fantastic vacation and as a research vehicle for our desire to relocate. After her father's death, we had stopped talking about moving to a better place but recently we had begun to think about it again.

The Big Road Trip was a possibility, something I had always wanted to do. And we could do it in style this time, not in a '62 bug but in a loaf of bread motor home, the kind I'd been looking at in the paper for the last five years, always laughing with Amanda when I found one for two thousand bucks. We would joke about painting it all camouflage or white with Wonder Bread in big letters on the side. But there were a few draw backs with that plan.

Like why? Why spend the last days of your life driving around? Damn if I knew but it sounded a Hell of a lot better than sitting on the edge of Amish country watching my lawn turn brown and my tomatoes turn red. Maybe the answers to life's questions were to just experience as much of it as possible and I sure wasn't going to experience any more of it then I already had living in Lancaster County, Pennsylvania. It sounded a whole lot better to be moving then to be sitting in my energy efficient bungalow waiting for the reaper to knock on my insulated steel door.

And it wouldn't interfere with my treatment. Despite the arguments of my oncologist who took my decision to forgo his experimentation as a personal rebuke, I had said fuck that. Just give me some pain pills.

Mandy. I had to tell her, now, today. But I wanted to have a carrot to offer her after I was done beating her with the death stick. I knew she's stay with me even if I tried to drive her away, back to her mother or into an apartment, but there really wasn't any point in either of those choices—the house would be hers soon enough. She just had to stick around to the end. But how could I make that end worth while for her, the long run worth the pain?

I had always wanted her to go back to school, get a master's, do something with that marvelous brain. But she'd been hung up with me, her father and her own self doubts. We could use the road trip like the parents of a high school kid, taking him to his top three colleges during the summer of junior year. Only we could take a lot longer and visit a bunch more places.

I practiced my delivery, tempted to write down some notes. Do I start with the carrot, hoping to get her excited about the Road Trip or hit her with the stick and hope to ease the pain with the carrot?

The job she'd taken after she closed her and Jack's building business was fun and she loved it, managing an antique shop, but it was hardly a career choice unless she opened a shop of her own. We had discussed the possibility. Her job had given her the opportunity to learn the business side—she had all the product recognition she needed from her mother's collections. And she enjoyed merchandizing the shop, meeting the clients and networking with other dealers. She could easily make a living with her own store. Maybe she could open her own place in a college town and go to school too. I figured I'd better stick her first and use the carrot as a balm.

And it occurred to me that she had little chance of being alone for too long. She looked better now then she had when I met her, not so Biafran refuge skinny, up to a hundred and ten from my cooking. She could easily score a man—but I most definitely wanted a say in the matter, right of first refusal or something.

I know how that works. How many times in B movies have you heard the dying one say, I want you to find someone and start a new life. I want you to be happy. And how many times has the not dying one said, hey, no problem, I'll start looking this afternoon. There's an obligation to swear celibacy for eternity and I doubted that Amanda would be the first to break with tradition.

I felt like I was getting somewhere today as opposed to my scattered thoughts of yesterday. I was still scared shitless over Mandy's reaction to my news but I at least felt I had something positive to offer to go along with it.

Chapter Four

When Tex went down the second time and we went to the ranch to watch him die, Amanda had had no similar experience in her life.

I had gotten another Mom call at my work, this time from the courtesy phone outside the surgical waiting room. Tex had fallen again, just down from behind his walker but the result was the same only the other hip. They had done the replacement that morning, the only way to stabilize the break and give him a measure of comfort even if the prognosis for ambulation was bleak at best. He'd be in the hospital and rehab for three weeks and then she would need help. The last time she had given us the time line for recovery and left it up to us if we could come down and help out. This time she came right out and asked. That must have been hard for her—she wasn't used to needing any help and was temperamentally unsuited for asking for it.

She added one more thing. When they were prepping him for surgery, the doctor had questioned Mom about some abdominal problem Tex had been complaining of. The doctor did a quick exploratory while he had Tex under. He's full of cancer, she said. How long, I asked. Months at best was her reply.

And months it was. Two of them.

We flew in the day Tex came home from the rehab center, delivered by ambulance from Fredericksburg, thirty miles, Mom following in the minivan, Mandy and I arriving an hour after. Tex was propped up in a hospital bed and he looked like shit. He was pale and gaunt, needed a shave and didn't have his teeth in. But as soon as he heard that 'hey, handsome, how's my favorite man' in Mandy's happy soprano his lapis eyes popped open and a grin lit up his face. That's the first time he's smiled in a week, my mother whispered. She has that affect on me too, I said. You look fabulous, Amanda said to him, but your beard is picky. You need a shave. She marched into the bathroom, emerging a minute later with a hot towel, shaving cream and a Bic disposable and proceeded to make my father presentable, combing his hair when he was shaved and giving him his dentures. She cut about a hundred and twenty years off him and seemed to bring him back from whatever far away place he had been visiting in the process.

We got him into his wheel chair and took him out to the living room and I built a fire so he and Mandy could talk and be warm. Mom and I went to the kitchen and made drinks.

"How's he doing," I asked.

"He's in some pain. I have pills for him. He's mostly incontinent. He can feel it coming, he just can't do anything about it."

"That sucks. What are you going to do?"

"Keep him here."

"Until?"

"Until the end."

"Nursing home? Have you thought about that?"

"Long ago. I have insurance for that, for me. Not for him. I will not put him in a home as long as I can take care of him. So I never bought him any."

"The care giver usually goes first. You know that."

"Not in this case, I don't think."

"Yeah. Probably not. You're going to need some help. Not just us. Long term."

"Yes. The hospital gave me a number for an organization that supplies people and equipment," she said. "I haven't called them yet."

"Sounds like a job for Super Mandy," I said. "Give me the number."

We stayed for seven days. It probably wasn't necessary as the help Mandy arranged for was great and Tex got a bit better every day although the nights were a problem. We did a lot of laundry.

Fortunately the aid that we got was a wonderful, gentle man who treated Tex like his own father, constantly encouraging, always cheerful even at the worst of the job. Joe was Tex-Mex, second generation American. Before we went back, he brought his wife out on Sunday and cooked us all dinner. He was family from then on. I gave him a couple hundred when we left, every thing I had above what I needed to get our car out of the airport lot back home and told him to call us directly any time if he or they needed any thing at all.

We were home for three weeks when I got the last mom call. We landed in San Antonio and drove straight to the hospital in Fredericksburg. My sister Sheila the real estate mogul was already there. She started babbling about rehab centers and nursing homes and the day programs they had and the new friends Dad could make and how easy it would be for Mom to drop him off so she could shop or get her hair done.

I didn't tell her Tex was headed for the last round up but how she didn't see that for herself was beyond me. He was out, tubes in his arm, nose and penis. His color was about a shade better than the sheet and even Mandy's 'hey, handsome' didn't bring him around. She cried all the way down in the elevator. We went straight to a Stop 'N Go and bought a pack of cigarettes, the first we'd smoked in a year.

"He's going to die, isn't he," she said.

"Yes, Sunshine, he is. Soon I think." We went back to the ranch, Mom already there. Joe was going to spend the night with Tex, he insisted and none of us could convince him that it was okay to leave Tex alone for a couple hours. He set the tone though. Someone was with him till the minute he died, for the whole eight days he lingered there, all of us working it in shifts.

My other sisters, Sharon, Sheila's twin and an interior designer, Martha the home maker and Kathy the hippie chick, their husbands and their assorted children and step children trickled in over the next few days. We split up the day shifts with Joe working the nights. On the morning of the seventh day, he apologized to mom but told her he had promised his grand kids that he would take them camping so I got the last two nights. I made Mandy stay at the ranch.

After the seventh night I told my mother we should pull the pug. There was no point in helping him linger, nothing was going to bring him back and no matter how much they turned up the morphine, he was still in constant pain. The night of the eighth day, we did.

When I got to the hospital I sent the day shift home, Sheila's preppy kids from her first marriage. The night shift intern, a nice guy who had walked me through the signs of impending death, didn't come on till midnight and I wanted him with me when I gave the order. And it gave me the opportunity to say goodbye. I told Tex all that he had meant to me, repeating anecdotes from our life together, things that would make him laugh if somewhere in there his sense of humor was still lurking. I told him I would look out for Mom and take care of the ranch. I told him some of the things I might want to do when I had the time and the money and I promised him I would maintain his design integrity which made me laugh out loud because of the way we had winged it on most of the stuff we built, the design as often as not sketched in the dirt with a pointed stick.

We turned off the respirator at one thirty and by a quarter till two he was gone, his color fading from pale to palest in a few minutes, other than that, no sign of pain or struggle. I got the intern on the room phone and told him that my father had died and he said he was sorry. I went to the nurse's station on the way out and thanked them for helping him then went outside and smoked a butt before I called my mother.

The funeral home had been on call for a week and they picked him up that morning. The next day mom, Mandy, Kathy and I went in to process the paper work and pick out the coffin. We settled on a pecan box with a slide out drawer where we could stash mementoes for the loved one's use in the here after. I suggested a flash-light just in case but no one saw the humor.

The funeral was private but the memorial service was not and mom's church was so crowded that not one more withered ass could have been crammed into that room with a crow bar. The post service party at the ranch was a boisterous, rowdy affair, the booze flowing, lots of Tex-Mex food and a million tall Tex tales.

By dusk we were down to just family and everyone was about shot. At eight the phone was passed to me by a brother-in-law and I heard sobbing on the other end then, 'John is dead. Tell Amanda John is dead.' Clara, I said? Clara, I don't know who John is but she was crying again and I covered the receiver and said to Mandy, it's your mom. Someone got killed I think, then I handed her the phone. I watched her whiten then saw the tears begin to flow. She murmured to her mother for a few minutes then handed me the dead receiver.

"Sam and Judith," she said. "Dad's painter. We went out to dinner with them, to the seafood buffet in Maryland? Their son John was killed this morning in a car accident."

"Jesus Christ," I said. "How old?"

"Twenty two. He was hit head on by a dump truck coming home from work. They think he fell asleep."

"Do you know anything else, details?"

"Mom thinks the funeral might be Wednesday," she said flatly, tears running.

Great, I thought. Just exactly what Mandy needs right now. More death. And a young one at that. It took me a little longer to get good and pissed off at Clara. Why did she have to play the storm crow, calling Mandy in Texas to share her bad news when we were coming home the next morning? Couldn't she let Amanda have one night of ignorance of this tragedy that neither of us could do a fucking thing about? But that was Clara. If there was misfortune, she sure as hell was going to spread the news as fast as she possibly could regardless of the consequences to the recipient.

Chapter Five

Thinking back on it as I have since my diagnosis, after Tex and John, Mandy had all the experience anyone her age should have needed with death. She had witnessed first hand the decline of an old man who had lived a full life and was ready to go. And she had seen the exact opposite. Why she needed another lesson in life and death I can not say but she got one not five months later when her father died in her arms on the kitchen floor of his home.

His funeral was a grim affair and the hardest thing Amanda had ever had to endure I'm sure. But Mandy, my beautiful, skinny, emotional flower, was the bedrock where the gnarly roots of this family tree took purchase and without her, Jack might have languished unprocessed for weeks. She called the funeral home and made the arrangements for the cremation. She spoke to Clara's minister and scheduled a memorial service, rented tents and chairs, hired some local folks to help with the post-service food and clean up and dealt with the friends and neighbors who dropped off more casseroles and cold cuts than we could store. All without any assistance from her brothers, either emotional or financial and with almost none from Clara.

And then, in the greatest act of personal courage I have ever witnessed, she took out her father's address book and called every single friend, relative and business associate in the entire book. It took her almost two days, calling back when she got a machine, calling into the evening, telling hundreds of people that her Dad had passed. Each time she said it, the pain must have been a twisted shaft in her heart. I sat with her, watching as she preformed this miracle of inner strength again and again, tears streaming down my face even when hers were dry, hour after hour of torture. She would not let me help, it had to be done by her, for her Dad. I weep even now as I think of her pain but it reminds me that she is so much stronger then she appears. It gives me hope that she can survive my demise, make another life, maybe even thrive.

It's been a year since Jack died, a year of counseling and medication, a year of nurturing and support to the best of my ability and she's a lot better but by no means healed. She never will be, they were too close, too much alike, far too important to each other for her to ever forget. We can talk about it now and we can talk about him, about what he wanted for her, about how much he longed to see her happy. He must have gotten the same pleasure as I do when she lets loose that wicked, musical laugh, the lust for life so overt and requiring so little to spill forth. And that full speed ahead enthusiasm for anything new, no challenge too daunting, a still gawky colt galloping just for the joy of motion across a flowered meadow. My beautiful, amazing Baby.

It's also been an ugly year in many ways, the mother so long supported so far beyond her worth by Jack now looking for Mandy to fill the void, take care of anything unpleasant, be there for her capricious needs. And the brothers of negative assistance in closing the open loops of Jack's business and Clara's life, all left to Mandy, me helping as much as I could without quitting my own job out right. I had to be constantly on my verbal guard with Clara, my desire to tell her what a waste of Jack's life she had been constantly running up against my understanding of how any such eruption would affect Amanda who her mother would blame. And punish.

Chapter Six

And even after Jack's, the deaths continued like famine after war, a maiden aunt of Jack's, a nice one of course, that had been a strong and nurturing influence to Mandy, the antithesis of the herd of bitches that dominated Clara's side of the family. Mandy cried at the funeral, me holding her in my arms as we exited. Next the father of a recent client, the son having an in-law's suite built for the man's declining years, Mandy wheeling the old guy through the addition each morning, explaining what they were doing and how it was all going to look when it was done, keeping him involved in his new home. She would tell me how much he reminded her of Tex and how happy he was to see her each day. He died two months after Jack, living in his new rooms for all of four days. She cried at that funeral too, by now really gun shy of the whole genre, avoiding all but the son.

Another old man went right after, a neighbor of Clara's, the son an acquaintance who was living with his father as caregiver, the son always confiding his problems to Amanda when they ran into each other, the worthless brothers they were each burdened with the only real common denominator other than age. We were in and out of that viewing in ten minutes, Mandy only tearing up when she hugged the son and told him to call if he needed to talk.

And just recently another kid, the son of a couple that we knew from my work. The son was a problem child, the biological father a coke head with more money then either self-control or parenting skills, the mother over compensating by spoiling him. His friends had new cars, great clothes and one of them his own apartment. They were sixteen and seventeen and dealt a little of their favorite chemicals to make up the difference between their parent's largesse and their peer-driven needs. He was the hardiest partier and the biggest doper of the lot. He OD'd at a small party at the apartment. Eleven hours later, his pals realized he was dead.

Which brings us up to date on the death count at this point. There's also a large group of the nearly dead. On mine side there's the wife of a cousin who was diagnosed with breast cancer a couple years ago. They did the chop job and the chemo and told her to expect a clean report next time. Not hardly. After six months the supposedly no longer relevant mass had mysteriously spread to her limps, liver and brain. She was clearly terminal but no one had the audacity to say so. She was currently going through the entire gamut of cutting edge treatment. She was bloated from the steroids, bald from the chemo and exhausted from the combination.

Tex's aunt Gertrude was another one. Her husband had been gone for years but she was carved out of that rocky, frontier woman stock that creates an aura of invincibility around those possessed of its hardness. And she had survived unbowed until recently, finally catching a terminal case of whatever disease had killed her husband. She had looked a hundred years frail at Thanksgiving, the one before Tex's second hip, and Mom had filled me in when I asked. Now she was old so the expectation of death is never that far away. But when that venerable oak tree that's been in your backyard your entire life suddenly keels over one evening, it's a shock, unexpected, and even seeing the hollowed out, rotted core of the thing now that its shattered trunk is laying in pieces on the lawn doesn't mitigate the shock of its demise. Gertrude was like that. No way that tough old bark could be wrapped around a dying core but apparently it was.

Maybe it's just the demographics of the town we live in or maybe it's Clara's propensity to dwell on such things but in either event, Mandy was far too well informed of the medical condition of way more people than I thought was necessary, her mother a conduit of misery, of mortality, a news paper or a radio station whose clientele included only Amanda, a constant reminder of the status of all those who were scheduled to confirm death's ubiquity.

The man living diagonally behind Clara's house is a good example. He got the diagnosis and wrestled with his options, his prognosis similar to my own. Clara, of course was compelled to give Mandy the news minutes after gleaning the high points from one of her cronies. Mandy knew the man well enough to be saddened and also well enough to go through her mother's back gate and visit him. The hell with it, he told her, if I'm going to die, I want to go in one piece, not after six months or a year as a wasted invalid.

His wife must have beaten on him some because a week later Bill told her, I'm having the damn surgery. Mandy told me he wasn't happy about it but he was going to let them take a 'look see' anyhow. They scoped him two days later and three days after that he was back in his yard farting around with his flowerbeds. Bill, what happened, Mandy asked, seeing him home days sooner then he should have been. They took a look, he said, and told him it was inoperable. And they convinced him to take the radiation, start the chemo, all the shit he didn't want to suffer through. In a month, he lost thirty pounds, most of his hair and all of his vitality. And his will to live it seemed like. He sat on his back porch and lifted a finger at you if you noticed his shrunken form seated in the shade and called out a greeting. He was too exhausted to even work in his yard. His condition confirmed the correctness of my choice. Quality is better than quantity.

And as if all the human death and near death wasn't sufficiently traumatizing, the animals were going too. Tex had a big scruffy brown cat he called Bear for obvious reasons. He was as irascible and independent as Tex himself and that was exactly what made him so lovable to me. He was at least fifteen when Tex died and in about as good condition. On his bad days or just when he was feeling lazy, he wouldn't move even for food, laying on Tex's lap or on the floor beside him for hours, following Tex into the bedroom in the evening where he assumed his rightful spot at the foot of the bed.

We all thought he was far past what ever wanderlust had caused him to disappear for a week or two every few months back in his youth, a habit that had continued for years after the removal of those appendages that are normally to blame for such behavior. But that last Thanksgiving weekend, the one just prior to Tex's death, as Mandy and I were crouched in a deer stand the Tuesday before the big day, way out at the end of the property, I caught movement in the brush. I scoped in on the area, expecting to see a raccoon or a skunk, the movement too low to the ground to be a deer. Stalking slowly through the grass, head raised, nostrils working the afternoon breeze, a good half mile from the house, was Bear. I didn't think the damn cat could walk from the kitchen to the bedroom without resting and here he was out for an evening stroll. He came back Thanksgiving day, ate a helping of breast meat and slept for twenty-four hours. He died a week after Tex's funeral, Mom calling me to say we should have euthanized him and buried him with Tex.

Just another death. I'm so jumpy from it all that every time the phone rings I expect some stranger or relative to tell me that either my mother or Amanda is dead. Or one of my children or my grand daughter. At the very least, some close friend or obscure relative. With any luck, I beat the next one to the punch, finding out the answer to the big riddle first, hopefully be there to meet them when *they* come knocking on the Pearly Gate. I sure hope there is one and that I qualify to get in.

Chapter Seven

I told Mandy that night, without a lot of subterfuge, just came out and said it—I'm dying. She went through the whole spectrum of death responses in about five minutes. What? I repeated myself, followed by laughter to which I responded, I'm not kidding, Sunshine, followed by tears during which I held her and murmured words of optimism. Followed by anger. How could I be dying, she demanded. I looked fine, a little over weight but we had both stopped smoking, again, finally, and neither of us had had a drink in a hundred and fifty four days. Plus we were exercising, Mandy running again, not as vociferously as she had when we first met nor was I an every morning jogger like I had been when the Hell Bitch left, but still way more active then we had been during the years of death and depression. Shouldn't that have been enough to hold the big C at bay, even suppress the alien cells that must have erupted in my ravaged lungs and beaten liver during all those years of Camels, Camel Lights, finally Carltons, 'lowest in tar and nicotine'? After all, my liver was okay despite gallons upon gallons of cheap vodka, good gin and excellent tequila that I had flushed through it, the quality improving with age and socioeconomic empowerment, the wine I liked with dinner and the beer I loved with everything following a similar pattern. We had quit, I should be fine.

It took me a while longer to convince her that I was neither joking nor misdiagnosed. Nor was I going to try to prolong things through the miracles of modern medicine. She withdrew from me for a time, contemplating the future I assumed and I let her be. After an hour during which I pissed around with a stack of paper work, she came back into the kitchen and put her arms around my neck, pulling my lips up to meet hers. I love you, she said and I told her she was the love of my life. We both cried for a while as I held her on my lap then I pushed her away enough to focus on her face and said, hey, I have some ideas. Do you want to hear them? Okay, she whispered, her head back on my shoulder.

I started with her financial picture. She interrupting almost immediately with a disclaimer, me saying shut up, there's nothing you can do about it. You will own the house out right and you can cash my 401K without penalty. We have so much cash and such and such a value in investments. I have no insurance so you *will* have to work eventually, I laughed, tickling her. You bastard, she said, laughing and crying simultaneously. I know, I said. I'm a lousy boy friend but I'm *your* boy friend.

I'm sorry, Sweetheart, I said then, squeezing her tight. I never wanted to hurt you, certainly not like this and then I really cried, shuddering sobs. She held me, a life preserver, whether for her or for me I couldn't say.

After a while I wiped my eyes on my shirtsleeve and, carrying Mandy in my arms, lurched over to the sink for some paper towels. I got us back on the stool at the island and tore off a couple sheets for each of us and we blew our noses.

Sunshine, I whispered to the side of her head, we need to talk. Her head moved, the curls bouncing, but I could not tell if it was in affirmation or negation. There's a couple things I'd like to do, I said. And I'd like you to be with me on the one hand. On the other, I want you to get away from me now, move on, you see? Fuck you, she said quietly, close enough to my ear that it didn't matter that her mouth was facing away. That's a good start, I said. I like that a lot, groping her for emphasis. She squirmed in my arms, my legs already asleep so the motion wasn't unwelcome, but she didn't say anything more. I have some ideas, I continued, about what you could do, what we could do. You interested? She squirmed again.

You know the motor home of my dreams, the loaf of bread? I found it, right here in the Burg. Want to go see it? She moved her head, this time I think meaning no. When she did it again I'd be sure. Okay, you don't have to but here's my idea. We buy it and take the Big Road Trip! We go look at schools for you, grad schools. Places where you might want to live, maybe open a shop of your own. Somewhere fun, on the beach. In the south. Come on, you've always wanted to go back to school, you like the antique business, you love the beach and the south, we can combine all of it. What'd you say, Sunshine?

"Alone," she answered.

"Not for a while, my love. You need a plan, Sweetheart. If you have a better one, let's talk about it," but she shook her head again, this time clearly no.

"Take your mother in with you," I said with some reluctance. "She has enough old shit to sell. We'll get a place with an in-law's suite," I said, guessing at the reason for her reticence, hoping I didn't have to spend the rest of my life with Clara. "Come on, talk to me," I said, taking her head in my fingers and turning her toward me. "Come on," I repeated. "You *have* to talk to me."

"I want to stay here," she sobbed, pushing her head back down.

"No. You don't. You never did," I said. "We only stayed here for your dad. Then from inertia or laziness. Whatever. It's time to move on, Amanda. Now, while I can help. *Look at me.*" She was red eyed but cognizant, no sign of a hazy withdraw, her strength surfacing with the anger. Good. Get pissed and stay that way, I thought. You can't survive if you surrender.

I called the senior partner in the company the next morning, bypassing my VP completely, talking to him pointless. I need to see him today, I said to one of his secretaries. Impossible, she insisted. I'm dying and I'm coming, I said. Tell him I'll be there at two. He was, I give him credit. My VP would have been gone two hours before just to be safe and not returned for two days after.

"Here's the deal, Bob," I said. "I have a year left and I'm not spending it building Seven Elevens."

"What do you want?" he said, not taking my implied threat as a challenge. Money gives you that privilege I guess.

"My accumulated sick time, my vacation pay, my summer bonus and six months severance. In a lump sum."

"Damn, that's a little steep, don't you think? You've been with us how long?"

"Going on eight years. Check the numbers, Bob. I'm the best senior PM in the company. I need this."

"Just so I understand," he said with a slight grin. "What happens if I say no?"

"I die on the job. I take the chemo, I drag my sick, terminal ass in here every day, no more job sites for me, Bob, I'm too decrepit. And I suspect that each morning, by the time I limp up those front steps, I'll be so nauseous and exhausted that I'll puke in the lobby. Not good for moral, dead people hobbling around the place."

"True," he said. "No one likes to look at the dead."

In about two seconds he beat me down to four months severance, sick pay, and half my bonus. Vacation time I got regardless. I thought I had done pretty well. This guy made zillions each year through his negotiating skills. I built Quickie Marts. And he could have called my bluff.

"Okay," he said with a real grin. "I'll have legal draw it up. When's your last day? I'd like to say goodbye as I'm sure your co-workers would."

"Goodbye. You can pass it along for me."

"I'm sorry," he said. "I really am."

I was about as euphoric as a dead man can be as I left the home office. I had been assured of about eight thousand in vacation pay when I walked in and I walked out with that plus another forty more or less. Things were looking up. To the extent that they could.

I drove directly to the little used car lot on the outskirts of town. They had been in that location for thirty something years and had as good a reputation as a used car dealer was likely to get. I had seen the little Winnebago that had been parked in the back of the lot for the last several days, no iridescent price painted on the windshield of this cream puff, no guarantee of low mileage or singular ownership either.

I said, let's take a look to the bored sales guy. He handed me a set of keys without getting up. Don't leave the grounds, he said. Twenty five hundred was the going price for similar vintage, retired grand pa cruisers in the Philly papers, the five hundred tacked on for negotiations, the two thousand an actual lump sum of cash that you could *do* something with. I poked around for fifteen minutes, the old bus idling the whole time, engine pretty smooth, mileage below fifty K. I didn't kick the tires nor did I pop the hood. The tires were getting replaced along with the brakes, oil, plugs, filters and fluids regardless and other than the amount of dirt, I would not have been able to tell more about the engine then the number of cylinders.

I'll give you five hundred in cash right now, I said. He didn't even look up. Sorry, no way. Too bad, I said. It's a cute little thing. You want my number in case you change your mind? He looked up at me now from his *Car and Driver*. What's your best offer, pal? Five hundred ain't gunna to get it done. I looked out the plate glass window like I was mentally scratching myself then turned back and placed my hands on his desk.

Let's not fart around. I'll give you seven hundred, no warranty required. I'll pay the taxes. Yes or no. Go ask.

He pretended he needed to, staying away for six or eight minutes, returning with a forlorn look, the inception of a counteroffer on his lips. Yes or no, I repeated, standing up. Don't waste my fucking time.

He looked at me like I'd kicked his dog, even taking a short step back. Jesus, pal, cool your jets. I turned to leave and he said okay, okay. As is, take it away.

I was nearly pissing myself I was so happy with my negotiating coup. I had been a price taker all my life, bickering over pennies undignified. But that had been fun. Hell, I would have paid two thousand if they had painted it on the side. That's what it was worth. Why was it a crime to just pay the asking price? I had no patience before, I was going to be a head strong motherfucker now! I didn't even mean to be, I just wasn't willing to deal with the bull shit. I drove home whistling, hoping Mandy was early so we could go back and get our new toy.

She was and I told her about my meeting with Bob, our windfall from that and my brilliantly determined stance with the used car guy. I was fired up, punctuating my re-enactment with rapid hand movements. What's the matter, I asked her. You don't seem too thrilled with the news. She looked at me like I was the dumbest man that ever mastered speech and after a couple seconds, I realized that I probably was. I'm babbling on about things that, to Mandy, were less then inconsequential, she's seeing me as her dying lover, she has to be thinking about her future, alone, father dead, brothers worthless, mother a parasite. A used motor home was small consolation.

Come on, I said, let's go out to dinner, something we had done a lot in our drinking days, an excuse to have a couple during the week even after I cut back, years ago now, on every day boozing, just a little on the weekends. Unless we were in Texas.

No, she said. We aren't going to start that again. Here was a quandary. On the one hand, what did I have to lose? My health? And anyone who has ever lusted after the bottle will tell you, the urge never goes away. I wanted a drink. Lots of them. And who has a better right to indulge their desires then a dying man? On the other hand, Mandy and I had nearly split up over the issue a dozen times, every time I got hammered after the first year or so of her failure to recognize the problem. She didn't want to be dragged down into that abyss with me and she was well enough attuned to her own inner amplitudes to know that the possibility surely existed for her as well.

I quickly reduced it to its barest elements—did I want to die alone, drinking, or die sober with Mandy at my side? The rationalizations started leaping at me like hobgoblins on All Hallow's Eve. Drive her away, it's best for her the Bad Angel screamed. You *deserve* a drink, he added. The Good Angel didn't need to say a fucking thing, I could see him sitting there on my shoulder shaking his head.

You are correct, I told her, death is no excuse almost spilling out of the Bad Angel side of my mouth. But it was a dilemma and I was torn, my mouth juices just flowing with the imagined rush of a double shot of gold tequila, the icy numbness of a Stoli rocks, even a luke warm Coors Light would have been okay. Fight it, I said to myself as I had twenty times a day for every one of the hundred and fifty plus days of my sobriety. God, I wanted a cigarette.

"You know," I started, giving it another shot.

"Don't even bother," she finished. "You wanna be a drunk, die alone."

Chapter Eight

Mandy had been having recurring female problems as long as I'd known her. We had gone through four gynecologists, the first never acknowledging that her complaints of constant abdominal pain and severe menstrual flows were medically significant, the second taking an internal look and tinkering with a cyst but refusing to perform a hysterectomy and the third removing the uterus but then turning a deaf ear to her complaints of continued pain.

The forth ran all the tests, eliminating organs and bowels, having her scoped from both directions and dye testing the kidneys. Endometriosis was all that was left. With her history of issues in that area, neither of us could figure out why he didn't start with a laparoscopy to verify his diagnosis. The procedure had been scheduled for weeks and was due to take place three days after I got my bad news.

Mandy had wanted to cancel it but I said no, get it over with. I didn't say you need to be able to lead an active life now more then ever, wanting her to be able to do the things a more energetic mate might find interesting. So we kept the afternoon consult and went in the next morning for the seven AM, thirty-minute procedure.

The new OB-GYN was a mellow, funny guy, way over educated, Ph.D. in biology from UCLA preceding the medical degree from the University of Pennsylvania. We had teased him about it after reviewing the bank of diplomas decorating his office wall. He came into the prep room, asking the last minute questions and getting the consents signed, Mandy in a back-less gown with her toes sticking out, an elastic cap stretched over her blond head and tucked behind her ears. She was beautiful, laughing with the nurses, both of us making funny faces at the grumpy anesthesiologist then cracking up after he walked away, asking her doctor how his golf game was and when he was teeing off that afternoon. An hour after I stitch her up, he said grinning. I'll come see you in a half-hour he told me. I kissed Mandy on the forehead and told her I loved her. I'll see you soon, Sunshine, I whispered and went to the waiting room.

A half-hour later I was starting to pace. After another thirty minutes I popped the double doors into the nurse's station and asked where Amanda Cassidy was. No one would tell me shit and the staid little surgie center in the quiet community hospital was a hell of a lot busier and the people a whole lot grimmer then they had been an hour before. My alarm bells were going crazy and I lost my composure after being stone-walled by a second nurse. I grabbed her arm hard and spun her back to face me. What the fuck is going on, Goddamn it! I yelled. She pulled free and spun on her heal, demanding that her coworker call security.

"I'm going to find my fiancée," I said to the remaining nurse. "Either you help me or I'm going through every door in this fucking hospital," giving her three seconds then turning and heading toward the operating rooms.

"Wait," she said. "There was a complication."

"What?"

"I don't know for sure," she said.

"You're lying." My heart stopped beating, I know it did. Nothing else could explain the feeling of absolute emptiness that overcame me. "Tell me what happened." She looked toward the surgical suites then back at the double doors. Then up at me.

"I'm not sure. Really. They called a code blue, everyone went into number two. But they came out a while ago, most of them." After a pause she added, "The lawyer's in there now."

"She's dead. Just say it." She nodded her head.

My anger came roaring back, filling me like steam from a boiler as I marched toward number two. I was intercepted at the door by a security guard coming up behind me. He grabbed my arm, not too hard and said hold on, sir, you can't go in there. I didn't even look at his face as I swung on him. He probably should have expected it but he clearly did not and I landed my fist right between his eyes, knocking him backwards until his feet gave out and he landed on his ass. I punched the wall plate next and was inside the operating theater before the double doors were half open. A body was on the table, two gowned figures standing over it and one man in a business suit. The suit came around to block me but I hit him so hard and fast in his paunchy gut that he was on his hands and knees before he finished oomphing out all his air.

I took the sheet in two fingers and lifted it. The woman on the table was clearly gone, drained and white, head lolling to one side, eyes open and vacant. She was about seventy and my knees buckled, the relief so palpable I almost shouted out my joy, catching myself as the scream was forming, slapping my hand over my mouth to stifle it. This was someone's dearly departed and they were going to be going through all those feeling of helplessness and loss that had been coursing through me seconds before.

One doctor came up beside me while the other helped the suit to his feet and then led him toward the doors which swung open and conked the groggy lawyer on the forehead, the security guard charging unsteadily in behind, knocking them both to the floor again, the doctor stepping out of the way as they toppled over.

"I am *so* sorry," I said to the first doctor as I lowered the sheet and turned to leave. I stopped to help the dopey two-some, apologizing again as I dusted off the lawyer and the bloodied guard. "I thought my.... This was my fiancée's.... I thought she was dead," I managed. "I lost control. Are you guys alright?"

The guard grinned lopsidedly at me and said, don't worry about it, buddy, rubbing his forehead and leaning on my arm as he guided me out of the room. The lawyer was silent until we reached the corridor then he grabbed my other arm and tried to swing me around.

"You're in big trouble, mister. Show me some ID," he growled.

"Hold on, pal," I said. "I thought my girl friend was dead and everybody was bull shitting me. I over reacted. I'm sorry."

"You over reacted yourself right into jail!" he shouted, his gut bumping me as he stood on his tip toes, his jowls a fiery red and quivering.

I backed up a step and put my hand on his chest. "Easy, partner. *You're* going to need a code blue if you don't calm down," meaning he was going to have a coronary but him thinking it was a threat.

"We'll see about that," he screamed as he hustled up the hall to the nurse's station, shouting at the woman who had mistaken the old lady's death for Amanda's to call the police.

"What's with that asshole," I asked the guard.

"He's a fuckin' lawyer. You might wanna get yer butt out a here," he added as we approached the attorney.

"I can't. My girl friend's having surgery. Somewhere in here."

"Let me try talkin' to the guy. You go find yer lady."

I found Mandy in a ward with two other women, recovering nicely from her uneventful procedure. Her doctor was there, trying to show her photography of the spectacular cyst he had removed from her left ovary.

"Nice," I said, leaning over his shoulder. "How's my Baby doing?" She smiled at me, a little unfocused but otherwise chipper. The doctor gave a frown then grinned slightly.

"She's fine," he said, "but it has been an interesting morning."

"I heard about the code blue. I thought it was Amanda," I said to him. "I made a bit of a commotion, I'm afraid."

"Ah," he said. "I should have come out to see you earlier but I got caught up in the, ah, situation there. I'm sorry. But I got the other things for you. A couple nice ones," he said

"Great. Thanks. And it's okay, Doc. As long as she's alright, I'm alright. I did smack a lawyer pretty good though. I think he's going to make an issue out of it."

"Jesus," he said. "*Never* hit a lawyer. They don't have any sense of humor about it. Where is he? Maybe I can intercede."

"Out in the hall ranting like a wet rooster. You can't miss him."

He left and I kissed Mandy, telling her how good she looked and how much I loved her. I didn't mention the mistaken identity or the fracas that had ensued and I couldn't stop touching her, watching her as she grinned sleepily, thinking I might have lost her, no God, don't ever let that happen.

Her doctor came back in with the security guy. "He won't budge," the guard said. "You hurt his little feelings."

"I told you, no sense of humor. The cops are on their way," the doctor added.

"Oh well," I shrugged. "If you can't do the time, don't do the crime. Thanks for trying, I appreciate it," I said as I shook their hands.

"I'll be around," the guard said. "To give the cops a statement." He waved to Mandy as he walked out.

Two state troopers came in a moment later and asked me to accompany them. I explained to Mandy that I'd be back soon, not to worry. "Give her the short form, will you, Doc," I called from the doorway.

He gave me a thumbs up, the cops on either side of me now. We marched out through the sets of double doors and met the attorney in the corridor outside the surgical area.

"That's him," he said, pointing a finger at me. "Not so tough now are you, hot shot!"

"I never was," I said. "The way you charged into me," I continued, thinking fuck it, I'm not going to play dead for this little shit, "you frightened me. I thought you were attacking me. You had that big IV pole in your hand, you were going to clobber me with it, weren't you," I said, cowering behind the cops. "Thank God you guys showed up," I said. "This person is unstable!"

"You....you liar! You hit *me*! An unprovoked assault! You bastard! *You're* the crazy man," his face so red, I really did fear for his health.

"You see?" I said. "You can see why I thought he was dangerous. The man is clearly unhinged. Was that your wife back there? Dead? I'm so sorry for your loss, no wonder you're so upset. Officers, this man has suffered a terrible tragedy. I'm willing to forget the whole thing," I said.

The lawyer was sputtering like a ruptured pressure hose, single words popping out. He advanced on me with his fingers bent and extended like talons. One of the cops grabbed his arm and pushed him back against the wall, saying calm down, sir, we'll take care of this now, the other leading me away in the opposite direction.

"That poor man," I said when we cleared the lobby doors and stopped under the roof outside the main entrance.

"You can stop that," he said.

"Okay," I said. "What happens now?"

"If my partner can convince the shyster to let it go, we all walk away. If not, we'll have to take both of you back to the barracks for statements. Either way my report is going to say that he was agitated and threatening, you were calm and cooperative. Give me your side of it."

I told him about Mandy and the nurse's mistake, leaving out my encounter with the guard and making my body punch to the lawyer sound more like two guys bumping bellies in a crowded bar. He took my vital statistics then told me to wait *here*, pointing down at the concrete with his index finger so there was no chance of me mistaking here for Mandy's room or my living room, he was going to see how his partner was making out with the lawyer.

Ten minutes later the cops came back through the automatic doors.

"He's going to think about it," my trooper said. "Go home as soon as you can and don't talk to the man. Do you understand?"

"Yes sir," I said. "And thank you," I added. "Hopefully you won't be in touch."

My cop grinned but the other one strode off toward the Plymouth Fury that was parked at the curb. "Good luck," my cop said. "I hope your girl's okay."

I waved as they sped off, laughing out loud when they were out of sight. Life is good, I thought. At least some of it is, some of the time.

Mandy was home by one, the miracle of modern medicine combined with the frugality of modern medical insurance guaranteeing that no one would be malingering in a room over night if there was less then a fifty percent chance of major complications. Mandy was fine, sore and tired. I rented a bunch of movies and we spent two days in bed, napping and talking. About the trip, mostly.

On the third day she wanted me to cart a bucket of water out to the motor home so she could clean it. I refused. She sulked. I gave in, allowing her to sit in it while I cleaned. I had picked it up from the neighborhood garage that morning, riding my bike down to the service station, my mechanic having declared it road ready, tuned and tired, all new fluids, greased up and purring like a happy cat. I was ready to roll on out of town but Mandy still had a week of work left.

We had argued some about our agenda. I wanted to go south then west then maybe up the Pacific coast and back across Montana and the Dakotas, check out the Great Lakes country. I also wanted to spend a fair amount of time at the ranch, visit my sisters along the way, a bunch of good-byes. She wanted to find a good beach in the Carolinas and linger there. We agreed to do both, sort of, time permitting, the beach first, then the ranch. The last think she wanted to do was hang around my family for weeks, our time together better spent just the two of us, my obligation to tell each of my siblings and my mother, dreading that one, secondary to us having quality time together, the limited amount of it left never spoken but never forgotten either.

On the fourth day after surgery, Mandy went back to work, light duty only, no lifting, lots of time sitting down she promised. I drove her and when I got home, planning to spend the day cleaning and packing, there was a check for fifty four thousand, eight hundred and twenty three dollars in the mailbox. Not bad. Now I was really primed to motor. I also got a jabbing pain under my right nipple, like I'd had a knitting needle thrust through me, the hurt front to back and continuous. After an hour of massaging myself, bent over like an old man, I called my oncologist.

"This is the first one," he asked? "The first shooting pain?"

"Yeah and it's a good 'un," I said.

"I'm afraid you're going to have a lot of that."

"I didn't....expect it so soon. And this bad. Holy shit, it fucking hurts."

"I know. I'm sorry. There are a number of treatment options, to mitigate it. You will never be completely pain free, I mean nothing will eliminate it entirely, not that the pain will be constant."

"I understand," I said, the burning subsiding as we spoke, cooling back to front now as if the dart impaling me was being slowly withdrawn. "It's easing some."

"Good. You'll need to come in here if you can. I can't call in narcotics over the phone, except in emergencies. Can you do that?"

"You bet. I'm on my way," and ten minutes later I was climbing gingerly into my car, afraid that some jerk or bump would stick the hot poker back in my chest.

He took me into an exam room as soon as I arrived and displayed a fan of prescription slips, explaining the what and the why and the how of each medication. Percocets for every day use, Oxycoton in several strengths as things got worse. And a morphine patch, like the nicotine substitutes I'd used with varying degrees of success while trying to quit smoking. Several dosages of them.

"Start with the Percocets," he said. "They'll make you a little wifty at first. Move on to the Oxycoton when the Percs don't work. You can switch back and forth. That will help some with your body's tendency to compensate. Eventually you will need the morphine patch. And then," not saying at the end but I knew what he meant, "you'll need both, patch and pills."

I looked at the number of pills on each script. "I'm planning a trip," I said. "A long one. I hope. Are these going to last?"

"I was assuming I'd see you periodically. Monitor your condition. And you shouldn't really be driving while you're taking any of this stuff."

"I know. My fiancée...." I started to explain, stopping as I realized how irrelevant the reference to a future marriage sounded. "My girl friend will do most of the driving. And it seems sort of pointless to come back now and than, don't you think? Not to be rude, Doc, but why bother?"

He didn't answer, holding my eyes for several seconds before looking down and then turning away, removing his pad and scribbling out another bunch of scripts. I thanked him when I left and he wished me a safe journey. I never saw him again.

What a shitty job. Most of your patients are terminal and you get to tell them. I'd rather build mini malls, at least the clients were happy with the product. But then again no Arab or Indian shopkeeper ever pulled a rotten cantaloupe out of your chest cavity and bought you another decade. Good with the bad. I loaded up on legal dope and went home to get happy. What the fuck, it's not like I was going to get hooked.

But the realization that my last months were not only irreplaceable, a nonrenewable resource of the most precious variety, but that they might not even be enjoyable, the pain or the narcotics rendering me an invalid, was sobering, the pun, unintended, making me smile. I'm not sure why it hadn't occurred to me, that I wasn't just going to live for a short time as if nothing at all of any consequence was going on inside me, that I was a more or less healthy guy who, by psychic dispensation knew that he was going to pass beyond in a year or so, happily splashing in the ocean one day, dead the next. I was beginning to see that there might be more to it then that, that it wasn't going to be so simple or so easy, that I'd have to suffer before I met my maker. That sucked. That wasn't fair. Why should I have to die young *and* suffer? One or the other should have been enough. I thought about that guy who drops dead just before his retirement, no foreknowledge at all, and decided that I'd take the extra ten or fifteen years even if it meant working like a dog at some bore-ass drone job six days a week. At least you had your nights and weekends and those two weeks off in July or August. So what if you came home every night too tired to do more then watch TV, eat some dreadful, foil packaged frozen crap, drink and sleep. So what if you spent Sunday on your back on the couch watching cars moving in endless, noisy circles, the beer cans piling up on the floor beside you. So what if you were too poor or lazy to do more than more of the same on your two weeks off, shuffling off to the corner tap room when you needed to see another human face, someone else as bored and miserable as you were, another wage slave without cause or hope. At least you were alive, right? Maybe not. Maybe that guy was just as dead as I was going to be, he just didn't realized it yet.

I put the pain pill that was clutched in my hand back in its bottle. I'd take it when I needed it, really needed it, not just to get high.

Chapter Nine

I called my kids that night while Mandy was dozing, work aggravating her soreness, me forcing her into bed with a pain pill of her own and a heating pad. I arraigned to meet them the next day for lunch at the restaurant where my youngest, Jessica, my blood kid with the Hell Bitch, worked part time and her boy friend Randy full time, the owner a half-assed friend of mine who had promised to hold a table in a back corner, some place where we would have some privacy.

After I dropped off Mandy at work, I drove across the state line to a branch of the Bank of Delaware and grinned as I slid the fifty plus thousand dollar check across the manager's desk. I can take a couple certified checks but I mostly want cash, I explained. I gave them the girl's full names, five grand for each of them, the balance in large bills. I thought it was hysterical, expecting him to frown and complain, thinking they might not even *have* that much cash but he simply looked at the check, me and my license then produced an FBI form for me to fill out, the consequence of any cash transaction over ten grand in either direction.

He was back in ten minutes. It took me almost that long to explain my whole life to the federal government on paper. He had several stacks of bills, not nearly as impressive a pile as I had anticipated even though there was five thousand in both fifties and twenties, my request consuming every hundred in his inventory. I left with the checks in my wallet and a paper sack stuffed with bills, every one of which I had counted twice at the manager's insistence—his revenge I suspect.

The girls were already seated when I arrived, surprised at the reserved table they were ushered to almost as much as they had been when I called to suggest lunch. We hugged and kissed and talked about kids and jobs and school. We ordered food. I looked at their lovely, smiling faces, full of life, expectations sky high in the naïveté of youth, none of life's pratfalls sufficient to date to quell the fire, no amount of divorce or bad boy friends, weird family or weirder in-laws making them cynical or fatalistic. It made me never want to die, never leave them, be there for them when something did go so wrong that their happiness was threatened, protect them, not be the cause of their first really big dose of reality.

I did not know how to tell them. I rethought in an instant every plus and minus I had worked over in my mind, tell them to prepare them so they can adapt while I can be there to help them cope, don't tell them so the pain of loss is one sharp stab not a series of little pricks, tell them so they relish our time together as much as I would, don't so they're their usual uninhibited, joyous selves, the way you want your kids to be, not hand ringing and sorrowful every time they look at you. The 'don't' won out. I want happy, as much as I can get for as long as I can get it.

I grinned as I pulled out my wallet, relieved to have made the decision and just glad to be with them. "These are for you guys," I said as I handed over the checks. "I'm not going to tell you how to spend it but I *am* going to make some suggestions. And I will be way pissed off if you buy motorcycles or go to Cancun." They both looked at the amount then at each other then back at me.

"Thanks, Dad," Jessica said with a grin.

"Yeah!" from Gloria. "Thanks a lot! Why?"

"Cause you are great kids and I love you. And I've been a shitty father for a few years and I want to buy back your affection. How's that?"

"Works for me," Gloria said, "I can be bought!"

"Me too," Jessica added. "Probably cheaper than this."

"Okay, give 'em back."

"No way, dude," Gloria said, laughing and turning away with the check clutched to her breast.

"Good deal," I said. "Now here's the rules. If you lend money to your mother, I'll disown you. I'm completely serious. Let her get a fucking job for once in her life. Do you understand me on this?" They both nodded, so I continued. "And don't waste it. I suggest you invest it, put in an annuity that reinvests the interest. Hold it for ten years, add to it when you can. If you do that, I'll try to help." They looked at me like I told them they couldn't eat their Easter candy and I remembered being their ages and all the things I had wanted and could not afford.

"All right. I can see by your miserable looks that you had something else in mind. Jessica, you go first."

"I was thinking about school," she said with a half smile.

"This is not your school money, Angel. I'll still cover that. What else?"

"I need a new car?" she said.

"You can have mine. I told you that," I said.

"Dad! That car is a piece of junk," from both of them. They were right, it was, but cars are a bad investment and I had a history of buying them used, maintaining them very well and driving them into the ground. My Chevy was closer to dying then I was.

"That car is a classic, are you kidding me?" I said in horror. "Do you know there were only three hundred million of them ever made? And mine is one of only about fifty or ninety million still on the road? In another fifteen years you can put antique tags on it, it'll be worth more then I paid for it!"

"More then five hundred dollars. Wow," Gloria said, eyes big, mocking me right back.

"Okay, a new used car. What else?"

"Nothing important. Randy and I are in good shape at the apartment." She was living with her boy friend, a smart, hard working young man and I suspected they were really in love. There was nothing for me to complain about in the relationship and truthfully, I would rather see her attached then out dating even if she was only nineteen. Better piece of mind for a father once you get over the 'my daughter isn't a virgin' syndrome.

"Good. Don't get pregnant," I said, my usual admonition and the best fatherly advise I could possibly offer someone her age. I said it to her at least once a month. She always swore she had no interest in procreation but then don't they all right before they're stupid, late, worried, then married and a mother living in a crappy row house by the time they turn twenty one.

"Gloria. I know you have some things in mind, I can tell by that evil smirk on your mug. What? Talk to me. How's *your* car holding up?" Hers was halfway new. I'd been hit up for the short fall when she split with Paul and he took the good car, leaving her a piece of shit that made mine look like a brand new Eldorado.

"Furniture. At least a new couch." I couldn't argue with that. She and Paul had proudly shown off the new stuff they got shortly after the marriage, a sofa and matching chair so hideous that the sales man must have danced in the aisles when someone blind or dumb enough finally took it out of his inventory. "And I need to pay some bills." I knew that story too. Paul had been furious when she ran him off, cashing out their accounts and running up a big debt on their Visa then refusing to acknowledge any part of the bill. She was paying it down and might recoup his share in court but that was a ways off. She was still fighting with him over the child support, disposition of assets not even on the table yet.

"I never really disliked him," I said to her, talking about Paul, "but there really wasn't much to like either. What did you ever see in him," I asked, Gloria so happy and adventurous, Paul so miserable and staid. He was the youngest old man I had ever met, no curiosity, no interest in anything he hadn't already done, content to work in his father's bakery and go to the Eagle's games eight times a year. No hobbies, no nothing, a sad, boring life ahead—at twenty-eight. He was a lot like his father only duller. The father at least socialized a little and was active in Little League. And ate food. Paul only ate cheese steaks and pasta. That was his entire diet. I thought it a weird hangover from his childhood, his parents obviously not forcing him to at least take a bite as I had mine, the result for him the loss of a whole world of experience, food as great a pleasure as sex for me and capable of being enjoyed a lot more often. I thought he'd grow out of it, kept trying to entice him with various things I cooked but he never once even sniffed at one of my creations. 'I don't eat that' was always his response. My girls would suck down raw oysters and chase them with pickled jalapenos. At twelve.

The two of them had so little in common that the demise of the marriage was not a surprise. The vindictiveness of Paul, and the degree to which his father aided him in his quest for pay back, was. They would tag team Gloria, call her at work several times a day, canceled the house insurance, stopped their mortgage payments, took the good car and that was only the beginning

I told her to get a lawyer from the outset but she thought they could all play nice, reach a settlement without the aggravation. They offered her five thousand if she would sign over the house! Oh and no alimony, Gloria. And no child support. It's a good deal, they said, we'll send over the papers. When she got them, drawn up by their attorney, them thinking that it was all still in the family and she was a dumb bimbo, she got mad and finally hired an attorney who had been recommended to me by a friend who'd gone through a particularly ugly divorce. Gloria's lawyer laughed her head off when she read their stuff, Gloria and I sitting across the desk from her as she howled at the content, the typos, and the gall. These people are assholes, she exclaimed, my opinion of her sky rocketing. We are going to make them *pay*. Right on, sister.

Paul's income was about half in twenty dollar bills, the bakery a cash over the counter, Italian pastry operation and his father a second generation tax cheat who had been taught by *his* father that baking and fraud went hand in hand. They had been busted recently by the IRS, I didn't know how exactly but a disgruntled whistle blower ex-employee might have gotten them a quick once over from a local agent and it would not have been a stretch to realize that houses in the suburbs, Cadillac's and motor homes don't get bought legally on twenty five grand a year, not with five kids and a non-working wife.

They paid a fine and promised not to do it again but Paul's check never got any bigger and the pile of twenties never got any smaller. Gloria's lawyer was almost hopping out of her chair when Gloria explained that tid bit, especially when Gloria showed her the bank statements that indicated more was deposited each week than he drew in declared income. The down side for Gloria was Paul's straight faced declaration to the child support arbitrator that he only made two hundred and fifty a week and couldn't afford to give any of it to his kid. She took the maximum anyway but it wasn't very much, the IRS card making for a nice bluff but you could only play it once and not with the arbitrator at all.

Paul and his father harassed Gloria so much that she finally asked me to intercede, something that I had offered to do a number of times but that she had always declined, saying it will just make things worse, they're already mad enough. Fuck them, I kept telling her. They are *trying* to fuck you. I called the father at the bakery and told him that if he called my daughter again, ever, we would get a restraining order on both him and his son adding, I'm sure you wouldn't want that kind of publicity, not with all those IRS issues you just got worked out, right? He agreed that perhaps it was best left up to the lawyers at this point because obviously Gloria thought there was more money to be had out of them then there really was. Yeah, I said. Those new tax laws are a bastard aren't they, like he had not just called my daughter a gold digging little bitch. Hey, I added, if you need help with the government, I've got a golf buddy that does enforcement work out of the King of Prussia field office, I'm sure he'd be glad to look over your books for you. That ended the conversation, both with me then and with Gloria after that.

We had a nice meal and they left thanking and kissing me, thinking I'm sure, what a great dad we have, so funny and generous, what a terrific grand-father he's going to be now that we're all friends again. I felt like a shit, weak and indecisive, a coward for not telling them the truth. I paid our check, over tipping Jessica's friend who had served us, then walked up to the bar and pulled out a stool. If the bartender had been a little busier or a tad less attentive, I might have changed my mind, thought better of what I was considering, but she was on me with a big friendly smile before I had completely decided to sit down.

What can I get you, she asked and I said a double gold tequila up and a draft Bass as if I placed just such an order every afternoon at one, no hundred plus day break in my routine, nothing at all unusual. She drew the ale in an icy mug and then sat a tumbler in front of me with a flourish, tipping the little jug over it and running the amber liquid nearly to the top, a very generous double. My mouth was puckering and watering simultaneously as

I watched the little glass filling. I thanked her and she ambled off, leaving me alone with my new companions, old friends about to get reacquainted.

We stared at each other for several minutes, my rummy pal with the mismatched, miscolored eyes not much of a talker so I had to carry that ball. I told him all about Mandy, how much I loved her, how good she was for me and how I thought I had lost her in the hospital. I told him about the emptiness of that moment, the devastating despair that drained my guts as slick as an undertaker's pump and I told him how I never wanted to feel that lost and alone again.

I put a twenty on the bar, said goodbye to my drinking buddies and walked out of the place. One of the hardest things I've ever done, leaving those drinks there untouched, but damn I felt good about myself when I did, a big, stupid grin on my face when I turned my back on my Mexican-Limey pal with the goofy, watery eyes.

Chapter Ten

That night I told Amanda about the severance check and recounted my meetings with both the children and my old friends at the bar. Mandy teared up toward the end then leaned across the table and but her arms around my shoulders and kissed my lips. You're a good father she said, and a good boy friend. I took that as my cue to go for some late afternoon sex. She jumped out of bed right after and said let's go out, I'm starving and you're rich!

I took her to an Out Back Steak House, the meat store in our vernacular, and we found a miniature table in the bar, the only place you could smoke in the restaurant so we were familiar with the layout from our tobacco days. We went to them often enough that neither of us needed menus, Mandy an Outback Special well done, me the Outback Rack, lamb, medium. No Bloomin' Onion, thank you. I had read somewhere that that large, innocuous vegetable picked up something like eight hundred calories and a ton or so of fat in the dipping and frying process. Maybe it was in the sauce. I'm not sure but when I told Mandy about it, we had already eaten our last one. They were good but so were potato chips and they at least identified their content on the wrapping and you had choices in seasoning style and fat content. Plus you didn't have to eat the whole damn bag.

When the perky college kid server finally made it to our table, Mandy smiled up at her and said, a Foster's and a Bass, the big ones, then turned her perfect grin on me and said, what the hell, you only live once. I didn't really have a good response to that.

We drank a couple schooners of brew, each one served in a fresh frosted mug, the next easily more delicious then the one before. I expected a down to the toes, scrotum warming rush from the first one, certainly from the second it had been so long since any alcohol had infused my system but it was disappointingly missing. I don't know why. It used to be the first drink, after even a couple *days* lay off, would produce a very mellow if short lived buzz. Maybe it was the dilution of the medium, beer not nearly as concentrated as a shooter or a martini and not having that smack-you-in-the-head capacity even when hammered down in a hurry.

On the way home, Mandy laid out the ground rules. I've been thinking about this for a few days, she said. If you want to drink some beer once in a while, it's okay. No liquor. And you can't get drunk. It makes me sick, it repulses me, when you're loaded. Do you understand?

I did. Drunks repulse me too. I repulse myself, the next day. I asked her if she was sure about this. She said yeah. I said we don't have to, it's okay, I made my peace with it that afternoon. She said she was proud of me for that but really, what harm could it do me now? I'm more worried about you, I said. It's not that important to me any more, I lied. She responded, yeah, but it might be, in the future, you know? And you may....need a drink....now and then. Eventually. And I'm not giving you cart blanche. If you ever drink behind my back, I'm gone. Understand? I sure did. We were in this together. Like everything we did, we were a team. I get it, Sunshine. Don't worry.

We spent the weekend preparing, cleaning and packing, shutting off unnecessary services, cable and phone to be on hiatus for sixty days, I'd call to extend if required, and prepaying bills for her mother to send out with the appropriate statements. Mandy's cousin was going to stay at the house a few days a week, a sign of habitation for the local B and E guys if there were any. No one we knew had ever been robbed but I did not and never had believed in taking chances along those lines. Call me paranoid, Mandy often did, but I had never been burglarized and I wanted to keep it that way.

The cousin was happy to help. She had been in a stagnant relationship for years with a glad-handing bull shitter who, while not overtly abusive, was also not a loving mate by any stretch. He had another girlfriend somewhere, he swore it was platonic but no one believed that crap, and he would disappear for several day stretches every few weeks, like Bear, returning without warning or explanation. He used Tracey unmercifully, for money, cars, household repairs, and she didn't put her foot down, afraid of being alone I guess. She was forty plus and not unattractive but not a head-turner either. A partial relationship, even shared, must have been than none at all. I felt sorry for her but she wasn't the kind of person that you could offer advice to. Even Mandy would not risk confronting her on the boy friend issue. Tracey would get angry and shut you out, shun you like an Amish blasphemer. Too much risk, Mandy had said, no up side to ruining the friendship. She'll get tired of it eventually Mandy said but there was no sign of an impending breakup other than her perpetual willingness to house sit for people.

Almost no matter how the trip went, I figured we'd be back eventually, before the end, so there was no one locally I had any particular interest in sharing my story with. A few of my work buds had called to ask what the fuck I was doing, quitting without notice, but no one said hey, I hear you're dying and I picked up no under tones of ill-disguised pity so Bob must have kept the details of my resignation to himself. I doubted if I would have been able to be so circumspect. The urge to share such misfortune, diagnose and dissect it, tisk tisking about it in an effort to keep those dogs at bay, residing in someone else's tissues, would have been over powering in a lesser man. Rich as Caesar and noble as well. Quite a guy.

I had a week to kill, again no pun intended, while Mandy finished up her work requirements. I went to the bookstore and bought an up to date atlas and a couple Fodor's state guides and mapped out a back road itinerary down the Atlantic coast. That took one day. I debated buying a book on cancer but as I stood in the medical reference section with my head bent side ways perusing titles, most authored by various well respected, I'm sure, but living medical doctors and PH. D 's, I decided that in some cases, too much knowledge *is* a dangerous thing. I didn't *want* to know what to expect. I didn't need to know when and how the renegade cells in my lungs would reach critical mass, cutting off the flow of air, depriving my blood of oxygen and shutting down my system. It would happen when it happened and if I didn't anticipate it, didn't know to expect it *to* happen, maybe it would not happen so fast. I didn't *want* to be an educated hypochondriac, looking for the symptoms of the latest designer disease, afraid that every time I even *saw* a tick I was surely going to be infected by Lime's disease or that every whining mosquito was going to drill me full of West Nile. Call it the optimism of ignorance, I don't care. And I don't need to be reminded that I should not have ignored the subtle signs my body had been issuing for a year prior to my taking sufficient notice to get a physical, even then having to be almost forced by the GP to get a chest X-ray. That was stupidity. I knew what I should have done, I just didn't get around to it. Too busy at work, too many other things to worry about. This was my last stand and I wasn't going to arm my attacker with any more ammunition than he already had.

On the second day I started making lists, things I needed to do before the end. It wasn't nearly as easy as I thought it would be. I had a steno pad, purchased just for this list, the terminal collection of to do's, and I placed it on the island top and pulled up a stool. I wrote the date on the cardboard cover then started to write 'Last List' under that but decided it would be too macabre to have lying around for Mandy to see so I changed it to 'The List'. Simple, to the point, as all things should be for me now.

I opened it, flipped the cover back and stared at the first page. I have always been a list maker, the Steno note book my organizer, memory aid and Palm Pilot and I knew that the best way to create a list was to edit after memorializing, write down everything, then cross out the junk, rather than editing in your mind, expecting the list thus rendered to be some glorious document.

Nothing came out of my head onto the page. I thought of a will, mandatory in my situation but already done. Good-byes. I was going to do those later. But I needed somewhere to start. Funeral arrangements. Ah, that's good. Start at the end and work backwards. I had always assumed, when discussing this topic as everyone does at some point, in conversation, light heartedly as all of us know that we are never *really* going to die, that I would be cremated. It's cheap, easy, environmentally benign and saves your loved ones from having to make a lot of hard decisions that they are probably emotionally unprepared to make at the time that they need to be made. But since Jack's demise, I had come to recognize the importance of the tomb to the survivors. Jack had been primarily spread across the waters of his favorite fishing hole, a little pond on the edge of a rose nursery behind the house they'd lived in when I first met Amanda. It was a pretty spot and Jack and Amanda would walk over the hill and make a few casts either before or after work, father-daughter quality time away from the scowling countenance of Clara and the endless phone calls from subs and suppliers.

But it was someone else's property and the down side of that became evident even before the end. The nursery man who was Jack's friend had sold off the land soon after Jack and Clara had moved into town, down sizing from four bedrooms to two, moving closer to her lunch club friends and forever away from the borrowed land where Jack had hunted dove and deer, run his beagle after rabbits and aggravated the bass and sunnies in his neighbor's pond. We spread him there anyway, that wasn't the problem. Going back to visit was, not only because the new owner fenced the land and was preparing to subdivide the pasture and woods into three-quarter acre lots, but also because there wasn't really any particular place where Jack *was*. No head stone to decorate with flags and flowers, no little plot of tended grass to sit beside, just some swampy pond's edge that now you had to trespass on to get to. None of us realized the consequence of following Jack's request until it was too late.

Mandy swore later that had she recognized the problem, she would have disregarded her father's plan and had him planted in the local cemetery. As it was she had saved a pound or two of the remains for her own needs and she and I had buried most of that at the head of Jack's father's grave under a stone that at least had the last name right. As long as there was a place, an actual location where she could go and visit, say hello, bring momentous, then he lived on and she could cope. Your loved ones don't forget, so you might as well make it easy for them to remember.

I wrote 'funeral,' under lined it and then added a hyphen. Cremation? ashes buried, head stone(s). Where would the monument be? I'd like to be at the ranch, up on the bluff behind the locust wing looking down the fence line toward my favorite deer stand. Close to where the girls were asked to pee at Tex's going away party, the guests so numerous that mom was afraid we'd swamp the septic system in beer residue. They could sit on my head stone at future events and piss on my ashes. Hell, I might even get to see a little pussy, even if it was attached to a relative or a friend. But the ranch wasn't going to be ideal for Mandy. I doubted if she would ever go there again after I died. Maybe once or twice to visit Mom, but certainly not on a regular basis.

And I did not want to be in some cornfield in Lancaster County. I had no roots in the area, didn't particularly like it and wanted Mandy to get out ASAP. And stay out! That was the main reason for pushing the road trip on her, show her how to get away, help her to, force her if necessary.

There was room next to Tex in his little plot in Salado, purchased there because it had been the site of the first Barkley homestead, two hundred years back, but that was little better than the ranch for Mandy and not nearly as good from my point of view. Hell, I'd never lived there. And we didn't even know at this point where Mandy was going to end up living. The only solution that I could come up with was to split me down the middle, half levered into a shallow, rocky hole by the pee spot, half given over to Mandy for a burial spot to be named later. By then she might want to just be shut of me completely and she could hand the whole rendered sack over to my mother. That would be a good thing for Amanda, if she could get on with her life that quickly.

As long as I was on funerals and head stones, I thought I should take a wack at the words. Here was a good one. What am I? What have I done worthy of being carved into a block of pink granite? My name, that's a given. Husband, father, son? With the exception of my progeny, I wanted the world to forget the marriage that had produced them. Husband was out. Father to Gloria and Jessica? Kind of wordy. Space was going to be at a premium. I didn't want a grave marker like a sheet of stone plywood. Son. Good son? Only son for sure, how good was certainly a matter of debate. How about career? Builder of Convenience Stores! There was a monumental statement and yes, I did intend that pun. The blob of rock would last far longer then anything I had ever had a hand in contracting, no Hoover Dams or Empire State Buildings on this resume. I wasn't even leaving behind a house I was immensely proud of, the one we were living in purchased half complete from Jack's estate, too far along to be modified significantly, nothing of my design in the structure. The house I had built with the Hell Bitch was my design from sketch paper to roof shingles but had been sold and resold, modified and revamped so much that it was hard to see what was original and what was additions. Besides, working with her, not that she did one hour's actual labor, just bitched about the things she didn't like after I had already built them, was not a memory that I wanted to relive in this life let alone for eternity.

So I was a name with two kids, only one of which had my DNA not that it mattered in the slightest to me but in the immortality department, a stickler for the rules might draw a line through Gloria, a job—I had been a builder, of what we would leave blank—a son and a lover. To Mandy. I wondered if she would want to be stuck up there with me for a few hundred years—Lover of Amanda. I could add 'My Beautiful Baby' beneath, personalize the message a little more. I doubted that it would help.

What did other people have on theirs? There was a guy planted next to Jack and his dad whose head stone listed him as a PFC. When I first glanced at it, I thought he had died in the war and was buried as a soldier but when I looked closer, he had not only survived World War II, he had lived another fifty years! And the high water mark of that existence was apparently the two or three years he had spent serving his country, sky rocketing through the ranks all the way to private first class! And *I* felt bad about Seven Eleven's. This poor man must have retired at twenty two, never climbing out of his rocking chair or stepping off his front porch again after his victorious march across Europe, crushing the Nazis single handed. I was never in the military.

Friend. You saw that occasionally. I had friends, a few, none very close, no blood brothers, nobody I'd gladly jump in front of a beer truck for. Except Mandy and she was already covered in the lover slot. Acquaintance of Many, Liked by Most. Accurate if uninspiring.

I had forgotten Brother. That should be there with son, acknowledging my non-only child status even though as the youngest and only male, I had often felt like the only child, left out of the hair and make up rituals of my older sisters, all of them speaking some foreign language when we periodically ate in the same time zone. They were probably decent sisters to me although I could not swear to it but I *am* pretty sure that I wasn't the world's best brother. There was nothing much brotherly for me to do while we were growing up. Certainly they never needed me to defend their honor or run off some sleazy creep who wouldn't leave one of them alone. Not that I would have been particularly good at it anyway, the guard at the hospital being the first man I'd punched out since high school. We were more like residents of the same co-ed dorm then a big, happy Brady Bunch family. We were all too preoccupied with our own singular existence to be overly occupied with each other, Mom and Dad included. And we had none of the social or economic disadvantages that drive siblings, or siblings and parents, together. My folks belonged to a country club that hosted the PGA championship when I was in eighth grade. I met Sam Snead and Arnold Palmer that summer. We never suffered enough to be very close.

So my list was short—name, no serial number, son, brother, father, lover. Maybe I should forget the accomplishments and just go with a statement. 'Here I lie, Dead in the Hole, Died too Young to Reach My Goal.' Cute. What goal? That was the problem. I never had one. 'You Live, You Die.' Now that was depressingly accurate. Maybe something inspirational for others, don't do what I did.

'Life is Short, the End Comes Quick, Don't Spend it All, With Your Hand on Your Dick.' That needed some work yet. I couldn't see either Mandy or Mom passing those instructions across the counter to the stone carver.

'Life is Short, Follow Your Dream' would work, assuming you ever had one to follow. The idea apparently was to discover at an early age that which you were passionate about and then to work passionately at that endeavor. What if it was selling used cars or second hand homes? Or building gas stations? We've all heard our high school guidance counselor's take on that—what ever you choose to do, do it to the best of your ability, be the best. Well, I was really good at building gas stations but was it a worthwhile life's work? Not to me. I was disgusted with myself for having wasted my best years on something so irrelevant. I wasn't even rich from it, couldn't even redeem my worthless existence through philanthropy. I should have worked for Habitat for Humanity, palled around with Jimmy Carter in some urban ghetto somewhere, at least I might have improved the lives of some deserving minorities.

It was too late for social change on any kind of significant scale. I only had a few months and I needed to concentrate on the only deserving minority that I could realistically effect—Mandy. And my kids if they were willing. If the balance of their lives was improved through their indenture to me, that was good enough. My head stone would read, 'Take Care of Those You Love,' a statement and an admonition.

Now that I had a handle on my final resting place and at least some idea about what my marker might say, I needed to think about the actual act of dying. I could choose the where and if I wanted to, I could technically pick the when and the how. Suicide had not occurred to me till now, not that in any meaningful sense OD'ing on your death bed was actually suicide and I was pretty sure that I would not want to pull the trigger, hah, till the very end anyway so I doubted that even the strictest Roman theologian would fault me if that's what I chose to do. That was a bridge I'd cross when my feets brought me to the precipice.

The where, however, deserved some more thought. On the one hand, I'd want to be with Mandy. On the other, I didn't want to put her through it. I'd also like to be at the ranch at the end but was that fair to my mother who had so recently gone through just such an episode? Probably not. I could choose to be alone, I guess, but the thought of barricading myself in a flea-bag motel, surrounded by other dead and dying members of society's fringe was so unpalatable that I cringed at the thought. I was sure there were nursing homes that catered to the terminally indigent. At least I wouldn't be alone, someone would be there to kick the morphine up a couple notches periodically.

Tex's sister, my Aunt Mimi, had arraigned for her husband to die in his own bedroom, trucked home from the hospital when it was clear that there was not one damn thing they could do to prolong his life in the institution. He had been hooked up in a gurney bed and had the good taste not to linger more then a day or so, passing on in the presence of his wife and children, the way it used to be done, the undertaker on call. He was allegedly comfortable, as comfortable as a ravaged, bald, barely breathing cadaver can be, half his body weight missing, the tented folds of useless skin all that was left to remind the living of the man he used to be. There was a pleasant sight for the kiddies. Put a body bag over my carcass before I get to that point, please.

The suicide thing was starting to look better and better. Run it out to near the end, while you were still ambulatory, still able to get to the bathroom before you shit all over yourself, before you looked days past dead even if you officially were not, then pull the plug. Doctor Death was right. There was no dignity in Nature's course if the result was a living death.

Fly down to the ranch, hey Mom, how you doin', then call the funeral director, tell him to bring out the meat wagon Tuesday or Thursday morning first thing, whenever you wanted to end it, say good night, then load up on every drug you had, maybe chase it with a fifth of hundred proof vodka just to be sure. And put on the rubber sheets. I could even pick my own last outfit as long as I didn't stink up the Levi's too much in the death throws.

I was really smoking now! Head stone with epitaph and 'place'. And 'how.' 'When' would reveal itself. So what came next in my reverse directory? Living from now till then. Christ, I had three days left till Mandy was done working. What was I going to do? I couldn't just waste them, sitting around watching soap operas. I could have before but not now, not three whole, long, precious, irreplaceable days!

I spent the first one baby sitting Celina, Gloria speechless when I called to ask if I could be her daycare for the day. Why, she asked? Just because I want to, okay? She was suspicious that something was wrong, asking point blank the next morning before she handed over my grand daughter. Is there something you're not telling me? I lied like a lawyer, grinning at her and swearing I was fine. You can't lie to women. I should know that by now. She called Mandy at work from work and Mandy told her the truth. I couldn't lie to her she told me when she called me at Gloria's house right after.

Shit, I thought. She'll be here in fifteen minutes. It took maybe twenty-five but I heard her screech into the driveway and slam the car door while I was cooking a hot dog for my littlest girl. Gloria ran into my arms, tears flying and then almost immediately pulled away and punched me in the chest.

"You weren't going to tell us, were you!" she said. "How could you *do* that! God damn it, Dad, we deserve to know!"

"Well, now you do. Do you feel better or worse then you did before?"

"I feel terrible! How do you expect me to feel," she yelled.

"I would like you to feel good. To be your usual smiling self," I said. "That's why I wasn't going to say anything. There's nothing you can do about it so why burden you with all that grief? You see? I don't want you to be unhappy. There's no need."

"Mandy said you were leaving. Were we ever going to see you again?" she said, accusatory.

"Of course. And I *was* going to tell you, just not right now. Do you think you can keep this from your sister?" I asked. She said, don't even ask.

"Okay. I'll tell her." We talked for a while, all the usual questions, then we packed up the baby and went to find Jessica. She was off on Wednesdays but Randy worked so Gloria felt there was a good chance she would be home. She was.

I gave it to her fast but as tenderly as I could. Jessica is a tough kid, a Capricorn like her father and not real emotional, so she took it without a lot of wailing, none in fact, quiet tears and long hugs more our style. I answered all the same questions then told her Mandy and I were going on the road for a bit. She wanted to know why, why was I leaving them? I said I have to get Mandy established somewhere where she can make a life for herself. I could see the unspoken 'what about us' in her eyes. I love you girls. You know that. And I love Mandy, too. You know that as well. You guys have your lives on track, you're both smart, beautiful kids. If I asked you to move away from here, would either of you want to go? They looked at each other and me but didn't answer. I want you to think about that, okay?

Mandy is going to be left with no one, I continued. She isn't nearly as, oh, resilient as you two. I have to help her. Please don't be angry with me for that. Or with her. You know she loves you guys, and Celina, and I hope you'll be there for each other, not adding the when I'm gone that was implicit in the conversation. They both said they would.

"She'll need you. And you two could stand to have a normal woman in your lives. Promise me you won't abandon her. Actually, she's my executor so you won't be able to," I grinned. "Not completely."

"Are you going to get married?" Jessica asked.

"I don't know. We haven't talked about it. Why?"

"Cause we'd want to be there if you did."

"Oh. Okay. I promise I'll give you forty eight hours notice," I said. "Kidding. I don't really see the need but maybe." We had a big group hug and I promised to call at least once a week, then we all cried, even Celina although she didn't know why, just that everybody else was.

As I drove home that evening, the mutual support aspect of life after death, life for the living, kept creeping back at me. I wanted to get Mandy away from her grasping mother, worthless brothers and sniping aunts. But was that necessarily a good idea? Would she be better off having familiarity around her even if the familiar people were going to be of no help to her? At least they were around. There was a certain comfort in knowing you had a family in the area even if you never spoke to them. And if I moved her, how often would she see the girls? They would probably not hang out together regardless, see each other a few times during the death aftermath and then maybe never again but if she was ten hours away, there was no maybe about it. They would talk on the phone at increasingly longer intervals and then stop at some point. That would be bad for all of them in my opinion.

What would be ideal would be to get *all* of them to move. Jessica was certainly young enough to be footloose and the Carolinas were full of good colleges. She and Mandy could go to school together! That would make for some step mother/daughter bonding. And drive the Hell Bitch just crazy. I'd have to talk to Randy, see what his long-term plans were. I knew he loved the restaurant business, had talked about having his own place some day. Maybe he'd want to try it in the South.

Gloria might be willing once the divorce crap was ironed out. She had a bunch of local friends but she was adventurous, not at all like Paul. She might think a fresh start in a new place was a great idea. And she and Mandy had gotten much closer in the last six months, talking decorating and antiques on the phone, Gloria asking kid questions, advise that you would normally go to your mother for. If you had a normal mother. Gloria sure didn't, not until now, but Mandy was friend and mother combined. I'd have to find out more about the new boy friend. Gloria'd been playing that one real close to the vest—just friends, that kind of thing.

I said to Mandy that night, will you take care of the girls, you know, after, thinking how subtle I was, laying the groundwork. Of course I will, she said. You know I love them. And they love you, I said but I'm worried about all of you. You're going to need each other. I wish there was some way to, oh, combine the family. What do you mean, she asked and I said I'm not sure, maybe if we got married? It would make your relationship to them more concrete. You see what I'm getting at?

She stared at me, her brows scrunched up, the thought wheels spinning. Okay, she said. If that's what you want. Yeah, I said, that's what I want. Besides, I thought, that whole widow thing plays really well in the South. I only wished I'd been a military officer as well. That would really jazz up her reputation, the widow Mrs. Major Barkley. I could picture Mandy in a long Scarlet O'Hara gown with a mint julep in her hand, some one-armed, gray uniformed bearded gent telling her proud he was to have served in her husband's regiment, what a great soldier he had been, an inspiration to his men. Tragic lose. Tragic indeed, particularly for me.

How do you want to do it, she asked? On a beach somewhere maybe, I replied. We'll see. Something simple, us and the kids.

And your mom I added hastily when I saw her look. And yours, she said. Maybe, maybe not. Depends on the time and place I should think. That was the end of our wedding planning which was about as far as we'd ever gotten.

She has the ring, has for a few years now and there was some hazy discussion about a back yard wedding in Jack's marvelous garden but his illness put that on hold and then Tex and then Jack's death. Planning a marriage during all that mourning, there's no way to do it. We were on permanent hold until now. Now it was now or never and there really wasn't much of a down side for Mandy. It was like the best pre-nup you could have, a year of marriage and then you get it all, no wrangling over assets, no custody fights. No alimony of course but she would never be able to complain about how shitty her ex-husband was to her, what a cheap prick and lousy father. And she could be the demure widow lady if she wanted. Personally, I hoped she went line dancing in a country-western bar on each anniversary of my demise, drank a little too much and laughed till she was hoarse. Remember me with your boots on and a long neck in your hand. Yee hah!

The next morning I called Gloria before she left for work and said I want you to think about a couple of things and then explained my concept in a broad out line, she and Mandy opening a business together. And maybe her doing Mandy and I a huge, unusual favor. For a fee of course, I added. Just think about it, I said. And don't say anything to Mandy, I want to flesh it out a little more before I talk to her. She's not thinking real clearly right now.

Where, she wanted to know, me hoping to postpone that information until after she started to like the idea. In the South, the Carolinas probably. Why not here, she asked? Cause here sucks. The Carolinas are much nicer. But I like it here, she said. Just think about it, okay, I said. No commitments, we can work out the details later if you agree in theory. I'll call you tomorrow.

I waited an hour before calling Jessica. She was a notorious late sleeper but I woke her anyway. Get up, sleepy head, it's after nine. I'm up, she said. Have you thought about where you want to go to school full time, I asked? She was taking classes at the community college, twelve credits last semester, but didn't want to go full time to a 'real' college till she knew what she wanted to study. Smart kid, saving me all that money.

West Chester I guess, she said. Have you looked at any schools in the south, I asked. Duke, Wake Forrest, North Carolina, there's a bunch of them.

Daddy, she said, as if she wasn't exactly sure who she was speaking to. Yes Angel, I responded. Why are you asking that now? Cause life is short and you need to get moving, Sweetheart. I want to see you squared away on college. Soon, I said, not wanting to add the obvious 'before I croak.' I'll send you brochures and stuff, if we see a cool place, is that okay? Sure, that would be fine, she said then yawned in my ear. Okay, sorry to wake you. I'll call tomorrow. Bye Angel, I love you.

That afternoon I got on the net and down loaded about fifty pages on southern schools, stuffed it all in a manila envelope with a short note and mailed it to her. She'd be amazed at how far we had traveled so fast if she didn't look at the Pennsylvania post mark.

The next day I packed a little, farted around with the motor home, then called a realtor I liked but of course didn't trust and told him I might be selling the house and wanted him to have the listing. I asked him to run the neighborhood comps and see what he thought I could get for it. He told me he would be out my way in an hour, could he stop and look around so I had to straighten up. He was on time, for a realtor, and did a quick tour, admiring Mandy's painting and decorating. No problem, he said. At a fair price, I can sell it in a couple weeks, this place is great. Yeah, yeah, I bet you say that to all the prospective listings, I thought but I gave him a key and told him we would be out of town for a few weeks, feel free to show it if you have someone really interested. I don't want it on the fucking breakfast tour, Chuck. You can show it personally but that's it. Deal? Deal, he said. We shook hands and he left. I thought of it as planning ahead. If we decided not to move, I wasn't contractually obligated. If we did want to, maybe he'd get a buyer interested while we were away. He had wanted to execute the listing paper work on it right then but I said I was busy, he'd have to trust me on it. If he had said that to me, I'd have thrown him out the door. Fortunately, builders have slightly better reputations then realtors.

The owners of Mandy's shop wanted to take us out to dinner that night and as soon as I saw their faces in the vestibule of the restaurant, I knew that they knew. There was no way they could hide the concern and pity that crept into their wary smiles and the hesitation, ever so slight, in the proffered hands, like whatever I had just might be contagious.

The meal was good, the conversation stilted, neither of them addressing me directly that I can remember, Mandy there to carry that load for all of us but she was straining by desert. She would glance at me occasionally with a look that was an apology, whether for telling them or for including me in the going away celebration I'm not sure but either way, it was clear that my inclusion with their knowledge put a blanket over the affair more suffocating then a funeral shroud. I was glad to be gone and Mandy said she was sorry in the car while we were still in the parking lot.

"It's okay, Sunshine. It's not a secret but it *is* probably best left unspoken. Christ, I felt like a leper," I laughed. "Those poor people may never go out to eat again."

"My lobster was good," she said.

"So was my rib eye, by golly," I said grinning at her. "And it didn't cost us a dime."

We climbed straight into bed, me thinking love, Mandy apparently thinking death because when I snuggled into her, she snuggled back but put her head into my chest and started to weep. Don't cry, Sweetheart, you're going to be okay. When she didn't respond, I said, I have a few ideas to help you cope. She still didn't answer and I thought she had drifted off. As I was scrunching around in the pillows to join her, she said, like what?

Well, I said, like opening your own shop. Maybe with a partner? She opened one eye or at least I could only see one and it was open. Who, she asked? Gloria. Oh. She'd do that? I think she might, if we work on her a bit. Where, was the next question. In the Carolinas probably, I said. I can't leave my mom alone. Yes you can and she's not alone. She has her sons. That got a harsh laugh and I laughed too, neither of us having to remind the other how much help they had been to her so far.

"Like I said, Mandy, if you can't get away from her, then invite her to join you. Send her out to shop yard sales and flea markets. God knows she's had enough practice buying shit."

"She won't move. Everybody she knows lives here."

"So that means you have to as well? Bull shit! What would your dad tell you to do?"

"Move," she said.

"Far, far away," I added, "to a place you like where nobody knows your business. Isn't that how it goes?" Jack had often complained that the little burg we lived in had the biggest population of gossips and busy bodies per square block of any town in America.

"Yeah, but he never did."

"Exactly. All the more reason why you should. Make her the offer. If she says no, you have a clear conscience."

"Easy for you to say."

"Everything is these days," I said.

"I'm sorry," she sobbed, "but I'm scared! I don't want to be alone."

"That's why I'm trying to hook you and Gloria up. You can help each other. And she's full of life, not like your…" I let it go there, a few words too late.

"My mother. I know you hate her but she's my mom. I have to take care of her!"

"No. You don't! And neither did Jack. Now stop it! Live your own fucking life, not hers! And I don't hate her. I just don't like her. I don't like what she did to her husband and I hate what she's trying to do to her daughter. She's completely selfish and it's hurting you. I won't tolerate it any more. You're going to make her take responsibility for her own actions. No more sponging. It's time for Clara to grow up! So you can have your own life."

That was it for the night. We slept, tossing, waking each other more than once, me her when I took a leak and again when a pain sat me straight up with a shriek, her me with a garbled, vocal dream and when she peed some time after I did. I got out of bed at seven, Mandy gone already. I felt grouchy and unrested. There was coffee left, thank you, Jesus, but no significant other. She returned a half-hour later in her nightgown and slippers, looking glum.

"Where ya been, Sunnyshine?" I asked, grabbing her around the waist, trying for a grope and a kiss. She submitted but only for a second.

"I went to say goodbye to mom."

"And?"

"And what?" she said.

"And how did it go, what did you say to her?" thinking if ever there was a time to tell Clara something that she didn't want to hear, this was it. The Silent Treatment doesn't work for shit if you're hundreds of miles away.

"I told her we were thinking about moving, soon, far away."

"Let me guess. Did she pout first and then cry or go straight to tears?" I asked.

"She cried. But then she pouted."

"Good, good. I don't want to worry that she's losing her touch."

"No chance. She was in rare form," Mandy said.

"Had her game face on did she," I said, scowling in imitation.

"Oh, yeah. Big time," she said.

"Did she tell you to have a good time at least?"

"Grudgingly."

"So you're not a hundred percent convinced she really wants you to go, eh? Shocking, shocking I say."

"She was just a little bit pissed," Mandy said, showing me a pinch of air between her thumb and index finger.

"Did you offer to take her along?"

"She pretended not to hear me."

"She's good at that. Don't tell me bad news cause my ears clog up. That's my girl. Can't say I'm going to miss that smile. What's that you say? What smile? Good point. I must be thinking of someone else.

"Hey, Sweetheart, you tried," I said hugging her. "This will give her something to think about at least, while we're away. Maybe she'll realize she can't dictate to you any more, you're going to do what you want for a change."

"Fat chance. My mother?"

"Come on," I said. "Let's go have an adventure."

Chapter Eleven

We rumbled out of town in our bread box at ten that morning. It took an hour before hand to shit, shower and shave, another to put on our make up and set our hair and still another to load coolers, back backs and nap sacks. Our itinerary was carved in stone all the way to the Maryland line, about fifteen miles south down U.S. One. After that we were going to wing it. I would have wandered through Delaware then back into Maryland and Virginia and taken the Chesapeake Bay Bridge Tunnel over to Norfolk but Mandy wanted to bypass all of coastal Virginia, saying she didn't want to live there so why waste the time. I had to agree with her time wise, so we jumped on I-95 like we were off to Florida, this time though, having to go all the way around Baltimore because motor homes and their gas bottles had a HASMAT restriction designed to keep people like us and/or retired school teachers from blowing themselves up under Baltimore harbor.

We bypassed Richmond on 295 then cut east on I-64, ending up in Norfolk hours, maybe even days, sooner then we would have if we had taken my scenic route. I-54 turns back on itself south of greater Norfolk then disappears completely so we took 464 south from there, regressing from interstate, to interstate under construction, to interstate of the future. By the time we crossed into North Carolina, we were back on a U.S. One style highway with lots of stops in little towns and speed enforcement again delegated to local authorities. We spent the night, several hours of the night anyway, in the parking lot of a Denny's just outside of Maple, having passed up similar accommodations in Currituck and too tired to press on to Coinjock. About four AM we were politely asked to vacate the parking lot by a member of the Maple Police Department, the only member I suspect based on the old station wagon he was using as a patrol vehicle. Despite its proximity to the ocean and the good manners of its constabulary, we decided Maple was not going to be our future home.

Some time during the night, state highway 168 had morphed into federal highway 158 but as we were still heading south along the coast and there were no other roads available, we pressed on, stopping an hour after our eviction between Kitty Hawk and Kill Devil Hills to climb up a sand dune and watch the sun rise.

We were facing another travel decision, this one whether to stay on the barrier islands of the Cape Hatteras National Seashore or cut back inland and wend our way around Pamlico Sound on the bay side. Mandy had two opinions, one being that we probably could not afford to live anywhere near Cape Hatteras even if we found something suitable for sale and, as a corollary, the place was so fucking remote from any source of supply for anything one might reasonably expect to sell, that it made a business location for anything other than suntan lotion seem far fetched. The other opinion was that the bay side was too, well, weird. Like the upper reaches of the Chesapeake Bay, too remote and too rural, hill billyesque almost. Having no direct experience with the area, I had taken her word for it. After looking at the map though, with towns like Gum Neck, Stumpy Point and Lowland scattered about and seeing all the areas shaded in with blue lines and little grass symbols that indicated wet lands and swamps, I was inclined to skip the bay side too.

We did, staying on 158, then Branch 158, the really scenic route. We even resisted the urge to turn west on U.S. 64 when it popped up below Nags Head, the relationship between this 64 and the indecisive one that petered out around Norfolk unclear.

Route 12, two lanes of asphalt paved on top of a hundred miles of sand with a short ferry ride at Hatteras Inlet near the end, gets you from Nags Head to Ocracoke where you get to take a long ferry ride to go back to the main land. It's a beautiful drive, the ocean on one side and the bay on the other, sometimes so close together that you feel like you could dip your hands in them simultaneously. The little towns on the way, all seven of them, were far too nautical cute and summer home wealthy to be in our price range but they were fun to look at. That long ferry, we discovered, takes *reservations* and that coupled with our non-car status nearly had us stranded on Ocracoke Island but I persuaded the captain, my twenty may have helped, to lug us out of there when he ended up with an extra slot on the deck of the old, flat bed tug boat.

We landed on Cedar Island an hour later and drove slowly through a time warp so complete that but for the crop of current vehicles scattered about, the whole peninsula could have been a nineteen twenties movie set. There were a half dozen tiny villages hugging the coast, each looking much like the others and all of them looking like one decent storm would send the white man packing, opening up the area for resettlement by the Indians. It was a tranquil, time-forgotten kind of place but I did not get a warm and fuzzy feeling from the locals that we passed. I felt more like an alien just disembarked from my saucer, the Earthlings wary, not curious.

The last bead on this string of pearls, Beauford, was also the largest and most urbane if that word isn't a stretch when used to describe a pre-civil war town of maybe a thousand. It seemed like every building had been completely restored to its original condition, all immaculately maintained, the yards and gardens perfect, the streets and sidewalks swept, even the tiny business district impeccably costumed in antebellum grandeur. And there was commerce, actual shops and stores, restaurants and museums. It was so quaint it almost made you suspicious, like who are they kidding, this place was built last year. They could seriously have set up a tollbooth and charged the out-of-towners just to drive through. Colonial Williamsburg in microcosm, without all the actors in costumes. We both loved it. And knew in about forty seconds that we could not afford it. We left town wistfully and then Mandy pointed out that maybe our children's children might be accepted as native Beaufordians but that we would have to out live every single one of the current inhabitants to be accorded the same status, marked as tourists by our impossible Yankee accents, never ridding ourselves of this most obvious, and damning, impediment to acceptance. It was a nice place to visit but I wouldn't want to live there, I said, both of us laughing as we began to detour around yet another inlet thrust like an irregular dick into the swampy low lands that made up most of the territory that we had covered since daybreak.

"What's next," Mandy asked?

"Morehead City," I replied. "A metropolis according to the map."

"Is that good?"

"Damn if I know," I laughed. "If it's a big Beauford it might be." It wasn't. It was more like any town outside any city anywhere.

"Nah," I said as we coasted down the west side of the bridge into the city proper.

"Me neither. Too industrial."

"Okay. Let's keep cruisin'." We turned south outside of town and crossed another bay, sound or river. I couldn't keep track of them all let alone the creeks, kills and streams that interdicted this country like the varicose veins on the leg of a skinny old woman. On the other side of town was a shore resort community completely different from the industrial port city we had just vacated. It looked like a fun place to spend a low-key spring break or to bring your pre-teen kids on your weeklong summer vacation. It did *not* look like a good place for either an antique shop or for higher education. We had lunch in a nautical brewpub, crab sandwiches and Lookout Lager, presumably named for the local lighthouse and not for its effect on your equilibrium. We brought our road map in with us, no sense standing out from the other tourists, most of whom presumably knew where they were going or at least where they were.

"Where are we going?" Mandy asked after we had received our beers.

"Back out on the main highway at….Cape Carteret it looks like. Named for Jimmy's daughter, what was her name, the homely one? Not Chelsea, she's Bill's homely daughter."

"Will you stop it," she said. "You are just evil."

"Come to think of it, who was the last president that had a decent looking kid? Kennedy? It sure wasn't Lyndon Baines. He used to pull on his daughter's ears after they got on him for yanking on the beagles."

"Good question," Mandy said, giggling. "Not Nixon. Did Ford even have any kids?"

"I couldn't say. If he did, he probably dropped them on their heads while they were infants."

"Yeah and he was only president for what, two weeks?"

"Maybe a hair longer," I said. "Two years plus or minus I think."

"Then came Carter and…Damn it! What *was* her name? I keep thinking Hillary."

"Then your buddy Reagan. He had kids, the weirdo son and the dikey daughter at least. Although I'm pretty sure Nancy was his daughter before they were married."

"Bastard!" she yelled. "I loved Reagan!" She told me that when we were first dating and I rarely passed on an opportunity to poke fun at our economically challenged, nap-prone former leader.

"I know, I know," I said. "He made us believe in ourselves again blah, blah, supply side voodoo blah, blah." Mandy gave me a two fisted finger, fingers, and told me to go fuck myself then called me a Clinton democrat which I knew was a mighty insult reserved for only the most fuzzy headed, wishy washy liberal types. "A great president," I said wagging my finger at her. "And a great man!" I continued, then we both started laughing so hard I was afraid they would ask us to leave.

We went over another bridge and descended this time into a giant shopping center. If Morehead City at the north end of the resort islands was where the locals worked, than this was surely where they came to shop. At least for food, beer and gasoline. We stopped long enough to get some of each then got out of there. But curiously, as soon as we cleared the last of the twenty-first century landmarks, we were back in the nineteenth. Just outside of town, the road was fairly littered with antique shops, vegetable stands and a few odd combinations that were offering for sale anything they had ever owned along with whatever they grew.

After driving slowly past a couple repositories of the old and the overpriced, we decided to stop at a few and check out the possible competition. I knew it meant the end of our progress for the day but I didn't care. Where were we in a hurry to get to? We drove from one little shop to another, browsing the merchandise idly and, after an hour or so, I was ready to call it quits. I got Mandy back in the motor home, hoping to find a place to camp, but we hadn't gone a mile when she yelled 'stop' at the top of her voice. We have to go in *there*, she said, pointing across my face at an old timber barn, huge, weather beaten and gray and seemingly under siege by an army of rag tag, cast off....junk. How else to describe all the crap that was surrounding the place? Isn't it beautiful, she exclaimed, me thinking if you're Fred Sanford but she was positively aglow so in we went.

The inside was exactly like the outside, so crammed full of *stuff* that it would have taken two days to even cursorily peruse all the merchandise. Mandy was immediately in deep conversation with a hoary old woman who she discovered in short order, was a native Down Easter as the Carolina territory we were about out of was colloquially known. And a pack rat, self described and unrepentant. She might have been called a garbage picker in a more urbane environment. Or an incredibly shrewd long-range investor if she was making enough money.

I thought at first she was mistaking Mandy for some long lost offspring as I watched them laughing and chattering but she apparently remembered who she was well enough because she started telling Mandy her life's story about one minute after we walked through the door.

I listened to enough of their conversation to realize that we were going to be there for a while and there was plenty of stuff to look at so I wasn't bored. Every ten minutes or so I'd circle back to the big slab of oak slapped across two whiskey barrels that served as the check out counter just to make sure that there was no chance they were wrapping it up. A brass National cash register and a small clear space on the wooden slab were the only indicators of the checkout function. That and Mandy and the old lady leaning in from either side, heads about twelve inches apart, both mouths and all four hands moving nonstop.

I spent two hours in that barn and I knew the entire conversation would be replayed for me that evening if I continued to abstain from the socializing so I wandered up to them at last and said, hey, you two know each other? What a coincidence. They stopped talking long enough for Mandy to introduce me to Greta and I stuck out my hand. She was smiling as she took it but her expression turned instantly to a deep frown and she dropped my hand like it burned her. She looked up at me, her expression changing from puzzlement to something like resignation. I'm sorry, boy, she said. It's okay I said, then added, you two should be well acquainted by now.

Isn't this fabulous, Mandy said. Yes it is I agreed, thinking how would you know, you haven't seen any of it but I guess Greta had been giving her an oral inventory because Mandy began to tick off dozens of unusual items that were allegedly residing some where inside this cavern of antiquities. I personally had found all manner of odd-ball treasures in there, most of them surrounded by a peanut gallery of crap, at least it was crap to my untrained eye, but I could see that with a week or two of sorting and organizing, with the aid of a chain gang of laborers and a forty cubic yard dumpster, Greta had the inventory for an extremely well stocked, huge and eclectic antique shop. The average person probably took one look at the disorganization and the dirt and backed out of the front door thinking of an immediate shower and a change of clothing. Mandy wasn't nearly so squeamish.

"Greta's thinking of selling the place," Mandy said.

"Ah," I replied. "Mind if I look around, ma'am? Outside," I added, having just spent two hours looking around inside.

"My name's Greta, not ma'am and you make yourself right at home, young man. Amanda and I will join you directly, I just need to show her a few special things I have in the back."

Wherever the back was. The whole barn looked like the back of something. Maybe a landfill. I walked outside, looking now with other eyes, not as a bored follower in Mandy's exploration of the Down East but as a savvy real-estate investor type looking over a plum property. I could see right away that this piece of fruit had a few rotten spots, had seen it inside as well, but studying the buildings and grounds now in this new light, there was also a lot of potential.

Greta's homestead must have been just that a couple hundred years ago, a coastal farm complex, a main house, a big timber barn and a bunch of out buildings, all wood clad, the Victorian house in clapboard, the barn in wide, vertical plank with batten strips, the out buildings in leftovers. Judging by the hedgerows of trees and brambles that formed a rough box around the buildings, she still owned quite a few acres of the original holding and even mowed it once or twice a season. The 'lawn' within the box and especially the area around the structures, was shadowed by dozens of live oaks, some pre-colonial with trunks five and six feet in diameter, their branches blossoming upward into massive, moss-laden crowns that created individual mushrooms of shade a hundred feet in circumference.

It could be a park with enough work and it didn't hurt a bit that the ocean was just out there beyond the farthest hedgerow, a hundred yards of grassy dune the only barrier between the long leaf and southern yellow pines that defined the end of the back yard and the breakers rolling onto a strip of sandy beach at the foot of the dunes. And the whole farm area sat up on a small bluff that probably explained why it was still intact this close to the ocean and this close to ground zero of probably a dozen hurricanes over the lifetime of the structures. It spoke well of their construction.

I walked from the view side all the way around the buildings, trying to visualize them without the infestation of un-priced antiques and junk that surrounded them like dandruff on a dark suit. The house needed a telephone book of sandpaper and a tanker load of paint but from the outside at least, it would be beautiful after that. The barn, I thought, should be left pretty much as was. It *looked* like an antique, rustic and charming, the faded and flaking red paint mostly gone, just enough still there to give the weathered pine planks a patina of color. At some point in the last ten years or so, Greta must have sprung for a new standing seam roof, the metal panels and vertical seams a muted red matching the faded siding nicely. Some new gravel in the parking area, lots of flowers in the planting beds and some good signage and the place would grab the tourists heading to or from the Crystal Coast beaches like a child sucked into the Magic Kingdom. And we wouldn't let them out till they were just as broke.

Mandy and Greta were coming out of the barn door as I came around the building. It was late afternoon by now and I was really tired. And hurting some. I wanted to lay down for a bit, snuggle with my Sunshine, maybe 'you know' a little.

"Greta," I said as I drew even with them, not waiting for a break in their never-ending conversation. "Would you mind if we parked here tonight," gesturing toward the motor home.

"Don't you two ever talk?" she said to Mandy, the two of them laughing at my blank look.

"We've already been invited, Chance," Mandy informed me. She rarely called me by my given name, one of them, the whole mess being Lassiter Chance Barkley, Chance Mom's maiden name, Lassiter some obscure cowboy ancestor of Tex's. I had been 'Last Chance' Barkley so long growing up that even my mother gave up calling me Chance and adopted Last. It didn't bother me as a teenager. It had a certain panache and was a hell of a lot better then being a boy named Lass which had been the reason for my last fist fight prior to the guard and lawyer, a class mate picking the wrong time on the wrong day to tease me for the millionth time. I beat him into an ambulance, remembering nothing after the first fully cocked right hand delivered with everything I had to the point of his wide, zitty nose. He was a lot bigger then me and a consummate bully. I lost a week of school to the suspension but he didn't return for another week after that, even then a raccoon eyed, puffy caricature of his former strutting arrogance. I was a fucking hero then, my rep made for the duration of my school years, always 'Last' after that, never Lass even to my closest friends, a berserker not to be trifled with. I wished I could remember the fight but it wasn't even a blur, only the accounts of the bystanders giving the event life in my memories.

"Invited?" I repeated absently.

"Look down there, son," Greta said pointing toward the ocean. "See that old picnic table under them pines?" I didn't but nodded anyway. "You drive that old bus a yours right in under those trees. There's a outlet nailed to the big one on the left. You can plug in there. There's a flood light on the other one, on a seein' eye cell, it'll come on at dusk. You want to, there's a path down to the water. Ain't nobody around, you can skinny dip if ya like. Come back up around eight, we'll have dinner on my porch," this time gesturing toward a screened in room on the back of the house.

"Sounds great. Thanks, Greta."

"Hush, boy. Take your lady and go have some fun."

I parked us in the designated space, out fitted as described and with a beautiful view of the breakers slapping pleasantly against the shore. Her uncle had a trailer down here for a few years, Mandy informed me. She finally 'ran his worthless ass off' back in the late seventies.

"He's dead now," she added.

"So, are you going to tell me about our hostess?" I asked as we sat looking at the ocean through the boughs of the evergreens.

"Let's go swimming," she replied, then swiveled in her chair and scampered into the back, pulling off her clothing as she went. I caught her at panties only and had them off and her down on the bed in a half second, my nudity lagging a minute behind. We made quick and noisy love, then she hopped up and began to rummage through our clothing for a swimsuit. I would have dozed off but she wasn't having any of that.

"I sexed you up, now you're going swimming," the price, I guess, for getting my rocks off. In the afternoon, on a week day. Small price indeed.

"Okay! Let's do it."

There was a clear path through the dunes as if someone came down here regularly. It ended in a straight line demarcated by a wooden slat fence, the kind used in the north to hold back snow-drifts. Beyond was a sandy beach, fifty yards maybe at low tide and not real fine sand but good enough to lie down on in comfort and terrific for shelling. And the water was lovely, as blue and clean beyond the breaker line as any I've ever seen. And warm, almost hot, delightful and soothing like a whirlpool. We splashed and body surfed for a while then flopped on the sand and baked in the setting summer sun. That's when Mandy began to tell me about her new friend.

"Greta's a bit odd isn't she," I prompted. She looked at me like I'd made another Reagan joke then grinned and nodded.

"Eccentric," she said laughing. "Okay, a fruit cake but I like her a lot."

"Our kind of people," I grinned.

"Yep. Only she's lived here I guess all her life and she wants to do some other stuff–she was a little vague about that–before she's....too old?"

"Or too dead," I said before I thought better of it. "What all did you talk about?"

"She's a little weird. She said she'd been expecting us, that it was about time we made it, real straightforward, not mysterious. I asked her what she meant and she said, I knew someone was going to come here and fall in love with the place, let her get away. Like she couldn't leave till her replacement arrived. Very odd but like I said, not hush hush mysterious, she just came out and said it."

"And we're the new care takers?"

"Yeah. If we want to be. She has it all worked out. I'll let her explain it but there's like a lease with a buy out, she knows how to deal with the existing merchandise, as opposed to new stuff we might have to sell, she has appraisals, all kinds of stuff. She has a whole plan, she was just waiting for the new owners to come. Weird, isn't it?"

"You bet. But kind of cool too. It's a great set up, would be with enough work. How'd she know you were the one," I asked?

"Us. She made that very clear. A couple. And she has the second sight. Clairvoyant. She knew it was us as soon as she touched my hand she said."

"When did you tell her about me?"

"I didn't. But I know why you're asking. I saw her face when she shook your hand."

"And she said she was sorry. I assumed you told her."

"Nope, not a word. After you wandered off, she said 'You are going to be just fine, Amanda. And he ain't as close as he thinks he is.'" I didn't say anything to that. We got up then and went back to the campsite. I got beers out of the motor home and we sat at the rickety picnic table.

"I thought maybe she *was* psychic," Mandy said after we were comfortable. "Until she said she saw me with children," this followed by a bark of harsh laughter. "She said 'It ain't real clear to me, there's something odd about the kids,' about their lineage she said, like either that was murky or her 'vision' of them was, I'm not sure what she meant." Mandy snorted again then said, "We know that's not going to happen."

"Ah, there's something I, ah, probably ought to mention?" I said.

"What?"

"Hold on," I said. "It's a hypothetical, something I've done some, ah, research on, that's all."

"What?"

"Well. We could have a kid, if you wanted to." She looked at me like I was a two-headed idiot so I tried to explain what someone like that might come up with. "Artificial insemination. Your egg, my sperm, someone else's womb."

"You are a moron, you know that don't you?"

"I've always sort of known that, yeah, but this is different. This is a moronic *plan*!"

"Okay. Let me see if I understand. First we harvest my eggs which I assume means another laparoscopy." When I just smirked she gave me a nasty frown and another hard 'what.'

"I, ah, we already, ah, have some. Compliments of Doctor Hardy." When her frown deepened I added, "Hey, he was in there anyway, I thought what the hell, can't hurt."

"Fine. Should I assume you jerked off on them and now they're in storage somewhere?"

"You make it sound easy. There's a whole big ritual involved. I had to wear a Polynesian fertility outfit and do this really complex dance while I beat off. Christ, I worked my ass off for that jism."

"And where was I while you were slaving away over your hot pecker?"

"Resting comfortably in the recovery room."

"Was this before or after you beat up the lawyer?"

"After. There was no sense going through all that work if Dr. Hardy couldn't get any eggs. But he did so after my conference with the state police, I went up to old Doc Hardy's masturbation parlor and suited up."

"Well that part was easy. I didn't feel a thing," she said.

"Speak for your self."

"I am. I hope you got blisters."

"Nah. It was fun. You wanna see?"

"Shut up. Who, might I inquire, would carry this love child, smart guy?"

"Gloria. Keeps it in the family. I thought that was a nice touch."

"You *are* insane. Why would she ever want to do that?"

"Because she loves her Daddy. And her stepmother to be. Besides, it's her only chance to have a little brother."

"Kind of a high price to pay for another sibling," Mandy said.

"I offered to pay her. I don't think she'll take it. So, what do you think?"

"That you're crazy, just what I said. You're creating a fatherless child. Have you thought of that?"

"Absolutely. But, well, look at it from the other side. You would make a terrific mother and you'd have…"

"Something to remember you by."

"Yeah. It sounds so egocentric like that but I guess there's really no better way to describe it. It would be a form of immortality, too, not that that's any less egocentric. More so even."

"He would be a wild child. You realize that. I don't think you're doing me any big favor here."

"True. The wild child part. I don't see you being big on discipline. Lots of love, though. I suspect Gloria would be a pretty active sister, considering. And he'd have Celina for a real big sister, big aunt, whatever. Think about it, that's all. It was just something to consider."

"Okay," she said as she leaned over and kissed me. "I will. Now, we need to get ready for dinner."

Greta greeted us with a shout from eighty yards out, the two of us walking hand in hand up the back yard in the twilight. "Y'all hungry I hope," she hollered.

She'd made fried chicken, spicy and succulent, garlic mashed potatoes and some kind of greens sautéed in ham fat. It was all delicious and I ate too much for health or comfort but not nearly enough for satiation of flavor. We were pushed back from the table on the porch, the dishes stacked off to the side, coffee laced with apple brandy just cooling in our mugs, when Greta looked me in the eye, hers twinkling like fire flies in the candle light and said, "so what'a ya think a my proposition, Last Chance Barkley?"

I was plump with the food, relaxed as a hot old lizard, gazing out at the surf sparkling in the moonlit distance. I saw her staring but the name use threw me some and I was slow to reply.

"Come on, boy. That ain't a stumper. Tell me what yer thinkin'."

"I'm thinking you are a damn fine cook and I'm feeling pretty good."

"Bullshit! You think I'm a crazy old woman who's runnin' some kind a con. Well, you're half right. You figure out which half after, once I'm done talkin'. Fair?" I nodded as she continued, apparently going to no matter how I reacted. "I told your beautiful girl here a lot about myself. She tell you?" Greta asked.

"Some of it, yes. You're clairvoyant, is that correct?"

"Paush," she said, waving her hand at invisible insects. "I know things. I see 'em in my mind, mostly when I touch people. But sometimes I just know 'em like you know your own name. I knew you were coming. You believe that?"

"I believe in the possibility, certainly. But how do you know it's us that you've been waiting for, not some other couple that might arrive tomorrow or next week?"

"You cut right to it, don't ya? I like that. But that's going to take an act of faith on your part. I can't tell you how my mind works, don't even know myself, I just know y'all are the ones I been waitin' for. Now, you want the details?"

"Sure. I'm fascinated, don't get me wrong. And I love your place. It's beautiful here."

"Good. You'll still have time left to enjoy it. More then you think. Here's what we need to do. Y'all take over here for me, run the place, sell the merchandise, live in the house. It's yours, you're going to buy it from me."

I started to protest but she held up her hand and shushed me like you might a noisy child in church. "Hear me out. I had the place appraised last month, three different outfits," she added, sliding sheets of paper across the table to me, produced from a manila envelope that was in her lap. "They're pretty much all the same. They're based on the as-is condition, what the place is worth right now, before you start fixin' her up like I know you're both dyin' to do," she said. "And they don't include the stock or the furnishings. We're going to sell that stuff, except anything y'all might like to keep for you ownselves. Or for your kids," she said, winking at me.

"That middle one," she said pointing at the appraisals, "that'll be the sale price." I looked down at a figure that struck me as extremely reasonable, cheap even considering everything that was included. But it was also far more then we could afford prior to my death, which of course was the irony in the situation. Once I died and my mortgage insurance paid off our house and she sold it, then Mandy could probably swing the deal, especially if the business was demonstrably viable by then.

"We can't," I told her. "We don't have the money."

"Yes you do. Enough anyway. I don't need it in a lump sum, don't even want it that way. I want enough to get me movin' and a income to keep me goin'. The income'll come from the antiques. Everything I have, that's worth a damn anyway, has a red dot on it. Markin' it as mine. You can charge what ever you want for the stuff, that's up to you. But we split the money. You take the time to clean somethin' up, you charge more for it, you make more off it. So do I. You're goin' to do all the work to get the place presentable, you're goin' to open a classy place and charge a hell of a lot more than I can get in this dump. People just won't abide high prices here. They think it's a junk shop. Y'all ain't gonna have that problem."

"Mutually beneficial gains from trade. Classic economic theory. I like it," I said. "But…"

"How much do I want now and how do you pay me off completely? Ten grand ought to do it for now. And you have options on the buy out. You could sell the place. Fix it up real nice, probably double your money. You make the shop work for you, you can get a regular mortgage. You might even piece off a couple nice ocean front lots to some Wilmington lawyers, just keep the road frontage and a few acres. Course you'd have lawyers for neighbors. I couldn't abide that but that'd be up to y'all."

"I'm not selling a square inch," Mandy said. "Especially not to some friggin' attorney!" We all laughed at that and then Greta asked if we'd like to see the house.

I was expecting a ramshackle collection of discards similar to the items littering the grounds, cleaner maybe but in the same basic vein. Ha, did she fool me. And probably everyone else that ever drove by the place. She had dozens of beautiful pieces, all waxed and polished, pie safes and dry sinks, hutches, cupboards and dressers, tables large and small, oak, pine and mahogany gleaming in the muted sconce lighting that decorated every wall. Mandy was open mouthed, gently running her hands over the glowing wood surfaces.

"Holy shit, Greta. This stuff's worth a bloody fortune," I said. "You don't need us for cash flow, have an auction."

"Screw that," she spat. "I don't want no pack a strangers pickin' through my stuff. They've got no respect. Let me show you the bedrooms."

There were five of them, plus three full baths up there, all of them furnished as impeccably as the down stairs rooms, two four poster beds, an unusual brass one, a dorm-style room with two sets of carved cherry bunk beds. Who would make bunk beds out of cherry, I thought? Why waste it on kids? Wouldn't they just beat the beautiful wood to shit with their penknives and bubble gum, jumping and rough housing?

The last room was Greta's, the biggest and the repository of the most impressive furniture I'd ever seen, all black walnut, all perfect, a canopy bed with ornate posts as big around as my thigh and taller than the top of my head by a foot, massive dresser-sized end tables, two armoires, a dressing table, even the plank floors and interior trim were walnut. A queen would have been humbled.

"Dare I even ask," I asked, "where this all came from?"

"My grandfather made it, in that barn, from trees that grew right here. I'm not sure I want to sell it," she said.

"I'm sure I never could," Mandy said, putting an arm around the old woman and pulling her close.

"No, me neither," I said. "There's nothing to replace it. Nothing would ever be adequate. It's just so…imperial."

Greta smiled and said let's have a drink and led us back to the porch where she mixed up some kind of toddy that was as good as her food and kicked like a share cropper's mule. We talked for an hour, each had a second drink, then I recognized the signs of Mandy about to go from dead sober to dead drunk, something that she did only occasionally and that had always baffled me. There was very little warning, just a break point that I had seen a couple times. We gotta go, Greta, I said. Thank you so much for a wonderful evening.

As I was helping Mandy down the steps, Greta called out, "Get your girls down here as soon as you can, partner. They're gunna love it here."

I thanked her again and it didn't occur to me till we were almost to the motor home that I hadn't mentioned my kids to her at all. Mandy must have. But why the reference to bringing them down? That was something I'd been pondering in a small room somewhere in the attic of my mind while our evening unfolded, not something I had spoken of. Another anomaly in an afternoon and evening filled with them.

I tucked Mandy in and went outside with a beer and a pain pill to contemplate all the weirdness. Approach it logically. How could this be a set up? Forget the 'why' for now. No one, including us, knew where we were going specifically when we left. I had told the kids, my mom, maybe some others in passing, that we were going down to the Carolinas for a vacation. I might even have been as specific as the Carolina coast. But that was it. No one could have known we'd end up outside of Hampstead, North Carolina and stop at an old barn that looked like a half way house for landfill-bound, big trash day uncollectables. At least on the out side. And even if we had planned and broadcast an itinerary that brought us past this very spot, how could they have guided us into this particular junk emporium? It wasn't like there was a big sign out front that said 'Mandy and Chance, stop here'. It had been random chance. There was no other possible explanation short of extraterrestrial implants. Or as unlikely, Greta's psychic Siren's song luring us in. I didn't get it. It just wasn't scientifically possible.

Not even my megga-millionaire ex-boss, Bob, could have marshaled the nefarious forces necessary to unwittingly bring us to this spot. He was the only person I knew rich enough to cast in the role of grand manipulator. There was no reason to assume he might have had anything to do with it but conspiracy theory requires a funding stream and Bob was the best I could come up with. But that was no more likely then aliens and still didn't explain how we happened to be here, now, when *we* didn't even know we were coming.

Which left only two possibilities as far as I could see—full blown, off the wall coincidence. Or divine intervention. Both seemed equally unlikely. We come five hundred miles south, or was it six, I'd have to check the odometer not that it mattered, looking for a possible place to live, maybe with the potential for an antique shop, and the whole thing falls into our lap because Mandy spotted a crazy lady's second hand store out of the corner of her eye as we cruised along a two lane road in rural North Carolina. If she'd been looking the other way or in the back taking a leak, or blowing her fucking nose for Christ's sake, I sure as hell would have driven right by. It was preposterous and that made me really suspicious.

Wasn't it far more likely that Greta was in fact a con artist, granted as believable as Ghandi, but none the less bent on shaking us down for a quick ten grand, disappearing into the sunset and leaving us to find out later that she was the hired help, cashier at someone else's junk kingdom, after we'd signed the bogus deeds and handed over the cash? Of course it was. A preposterous scam, so unbelievable it made you *want* to believe—that there *was* a Tooth Fairy, that good things did come to those who wished upon a star. I wasn't having any, not that easy. I went to bed determined to have a heart to heart with Greta in the morning.

She headed me off at the pass so completely that I was sure of one of two things but I didn't know which. Either it was such a good con that she had anticipated my reaction to her pitch, had run the whole game before and knew what a clever mark would ask and was prepared with the answers, or she was exactly as gifted a second sighter as she claimed to be.

She was knocking on the aluminum door of the motor home just after first light, something that didn't bother Mandy, she was up and dressed in a bathing suit, about to head down to the ocean for a morning dip. But the noise of her pounding on our metal home brought me up out of a sound sleep in a most disagreeable manner.

She was bearing gifts though, a thermos of stiff, chicory-laced coffee sweetened with just enough blackstrap molasses to make it a breakfast desert, Mandy wagging a mug of it under my nose, drawing me up like I was the snake and she was the charmer. I came out of the back after half of it had perked through me. They were sitting at the dinette when I joined them, Greta switching topics as soon as I sat down, saying to Mandy, your man has a couple questions. He's thinking I'm an old witch lady tryin' to get y'all's money. Tell me I'm wrong, Last Chance.

"No, Greta, you're not wrong."

"Last!" Mandy said. "What are you thinking?"

"He's a smart man, Amanda," Greta said. "And he's bein' prudent. That's what he should be doin'. He's protectin' himself and you and your children. That's a man trait, one a the few good ones," she added nudging Mandy with an elbow and laughing. "So Mr. Barkley," she continued, "tell me how you'd investigate somethin' like this. How you gunna find out what's real?"

I'd spent a lot of time on that question the night before, assuming I was right, the scam the only logical conclusion. So I wasn't caught off guard.

"I'd do a title search first of all, verify ownership of the land. Maybe talk to those appraisers. Maybe go see the sheriff," thinking that might end this whole sham right there, scare her off.

"That's good," she grinned, "but how are you going to prove I'm me? The title's in the name of Greta Anne Foy, the courthouse records will tell you that. How do you know I'm her?" She was right about that. Other than the word of the sheriff who I immediately pictured as a pot gut, Rod Steiger, *In the Heat of the Night* look-a-like, how would I prove it if I had too?

"I don't know. Finger prints?"

"Yep," she said, grinning at me. "That ought to prove somethin'. Y'all got any tin foil in this bread box, Amanda?"

Mandy nodded and produced a roll, not even having to get up to reach it. Greta peeled off a foot and smoothed it on the tabletop then looked up at me with a mocking smile.

"Pay attention, boy," she grinned. "Nothin' up my sleeve," laughing, rolling her hands over so I could see her callused palms and the worn and wrinkled tips of her fingers, then over to show me the veiny backs and the yellowed nails, a gardener's hands. I could not help grinning back at her. I really liked this old broad, didn't really care if she *was* trying to cheat me. As long as I didn't give up Mandy's inheritance foolishly, taken like some country carnival rube at a rigged dice wheel, then what was the harm in humoring her? She was more full of life then a dozen of my coworkers combined on their best, most animated day, as mischievous and sparkle eyed as my beautiful Baby when she was at the very top of her happy game. I was tempted to say forget the whole due diligence thing, I'm in, but after a beat or two, my conservative side won out.

"Okay, Greta. I'm with you. Go ahead."

She very carefully rolled each of her fingertips on the flattened foil then slid the result over to me. Even without magnification, I could see that all the whorls and spirals necessary for a fingerprint ID were there.

"Greta," I asked, "why are you doing this?"

"Because you *are* the ones," she said. "This is where you belong, all of you." After a long time spent staring into each other's eyes, she added something that cut right to my core. "A man in your position needs to have faith. It ain't all science and logic, boy."

"Greta," I said, "you're scaring me. And why do you call me boy? I'm fifty-three for God's sake."

"How old do you think I am?" she asked.

"About seventy," I said.

"Amanda, this boy is polite, I will give him that," then she turned to me and said, "Liar. Your face might be sayin' seventy but your heart says eighty and don't I know it. Well, your heart's closer to right. I'm eighty-three and that makes me old enough to be your momma and *that* makes me old enough to call you any damn thing I want to includin' boy.

"Now *boy*, you take those finger prints into town and you verify my bona fides, you understand? You know how to get to Wilmington?"

"Delaware?" I asked with what I thought was an innocent look.

"Last, you are a jerk," Mandy said.

"If you like," from Greta, "but the one down the coast is a lot closer and you could probably get your information there a little easier. Now, Mr. Jokester, go to the federal courthouse. It's down town, by the river. Find yourself a nice clerk, someone who might do you a favor and have them finger prints checked. You might want to let her do it," she added, thumb cocked over to Mandy. "She's more likely to get helped then you are. Do that title search while you're at it. Do what ever you feel needs doin'. I expect y'all should be back here in a day or so with all your questions answered.

"Mean time, I'm gunna go start packin'," she said as she got up. At the door she grabbed Mandy in a tight embrace, kissing her on both cheeks. "Hurry back, child," she said, "but make sure he's satisfied first." Then she turned to me and aimed one of her working woman's fingers at my chest. "Did you call your girls yet?"

Chapter Twelve

We took a swim then cleaned up and drove our house up to Greta's. She came out before we could disembark and walked up to my side.

"Y'all know where you're goin'?" she asked.

"Yes ma'am," I answered. "The Wilmington to the south. Thank you, Greta," I added. "It's been a real pleasure meeting you."

"You think you ain't comin' back, don't you, Chance," she said smiling at me. I grinned at her but said nothing more. "We'll see. Goodbye, Amanda," she called across me, then looked me in the eye and said, "You take care of that precious child, you hear me, boy?" When I nodded she handed me a piece of folded paper and said, "This might help," then waved and walked back to the house.

I knew from past map studies that Wilmington, the North Carolina one, was south of Hampstead but I didn't realize how close it was or how big. It proved to be a regular little city with a grid of opposed named and numbered streets, a central business district, a waterfront, even a mini-skyscraper. I thought Greta had meant 'county' when she'd said 'federal' courthouse but Wilmington was the hub of a federal judicial district as well as the county seat. Plus it had all the southern charm of a little Charleston or Savanna, the wonderful Georgian and Federalist homes, some colorful ginger bread Victorians and a bunch of tree lined, restored cottage laden side streets giving the whole place a human scale. And it had a university, a branch of the North Carolina system of higher education, like the University of Texas had El Paso. I thought of Jessica immediately.

We toured the town, left, right, left, right, right again, going around and around the blocks of homes and churches and store fronts, gawking like the Yankee tourists we were, finally parking by the water to walk a few blocks of the restaurant and gift shop dominated river front, eating lunch at a place that had private, second floor balconies cantilevered out over the street, open air, the view the Cape Fear River and the battle ship North Carolina docked on the other side in a little cove. Very cool, a beautiful town with enough of a college crowd to keep the entertainment venues alive and youthful. I was pretty sure Jessica would like it. I did, very much.

After a quick tour of the campus we went back to the Federal courthouse which was down by the river just as Greta had said. I confessed to Mandy that I was proceeding reluctantly, pretty sure we were wasting our time, that one way or the other, Greta was a fake and the whole thing was too good to be true. We should probably spend our time looking more closely at *this* place, I said, this was reality, just the kind of town I had hoped to find when we set out.

She quoted Greta, telling me to have some faith, all we were losing in a worst case was an afternoon and hadn't I enjoyed myself regardless? Hadn't it been a hell of an experience? I couldn't argue that. Greta's picture was probably in the encyclopedia under 'strange old ladies'.

We went up the grand marble staircase, between the huge Doric columns and into the lobby, then circled around the interior, not sure what we were looking for, finally discovering an old fashioned, slotted directory behind a hinged, glass cover.

"Okay," I said. "What looks good for eccentric identification?"

"How about the FBI," she said, pointing at the second floor listing for the Wilmington field office.

"Is your name Hoover?" I said laughing. "I don't see them running prints for a couple of curious tourists. Maybe as a last resort."

We looked at the listings some more, judges and courtrooms, bailiffs and court reporters, finally settling on the information desk listed as residing on the first floor in the lobby. I hadn't seen it but we walked around the vaulted space again, finally discovering it by accident, tucked under the main stair.

An elegant white haired man was on duty, Robert E. Lee in a guard's uniform, a hundred and thirty years later greatly reduced in rank but no less courteous or dignified. Mandy started to explain but she soon had *me* confused and *I* knew what she was trying to accomplish. Let me try, Sweetheart, I said.

"It's a little unusual, I'm sorry," I said to the man, "but we're trying to verify the identity of someone who wants to sell us some land. She suggested we try here, the federal courthouse. I don't know why. She gave us her finger prints." He pondered that for a minute before he spoke.

"She," he said, almost a question. "Was she ever in the military?" When I said I didn't know, he continued. "If so, her prints might be accessible through the recruitment offices on the third floor. That or the FBI." Mandy frowned at this last and he caught it. "What's the matter, young lady, not a fan of the G-men?" he said.

"It's not that," she said. "It's more just government in general."

"She was a big Reagan fan," I explained. "States righter and all that."

"Then you'll fit right in down here," he said.

"For a Yankee?" she said grinning.

"I'm not allowed to discriminate by race, creed or state of origin. I took an oath," he said straight-faced but with a wicked twinkle in his eye. "I'll tell you what. Go up and see Master Sergeant Hines. Army. If he can't help you, come on back and I'll take you to see the Feebs."

We thanked him and marched up the stone stairs to the third floor. The army recruiter was stationed in a fair sized room with two World War II vintage desks topped incongruously by colorful I Mac computers. Behind one of them, feet propped up, was a life-sized poster of a decorated noncom, crew cut, starched and fit. My appearance didn't seem to phase him, too old to be of interest I suspected, but Mandy's arrival right behind brought him to his feet at parade rest.

"Good afternoon, folks. How can I help you?" he asked in a gravel voice that must have called cadence to a hundred thousand boot camp recruits.

"General Lee, down stairs, sent us up," I said. "He thought you might be the best place to start."

He grinned at my reference, apparently knowing who I meant cause he didn't ask. I went on to explain our mission, expecting him to nicely tell us to go fuck ourselves but he didn't. Instead he pointed at chairs in front of his desk and sat down, pulling his key board toward him and, with a dexterity that would have shamed a ninety thousand dollar a year New York secretary, began to make music on his computer.

"Greta Anne Foy," he said after a couple seconds, "of the Down East Foys I assume," he added.

"Damn if I know. She's eighty three and crazy as a shit house rat as far as I can tell."

"Eighty three," he said, looking at me like I was Mandy's two-headed idiot again. I was getting tired of people looking at me that way, mostly because every time someone did, I deserved it. "I doubt if our records go back that far."

"Can you check anyway. Please," Mandy asked. I could never turn her down so I wasn't surprised that he didn't.

A few seconds later he said, "Greta Anne Foy. *Colonel* Foy. She out ranks me," he said with a grin. "WAC, 1941 to '45, then regular army, 1950 to 1971. Retired as a full colonel. I wonder what she did from '45 to '50? Doesn't matter. They probably disbanded the WACs after the war and didn't let women back in till Korea. Let's see what she did." After another pause, longer, he looked up at me and then over at Mandy.

"A problem?" I asked.

"Yeah, maybe. She had a security clearance. A real good one. This isn't some pencil pusher you're asking about. You know that don't you?" he said.

"Sergeant, I don't give a damn what she did for her country. I just want to make sure our Greta is the real Greta. Can you access prints? I'll take your word for it that they match or don't. I don't need a copy or anything."

"Let me poke around here a little more," he said, then clicked rapidly on the keys again. "Overseas in W.W.II, duty classified. OSS I bet. Funny they still have that stuff covered up. Korea, duty overseas, classified again. Nam, two tours, duty classified. You got yourself a real mystery woman here, folks. And I can't help you. Her prints are, guess what? Classified. Not in my files. Sorry," he said pushing back from his desk. "Try the FBI."

We marched back down the steps and than right back up with the general in the lead this time. I noticed he had a gun and not some old highway patrolman's revolver either, a fat-handled, mega-shot automatic in a cut down, quick draw holster. Kind of potent for a rent-a-cop I thought. He led us to the FBI offices and walked in like he worked there, saying good afternoon to the receptionist who smiled and said, hi, general. Off the lobby detail already? He smiled but kept walking, around her desk and into an office to her right, waving us in behind.

"Sit down," he said as he pulled out the desk chair and flicked on the computer.

"I take it you're not the regular lobby guy," I said.

"We take turns," he said with a slight grin.

"Budget reductions?" Mandy asked.

"Something like that," he said. "Now, what is the lady in questions full name?"

I told him and he gave me a long stare before he punched it up, playing with the keys for a while then giving me the same look the Sergeant had, probably when Greta's security classification came up.

"I know," I said. "She did something, ah, special for the army. I'm not interested in what, I just need to know if this is the real Greta."

"You say you have her permission to make these inquiries. Do you have any proof of that?"

"Her note," Mandy said. "Did you even read it?" she asked me. I hadn't. It was still folded in my shirt pocket and I pulled it out and handed it to him. He read it, then started to chuckle, finally laughing full out as he handed it back.

"She's an interesting woman," he said, still laughing. He began to fiddle with his computer again as I looked down at Greta's message. 'Tell these two any damn thing they want to know, General Lee. I don't care if you have to violate the Official Secrets Act, you hear me, boy?' It was signed 'Greta' with a PS. 'I'm probably going to miss the reenactment this year.' I passed it to Mandy and looked up at the Special Agent security guard just as he swung the monitor around to face us.

"Holy shit," I said. "Look at this, Mandy." She was still studying Greta's note but glanced up, then back down, then up again, this time really looking at the image on the screen. It was Greta as far as I could tell, a lot younger and with a scowl on her face that would have frozen the waters of Hell. The uniform helped the nasty look considerably. It was so much more intimidating then a pair of old cut off jeans and a tee shirt

"Wow," from Mandy. "What a hard ass. Are you sure it's her?" she said to the agent.

"As one Reagan fan to another, off the record you might say," he added, "I'm as sure of that ID as I am of my own mother's. Miss Greta and I go back a ways."

Mandy clapped her hands together and let out a burst of her best laughter. The power of it always brought a goofy smile to my face and I'd seen the same reaction from a hundred others. The FBI guy was not an exception.

"I *knew* it," she exclaimed. "I just *knew* she wasn't a fake! What do you say now, Last? Any more negativity to interject?"

"Whoa, hold on," I said. "I'm not being negative, just cautious. Give me a break, Mandy. How often has someone offered you their home and business for ten grand?" She didn't respond but the General did.

"You're the ones," he said. I nodded and said I guess. "She's been telling me for two years that someone was coming to help her out with the place, someone to set her free so she could travel again. I'm glad to see y'all finally made it."

"Can I ask you a question? Several actually."

"Be my guest," he answered.

"Why were you working the lobby today, dressed as a guard?"

"We take turns. A surprise for the terrorists that are swarming all over Wilmington. Orders from Washington," he said without any hint of humor but with that lighthouse twinkle again.

"I described you to Sergeant Hines as General Lee. A joke I thought, my own witticism, but it seems like everyone else has the same idea."

"I'm a re-enactor. I play Robert Lee. I'm almost famous for it."

"Are you a student of history?" Mandy asked.

"Yes. And you?"

"My degree is in military diplomatic history," she responded.

"With honors, from UNC," I added for her.

"I am impressed. Did you focus on the War Between the States?" he asked, smiling slightly now.

"No," she said. "I prefer more current conflicts. The Middle East in particular."

"How prescient of you," he said, this time with an actual smile. "If I had done that, I might be somewhere more, oh, relevant at this stage in my career."

"But Wilmington is so beautiful," she said.

"And so dull," he replied.

"I'm sorry. I guess it isn't exactly a hot bed of crime."

"Not even a water bed," he added. "But you're right. It's a lovely place to live and there are a number of advantages."

"Like being able to wear a beard?" I asked. My entire experience with the FBI was based on TV, that and a girl I had dated in college that supposedly had gone on to become an agent. She didn't have facial hair, not much anyway, and neither did any of the blue suited stereo types you saw on '*Law and Order*' or '*The FBI Files*'.

"Yes," he said, "there is that. And I have a certain, ah, flexibility in methodology."

"Like being able to help us with Greta."

"And vise versa."

I didn't know what he meant but I had other questions in mind. "Can you do one more thing in that regard?" He nodded. "Pull up her finger prints and compare them to this," I said as I slid the folded tin foil across to him. He did his typing thing again, the monitor back facing him, then opened the folded sheet of aluminum and looked at me without speaking. He got up and left the room, returning in a half minute with what looked like a woman's compact and a fluffy brush. He very carefully dusted the black face powder across the tin foil with the big brush then held up the result. The ten sets of natural oil lithographs were now clearly discernable on their reflective background. He studied first the foil and then the monitor and then returned the sheet to me and spun the monitor around to face us without a word. Obviously I'm no expert but it didn't take one to see that Greta's fingertips were represented on both mediums.

"Satisfied?" he asked.

"You bet," I said. I also had about seven hundred more Greta questions but I didn't want to wear out our welcome and he had answered the biggy.

"That old lady is a national treasure. Are you starting to get that part yet?"

"Not in detail but I've got a good imagination," I said laughing.

"Well let it run wild then add fifty percent and you might be in the neighborhood. Good luck to you both," he added, standing and offering his hand.

I shook it but Mandy came around the desk and planted a big kiss on his cheek. "You are so nice," she said to him. "Thank you. I can't begin to tell you how much this means to us."

"I have an idea," he told her. "Keep me in mind."

I didn't know what for but it would be hard not to in any event. It isn't every day you meet a legend. Or the reincarnation of one who helps you out.

We went back down the grand stair, me checking to see if there was another bogus rent-a-cop on duty under the stairs. There was, this one looking even less like an eight dollar an hour, semi-retired shoe salesman, thirty maybe with an almost bald head and muscles interfering with other muscles bunched on his fore-arms and biceps. And hard, squinty eyes, ambitious and alert. A junior G-man I was pretty sure, hoping for some Arab, any Arab, to come through those massive oaken doors. He better not have his hands in his coat pockets, I thought. Or be carrying a nap sack.

"I want to do the title search anyway," I said to Mandy as we cleared the sniper's domain. She rolled her eyes up out of sight like I was asking for the hundredth time to go find the pot of gold at the end of the rainbow. It should only take a minute, I said, don't get your thong stuck in the wrong crack. That got a reaction, but I didn't expect her to hit me so damn hard. Or so fast. I knew I was getting too old for that kind of banter when I didn't even see the punch coming. Wouldn't matter soon but I was starting to bruise too easily. I have to shut up more, I thought.

We went from the federal to the county courthouse on foot and with a little help from a nice blue haired lady and our road map, had soon located Greta's homestead on the plat maps. It was right there, Greta Anne Foy transferred from Francis Arnold Foy in 1956 through the senior Foy's executor, some southern sounding name followed by an esquire. The only thing left that I could see, if we wanted to be completely sure, was a title search to see if there were any encumbrances on the land. Mandy was about fully fed up by now but I prevailed with my winningest smile and a wheedling delivery. Fine, she nearly shouted. Go find a fucking abstract company.

In the spirit of paranoia, I thought it best not to use one of the offices associated with Greta's three appraisals and there were numerous others listed in the Wilmington yellow pages, the book on display at a pay phone in a booth at a Quicky Mart on the main road out of town. That was statement enough about the lack of vandals and ruffians in the local economy. An intact phone book was more scarce then an unbribed building inspector in greater Philadelphia.

I picked one at random from the middle of the listings and in twenty minutes we were sitting across the desk from a paunchy, balding realtor type with a big cheesy smile. Can you run this property for us, I said, handing him the legal description from the courthouse. While we wait, I added. He looked at the printout frowning and shaking his head, mumbling to himself. I'll pay cash, I said, quickly easing his conundrum.

He came back in about ten minutes with our papers and a couple more sheets. There you are, he said. The whole history of the property. I gave him fifty bucks and we left, reviewing the papers in the comfort of our own home which was parked right outside.

"Are you happy now?" Mandy asked after reviewing the results and handing them back to me.

"Let me see, I'll let you know." Even I couldn't find anything wrong with Greta's title report. There wasn't anything to find fault with. The land had gone from father to son, son to daughter, and since Greta had taken possession, she had neither subdivided or borrowed against the property. There were no encumbrances, no second mortgages, no notes, no liens, no nothing. It was her land free and clear just like she said.

So why give it to us? Where were the siblings, nieces, cousins, anyone with better claim then we had? Let's go back, I said to Amanda. I want to talk to the Colonel. She just rolled her eyes again.

We turned into Greta's barnyard well before dusk and I wanted to park up by the house, make it clear that I wasn't rolling over completely, settling in to our new abode without another question but Mandy pointed to our camp site and said 'go' without the possibility of argument. She was in her swimsuit and out the door before I could even grope her let alone try to wrestle her into the bedroom for a quickie. I figured I might as well join her, maybe I could get lucky in the ocean. No way.

We splashed around for a bit, Mandy telling me how wonderful it was to be near the ocean, like I couldn't tell that for myself or as if to remind me what a golden opportunity we were being handed. Either way, she was not about to lower her bottoms and let me slip into her wonderful sweet spot, not until the whole Greta thing was resolved.

I got out first, a little frustrated, but also a little sick, a strident shaft of pain interdicting my upper chest. I went back to our camp and got a Percocet and a Corona and parked my butt on the grass under the pines, facing the ocean, waiting for Mandy to come up and join me.

Greta came down first, noiselessly, no premonition of her arrival until she tapped me on the shoulder, this before the pill could have dulled my senses. I jumped about a foot straight off the turf, turning in midair to look into Greta's benign smile.

"Back so soon?" she asked with a big toothy grin, false toothy I hoped looking at that smirk.

"Yes, Colonel, we are at your service. Cop a squat, there's a couple of things I'd like to clarify."

"I bet there are, you doubting Thomas. Didn't I tell you to have a little faith? But no, you had to—"

"Shut *up*, Greta! You've made your point. So, is the General your son?" I asked. "How'd you know we'd meet up with him?"

"He's the agent in charge. He's always there. Are you satisfied yet, boy? We have to move this thing along."

"Why?"

"Cause I've got reservations on the Concord in a week. When are the girls coming?" she said as if the two thoughts fit together like a foot in a shoe.

"Time out. What?"

"You're going to get married before I go and I want the girls here. So did you?"

"Of course. How could I have not known that?"

"Cause you're an obstinate male just like most all of your kind. *Did you call them?*"

"*No I did not,*" giving it back to her.

"God *damn* it, boy! You are hard headed." She reached into her jeans, the back pocket, and pulled out a tiny flip phone. "What's the older one's number," she demanded, looking down at the punch pad, waiting for it to register an active line, something I thought was a remote possibility out here in the boonies. My Nextel sure didn't work.

Her whatever make miniature model sure did, beeping repeatedly to indicate its willingness to communicate with the outside world. I thought, what the hell, this ought to be interesting, and gave her the number. It rang a few times, I could hear the tiny bell-like sound, then I heard Gloria say hello.

"Billie," Greta shouted into the baby phone, "is that you?" Gloria was apparently as taken aback as I was to hear this stranger use her adolescent nick name, something she hadn't been called in over twenty years to my knowledge, the Hell Bitch having none of Gloria's desire to be known by the colloquial form of her first name, maybe even because she preferred it to Willonia, the grand mother Hell Bitch's moniker and an even more hellish thing to burden your own flesh and blood with then Lassiter. They had compromised with 'Gloria', her middle name.

"Who *is* this?" I heard Gloria say, clearly and with some heat.

"It's Greta, girl. I'm here with your daddy in North Carolina. How soon can you get your butt down here? They're fixin' to get married and we need you to witness the grand event. And your sister."

"*Who* is this?" Gloria repeated as I held out my hand for the phone, catching a glimpse of Mandy coming up through the dunes and wanting some semblance of order instilled in this craziness before she arrived with her questions.

"Gloria, it's your dad. What it is, Princess?"

"Who the hell is Greta?" she asked.

"A friend. The bottom line is, can you come down here? Soon. Things are moving kind of quickly and I'd like your input on something. It requires an act of faith, I know, but can you?"

"Daddy," she said solemnly. "You are insane."

"Yes, Sweetheart, but I need you to go with me on this. Can you?" After a long pause during which I assume she was running the scenarios, she came back to me.

"Yeah, I guess. When?"

"Now. Tomorrow. Right away. I'm going to call your sister. I'd like you to come together. And bring Celina."

"No, duh," she said to the two-headed idiot. "I was thinking I'd give her a big bowl of food and a cat box and leave her here."

"No, bad idea. Bring her along," I said laughing. "I'll call you later," then I hung up.

"Was that so hard?" Greta asked, Mandy now seated at her feet, the old woman's arms wrapped around my Baby's shoulders.

"He's a total butt head," Mandy said, smiling up at Greta.

"Sometimes," Greta said to her like I was in Nova Scotia. "But mostly he's a sweet man. I like him a lot."

"Me too," Mandy said, two girls discussing a first crush. I started to tear up and had to go into the motor home for more beer. "Us too," Mandy called out as I climbed the steps.

I came back out with my own phone and three Coronas but mine didn't work, Greta watching me dial up Jessica twice, all of us hearing the tinny busy signal, too fast to be a real indicator of someone on the line at the other end. Try this, she said, tossing me her Cracker Jack prize phone. I dialed, it rang and Jessica answered almost at once.

"Can you take a week off and come see your father marry the woman of his dreams?" I asked.

"Is it Mandy or Greta?" she said.

"You two are quick," I said. "You must have each other on speed dial. It's Mandy of course, you dork. Here, talk to her," and

I handed the phone over, Mandy now resting against Greta's fore-
legs like she was relaxing in a short beach chair, Greta propped
back on one arm and against an oak, the other holding the neck
of the beer bottle.

Mandy was her incredible self, going on and on about Greta
and her amazing abode, Greta listening in, Mandy cocking her
head and the phone back to make it easier on the old woman.
After what seemed like an hour, Mandy gave me back the phone
and said, she's coming. Can you swing it, Angel, I asked and she
said, yeah, if Gloria can and I said cool, I'll call you back and hung
up on her too.

"So," Greta smirked at me, "all it took was two calls. Good. Now
we can make some plans."

"Hello, Greta. Are you still on planet Earth? What the fiddley
fuck is going on around here?"

"You two are getting married next weekend and I'm going to
Paris. Duh. Get with it, boy. You're all mixed up."

"I guess so." I was dumb after that, too much stuff going through
my mind too fast. After a few minutes I regrouped a little. "You still
owe me a couple answers, Greta."

"Shoot," she said.

"I'd like to but your FBI pal would probably figure it was me.
Okay. What did you do in the army, Colonel? You apparently
have one hell of a security clearance and your activities are still
classified."

"Idle curiosity, I assume?" When I said yes, she said, "The same
thing I still do. Listen to people. With my mind."

"You were a military psychic?"

"Pretty much, yep. I put down 'second sight' under 'other skills'
on my WAC application. After about a year, somebody in the intelligence office must have noticed. The Nazis were supposed to be
all interested in things like that so I guess that got our folks thinking about it too. I was interviewed about twenty times, checked

out I imagine about as completely as somebody can be, then they shipped me to England to interrogate prisoners. Germans mostly but also some of ours that they thought might have, oh, mixed loyalties. Those poor Germans. They can't lie worth a damn."

"Too self-righteous," Mandy said. "They were convinced of their own superiority."

"That's exactly it, child. Terrible at it. They didn't need *me* to see through those fanatics. Now the Koreans, north and south, they were a whole different ball game. I had to learn the language before I could make heads or tails a what went on in their minds. Much tougher race of people. We were lucky to come out with a draw on that one. And of course Vietnam. We got just what we deserved I'm sorry to say."

"Did you have to learn that language too?" I asked, thinking this is a tall tale.

She rattled off a sing song monologue of about a thousand syllables which I took to be an affirmative response. "It's a beautiful spoken dialect, so musical," she said in conclusion. "And I told you you were an imperialist running dog lackey of the occupation army in case you wondered. That and a few insults. No offense."

"Oh, none taken of course. Some of my best friends are running dogs. Well, Greta, it looks like you are who you say you are and I've got to tell you, that's a damn tall order to accept."

"Don't never judge a book by its cover, boy. You ought to know that at your age."

"You're not your average Reader's Digest condensed version, Greta. You ought to know that."

"I do, oh believe me, I surely do. But can we move on now? There's a whole lot of stuff to get squared away." I could not have agreed with her more.

We sat on the sandy ground talking and drinking good Mexican beer for another hour then moseyed up to her porch as the sun was setting for a dinner of leftover chicken, fresh potato salad and some garden greens tossed with tomatoes and onions. It was great and I got a bunch of answers just by keeping my mouth shut and letting the two of them plan my future.

I was to be married the following Saturday with my daughters in attendance and Greta the maid of honor. Mandy had insisted, Greta suggesting one of the girls. The best man was up in the air, no one I knew capable of dropping everything and driving nine hours for something as transitory as my marriage.

"How about the General?" I suggested as a joke. They both thought that was a great idea so I didn't mention that I'd been kidding. When there was another half-second break in their chatter, I threw out another question.

"Greta," I said, "don't any of your relatives want this place?"

"Oh, sure, some of them would like to have it given to 'em. So they could sell it off real quick as soon as I'm in the ground. But none of them need it and none of 'em want to buy it off me. They all got their own, what's left of 'em. They don't need nothin' from me."

"But we do," I stated.

"Need? Not really. Want? Yes you do. The need is more on my end. I need to see somebody that cares livin' here. That's y'all, especially this lovely girl here, no offense Mr. Chance."

"Don't worry about offending me, Greta. I agree with you about Amanda surely. So you think she wants the place and cares and I'm sort of along for the ride?"

"Nah, there's a lot more to you then that. Your needs are important, they're your family's needs and you want to see them protected and secure. That's a real good thing. This'll work good for y'all, Mandy and the girls. The little ones will really love it. Great place to grow up."

I started to question who the little ones were but my window had closed, they were off again on important female conversation and I was left out in the cold.

That evening late, with Mandy tucked in, I took a moon light walk along the beach, going a half mile south until further progress would have required fording a tidal inlet fed, I assume, by another one of the million creeks that drained into the sea. I turned around and went maybe a little farther north, past our beach, the light from the tree-mounted halogen fixture glowing bluish in the boughs of the big pine, marking home, a security beacon.

I guess I was getting cold feet, until now caught up in the events despite my suspicions, everything moving so fast, which I thought was probably a good thing considering the importance of time to my condition. But the changes that we were rushing into were not inconsequential, new home, new business, asking my children to relocate, to procreate even, that was a biggy. It would be so much easier to just turn around and go back, let the inevitable unfold in the safety of our own home. So much less risk but of course, so much less gain as well. At least I was still looking at Greta's silver platter as a good thing. And it would be if it worked out right.

I retraced my steps down the beach, the sloshing of the waves, gentle tonight, the only sound, the false moon of the night-light bringing me back to the motor home and my Baby. I stripped and snuggled in behind her, wrapping every bit of her that I could in my arms, spooning like table behind tea. What the hell, I thought as I drifted off. Life is an adventure. Go with it.

Chapter Thirteen

The next day we went back into Wilmington to sign up for a legal marriage, all three of us in Greta's old Jeep Wagoneer, the kind with real fake wood on the sides, big knobby tires and fuel economy similar to a Sherman tank. Greta knew right where to go and seemed to know everyone we met, dozens of people greeting her either as Miss Greta, Colonel Greta or ma'am, the last not her salutation of choice because the couple young folks that called her that got an unceremonious introduction, my name's Greta not ma'am which was followed by yes, ma'am! from the victims both times.

After we got our application and instructions from the first courthouse, we reversed yesterday's tour and went back to the federal one to visit General Lee. He was off the lobby detail but in the office and the receptionist ushered us right in after hugging Greta.

"Company, Robert E. You awake in here?" she shouted as she pushed her way in. He looked up at her like, God rescue me from this place or these people but it was all down hill for him, Greta right behind his secretary, then Mandy, then me.

"Greta," he said. "To what do I owe?" he asked with a slight grin.

"Mornin', Bob. You met my friends yesterday," she said, indicating us with a hand wave, "and they were so impressed with you that they'd like to ask a favor. Another one," she added.

"What?" he said to all of us.

"It's odd, not that I think you didn't suspect that, considering," I said. He nodded, his grin widening. "We, Amanda and I," I said in case he thought I was planning to marry Greta, "are getting married Saturday at Greta's place and I need a male witness, to balance the two of them," I said with a nod toward my companions. "I thought of you and they liked the idea."

"A best man," he stated.

"Yes, sir. I know we're not exactly close, but we're closer than anyone else I know who's within a day's drive. Could you do that for us?"

"I'd love to," he said. "I'm honored, seriously. And it ought to be a hoot. If you're letting her help plan it anyway," pointing to Greta.

"Ceremony's at one, Bob, reception right after. Come early, I'll feed you breakfast."

"Can I bring a couple friends?" he asked her.

"I'm countin' on it. See ya, General," she waved as we trooped back out.

"Can we invite that nice Sergeant," Mandy asked, "from the recruitment office?"

We went up stairs and found Sergeant Hines who Greta knew by his first name of course and Mandy told him about the big event. He said he'd love to come, could *he* bring a couple friends? The more the merrier, Greta said and we went down and out to the car.

The ladies had a shopping list, the preparation of which I had not been party to with the exception of physical proximity, heavy on beer and barbecue it seemed, all three of us pushing shopping carts around the Food Lion, mine all beer, Gretta's all chicken and sauce fixings, Mandy's all kinds of odds and ends. My big contribution came at the check out line, three hundred dollars still a pretty cheap reception I thought but of course we weren't done yet, just done for the day.

We drove back to Greta's and she backed up to a pad locked sliding door on the street frontage side of the barn, her shop door around the corner opposite the house. She handed me a key and said, open her up, Last, the light's on a pull chain. The lock was rusted nearly solid and I had to whack it with a rock to get it to snap open. The door's wheels shrieked like a teenage girl at a horror movie when I pushed it aside, really having to put my shoulder in to it to make it go.

I found the pull cord, gave it a yank and got a pile of string on my head but not before it activated a bunch of industrial fluorescent fixtures hanging by chains from the timbers above. I was in a dusty old restaurant kitchen it looked like, an eight burner Vulcan range squatting like a greasy locomotive on the back wall flanked by butcher block wooden slab tables on both sides, two monstrous, ancient refrigerators, a wall of galvanized steel sinks, racks of vintage pots and pans and a sheet steel box, black with years of soot and burned sauce, big enough to grill every chicken in three counties simultaneously.

"I'm sure there's an interesting story behind this room," I said to her as she opened the rear door of her vehicle.

"Uncle Clyde's Folly we used to call it amongst the kin. 'Clyde's Famous Bar B Q' he called it. It might a got famous too if he'd a laid off the corn liquor at night and opened the damn place up every mornin' he was supposed to instead of sleepin' it off in the hay loft all day half the damn time. He'd only cook when he felt like it and a course you can't have people drivin' out from town expectin' chicken and getting' nothin' for their journey. They tend to not come back."

"How long since anybody used this stuff?" I asked.

"Years. You have some cleanin' to do. But the refrigerators work. I keep some stuff in 'em. There's a door over there that connects to the shop," she added.

We unloaded all the perishables into one and the beer into the other and then I started playing with the equipment, checking the water which worked fine after Greta told me where to find the proper valve, lighting the hot water heater which looked like it ought to be for sale in the shop it was so old, firing up the pilots on the Vulcan. Then I started to clean, directing the women to just leave me alone. Barbecue is man's work I said. I wondered if Randy would consider this too humble a start for a restaurant of his own. It wouldn't look so bad once it was clean and there was plenty of cooking stuff. The lack of seating capacity was an issue I thought, laughing to myself.

It took me all the rest of the day to make it clean enough that *I'd* be willing to eat something that came out of it and I wasn't all that particular. It would have taken Mandy a week but at the end, the Vulcan would have looked like an 'S' class Mercedes on the showroom floor, all the dented up aluminum pots so shiny you could shave in the reflection. The board of health wasn't coming, just my kids. And I hadn't poisoned them in all my years in the kitchen.

I dragged myself up to the house, knocked on the porch door and was hollered inside then told in no nonsense terms that it was my house now too so knock off the formality. Yes ma'am, I said, snapping off a quick British style salute and clicking my heals together which made the old girl laugh.

"Where's my Sunshine, Gret? Swimming or cleaning?"

"Dressing," she said, then 'sit' with a finger gesture toward a kitchen chair. Greta was working on something food-like, not talking for once, so I got a daylight chance to study the vintage country kitchen, everything I looked at since our return from town yesterday viewed as a project needing either repair, refurbishment or restoration. The kitchen was beautiful as it stood, stained pine cabinets, solid not plywood, glass fronts on the wall mounted ones with little waves and bubbles in the green panes, an immense butcher's block island, the biggest I'd ever seen, slate slabs like bisected pool tables for the counter tops. The fridge was way dated but it worked and I'd watched Mandy change the color on a couple that we'd bought second hand over the years. The stove was an amazing, nickel and iron wood-gas combination damn near as big as the Vulcan lurking in the barn. It made you long for that first cold autumn morning when you could build a little fire on the kindling side and perk up a pot of old fashioned boiled coffee.

I was thinking about painting the walls and maybe a quarry tile floor when I heard the whisper of quiet feet descending the main stair, the common sound muffled somehow and over laid with the whooshing of fabric in motion. Greta turned from the double bowled enameled sink and a smile lit up her wrinkled mug, the expression knocking twenty years off of her and revealing the beauty that she must have once been hounded for.

My eyes went to where hers were in time to see Amanda enter the room, Greta getting a peak before me from her angle at the sink. I hoped I looked as rejuvenated as she did cause my smile felt just as wide. My Baby was grinning coyly, perhaps a bit embarrassed to be wearing a magnificent shimmering lace and brocade wedding gown, floor length but not hooped, tight across her taught butt then dropping straight to her toes, a 'V' notched deep down between her breasts, the lace part looping the outside of her shoulders and covering her arms to the wrists. She was so beautiful, and so hot, that if Greta had not been in the room, I would have made an immediate attempt to hoist that dress and boink her on the kitchen island.

"Wait for the honeymoon, cowboy," Greta said the second she looked from Mandy to me.

"No fair reading minds, Greta. Not right now anyway."

"No need to read minds. I got eyes. I can see exactly what yer thinkin'," she laughed.

"Mandy," I said, "you are perfect." And she was, radiant, blushing pink, a Vera Wang ad or the '*In Style*' cover girl. "Where did you get such a fine garment?"

"That old thing?" Greta said. "I've had that in my closet I bet fifteen years."

"She made it," Mandy said. "Can you believe that? What do you think?" she said, spinning in a ballerina's circle.

I didn't need to say anything. "Why did you make a wedding gown, Gret? Great expectations?" I teased. "And which pair of my Levi's are going to go best with it? We're going to make an incongruous pair."

"I made it for my niece," she said with mock indignity, "then she ran off with the bum and got married in Vegas. Lasted about six months. And I got somethin' that might work for you, boy. If not, you get your ass into town and rent a tux quick."

What she had for me was a re-enactor's uniform, a Federal brigadier general's complete with campaign hat and sword. I'll need a blond wig, I said, and ten thousand Indians. Isn't this Custer's outfit from the last stand? We all yucked it up and then I tried it on. I guess the clothes really do make the man—it fit and I immediately felt like jumping on my charger and attacking Wilmington. I restrained myself but I couldn't help pulling out the sword and striking a few dramatic poses. Mandy told me I looked dashing.

Greta said that the difference in the eras represented by our attire was somehow fitting. Mandy was contemporary and I was an anachronism, I thought. Greta said it straight faced but I think she was making a rye joke. Mandy looked about twenty in her virgin's dress and I looked ready for my grand retirement ball, a salt and pepper haired military lifer ready to marry the babe and start a lusty new career. And family. We had to make that decision soon.

Chapter Fourteen

The kids were due any minute and with their arrival, things were going to start hopping around Greta's old homestead. I was looking forward to it, so was Mandy and it was clear that Greta, after all her brow beating to get me to call them, was fired up too. She had spent all afternoon cleaning by the smell of the place and there was some kind of feast in production as well, the scents of roasting meat and Mr. Clean commingling in the downstairs. I was reluctant to take off my general suit and Mandy was still in her gown, so when I heard the beep beep of a horn we both went outside like characters in some odd antebellum play to greet the girls. They already thought we were nuts so they didn't show too much surprise. My mom probably would have fainted.

We did a big hug dance in the driveway, Randy saluting me gravely then laughing before he bowed to Mandy and asked for the next dance. They had arrived in a four door, six wheel pickup that was vaguely familiar but I didn't make the connection, even when I saw the Harley tied in the back, until Bubba climbed down from the driver's seat and walked around the hood of the truck offering his hand. Bubba was Paul's half brother, a big, friendly, semi-biker looking dude with a rough edged, working man's body but a radio announcer's precise diction and melodious speech. I knew more by rumor than personal experience that he and Gloria were buds, that Bubba had been a moderating influence with his stepfather and half brother, had tried to be, and that he had been helping with Celina when he could, a father figure in place of Paul's abandonment. But his presence here meant there was more to it.

"You two come out of the closet?" I asked him.

"Yeah, pretty much. We don't rub it in their faces but we couldn't keep it a secret any longer."

"Good," I said. "I'm glad you're here."

"Thank you," he said. "I wasn't sure how you would react. Her mother flipped."

"She's a fucking psycho. That's her reaction to everything. Don't worry about it."

"I don't. She can kiss my ass." That gave me a good laugh.

"I hope you brought your work gloves. I could use a hand."

"Maybe you ought to change first," he said. "You don't want to mess up that fine uniform. Or is that everyday work wear in these parts?"

"No, your work clothes are the Confederate gray. Hey, speaking of which, why am I getting married in a Yankee suit?" I said to Greta. "I ought to be Stonewall Jackson or somebody." Greta was already holding Celina and hugging both my daughters at the same time.

"You *are* a Yankee, boy. Southern Pennsylvania don't count."

With the introduction made, the gaggle of females marched into the house behind the oldest goose carrying the youngest.

"How about a beer, lads?" I said to the boys. "There's something I want you to see out here anyway," I told Randy. "How are you at barbecue?" We went out to the barn kitchen and I explained its history and my expectations regarding the wedding. He said, I can make anything you want in here, his eyes luminous, a silly grin on his face as he wandered from stove to sinks to racks of utensils.

"How many guests?" That was a damn good question and I didn't have even the vaguest of facts on which to base my answer.

"I don't know," I said, knowing it sounded insipid, my own wedding and no handle on the quantity. "We bought a whole bunch of stuff. How many can we feed?"

He opened the refrigerators, pulling three beers from the first then reviewing the mountain of chickens and produce in the second. We could see him counting and calculating then he turned back to us and said twenty? Maybe thirty if nobody eats too much.

"Do me a favor, Randy. Go ask Greta. She knows something I don't because my count puts us around fifteen." He finished his beer, declining a shop tour which Bubba and I took after he went up to the house. Bubba's reaction to the shop was similar to my own first reaction. Wow! Lots of stuff, lots of work. This is where I need your help, I told him. I'm not sure I can physically move all this crap, organize it, you know?

"I'm really sorry to hear about your prognosis," he said, not the least bit self-conscious about saying it.

"Thanks. It's okay. I'm adjusting. Did Gloria talk to you about relocating? I want her to move down here with us, help Mandy with the business."

"Billie," he said. When I looked at him blankly, he explained. "She wants to be called Billie. That phone call from Greta the other day, it triggered something," smiling now and shaking his head.

"Okay. Billie it is." Greta had greeted her that way when Gloria arrived but I was trying to stop analyzing every off the wall, left field thing that came out of her mouth. It was consuming too much of my time. "So, did you guys talk about it?"

"Yes, sir, we did. I think it would be good for her and I told her that. I think she'll do it. And the baby if you want."

"The baby is still a maybe," I said. "But great on the move down. Thank you."

"No need. I told her months ago we should make a fresh start, somewhere else, anywhere. This looks good to me."

"So you're coming along?"

"If I'm invited."

"By me or her?"

"Both."

"Alright. You're halfway there. You have my vote."

"Then I'm in. I already have hers."

And so my half baked plan, a week before a half-assed gambit haphazardly designed to render a squandered life meaningful or at least give my last months some direction however vague or hopeless the quest might be, was taking on a life of its own. And my family had just expanded by three. Maybe four. And I was getting married in two days. Not bad for a man on his death bed.

Chapter Fifteen

G reta's feast was a Carolina ham as big as a medicine ball, baked in hard cider from an earthen jug she lugged up out of a basement I hadn't yet visited, more of the cider served chilled with the meal. A nice compliment to the collards and scalloped potatoes, oysters fried in corn meal, apple cobbler served with real whipped cream for desert along with that molasses laced coffee. It made a hell of a bribe, the food alone worth the trip. We all worked on the clean up and then Greta assigned the sleeping rooms, no pretext of separating girls and boys despite their marital status or lack there of. I wanted to go down to the motor home for privacy but Mandy wanted to sleep in the house. It's like Christmas, she said. Guess who won?

I woke early, not as early as Mandy but early enough that the sun wasn't up and I was disoriented, the illumination in the room muted by the mist that lay across the yard, knee high on the oak and pine trunks, the back yard my view from our bedroom window. As I lay on my stomach looking out toward the motor home and the dunes, I saw two shadowy figures cutting through the fog, one slow and misshapen, one lithe and nimble—Gloria carrying

Celina with Mandy sprinting on ahead, bound for the ocean, I'd wager. Looked like fun. I went back to sleep.

Some time later I was fairly slammed awake by coldness and wet and a winter storm of hilarious laughter as three moist and sandy, salty smelling females pounced on my body. I got up this time, no scented mug to ease the transition. It's downstairs, Mandy giggled when I croaked out my request. You better hurry if you want any before we go. Go? To town, she said, like you dope, how could you forget?

I tried to beg myself out of the voyage but it was hopeless. Mandy didn't even argue, she just said we're all going and you're driving, the motor home I assumed for that sized crowd. I wanted to sit on the porch in a rocking chair, drink a quart of Greta's wonderful coffee, maybe talk to our kids for a while, hang out.

We were out of there in twenty minutes, the whole boatload crammed into my house. At least I had a big plastic tumbler of coffee. Or I did until I spilled most of it turning onto the highway. I didn't know our destination or the purpose of the excursion and I began to realize that I was probably better off in ignorance, maybe even purposely spared the knowledge, easier just to go where I was told and hand over piles of money to whoever asked.

We went to a strip mall, I know because I had to park half way back in the lot to get two slots end to end. They all disembarked and split up, some heads heading left, some right, my view from the driver's seat obstructed by a hundred vehicles. I dozed off, the first ones back waking me. Jessica and Randy with arms full.

"You owe me ninety six bucks," she said after depositing her cache and plopping into the passenger's chair. I gave her two fifties and said keep the change, it's a tip.

"Gee, thanks, Dad. Last of the big time spenders?"

"I don't want to go broke till after the wedding." We laughed, Randy squatting in the aisle behind us. "So," I said. "You want to go see UNCW? It has a nice campus, brick buildings, trees, not too big. Did you read any of the stuff I sent you?" The Wilmington branch of the University of North Carolina had been represented in my packet of college info. Happy accident.

"Yeah," she answered. "We did. It's cute. Quaint."

"Very southern charming. The whole town is. So. What do you think or is it too soon to tell?" I could see that it was, her brows were wrinkled up, the thought wheels turning. "Just spit it out, kid. You can't hurt my feelings and bullshit is not allowed."

"It's a big step, Mr. B.," Randy said. "It isn't easy to just…move."

"Yeah," Jess added. "Not for us anyway. We're not as crazy as you and Mandy."

"Yes you are. You just haven't realized your full potential yet. Too young. Trust me, it'll come to you. It's in your blood. Seriously? I'm not trying to pressure or guilt you into this. It's more for me than you, I know that. At least at first it would be. But I think you'd like it here and I think it's a good opportunity. For both of you." I was into my pitch now, wanting to get it right because this might be my only chance to make it for days, maybe at all this trip if things continued to escalate, the preparations. And they obviously were going to.

"Here's what I'm thinking. You," pointing at Jessica, "can go to school full time, on me. You can live in the house, it's certainly big enough. Or in here," the motor home, "if you want more privacy. Some of each, whatever. Get your own place after while if it isn't right at Greta's. Hell, put an apartment in the barn. You'll have your own private beach, semi-private. Mandy and your sister were down there this morning already. You want your own restaurant?" now looking at Randy. "I just happen to have one. We'll have to get some licensing and you might have to start with take out, bar-becue, something like that, but there's room in the barn for that too, a dining room. We can put picnic tables under those big oaks, there's lots of beach traffic. You could build something pretty cool.

"And I'd have my family with me. That's what's in it for me. We'd all be together." I started to get watery eyed, tried to blink it away, looking out the side window to hide my face. I wasn't fooling Jessica and she climbed over and sat on my lap, a hundred and fifty pounds of six-foot child snuggling on her daddy's lap, the comforting going in the opposite direction.

"You have to do what's best for you and if this isn't it, I understand. But I want you to think about it, talk it out, check it out, then we can talk again. Probably after the wedding. Here comes the rest of the inmates," I said, seeing them returning, my vision through Jessica's hair over her shoulder.

Gloria and Bubba's mission only cost me a hundred and thirty. Mandy and Greta spent the big bucks. I gave Mandy the paper bag that we kept our cash stash in and said help yourself. We went to three or four hundred worth of other places, ran around campus for a half hour, Greta surprising me, well not really surprise, what didn't this woman know, by pointing out and naming most of the buildings, not only the doctor so and so hall but what went on behind the ivy clad walls, sociology or physics, student union or student sleeping.

Then back to the home place. Hey Greta, I shouted to her on the way, what are your hours in the antique shop? When I feel like walkin' over there and puttin' out the open sign she shouted back, all of us laughing at her laissez-faire approach to business. Mandy, I thought, will be open dawn to dark seven days a week, a dozen red, white and blue bed sheet sized flags announcing her readiness to help you with your shopping needs.

That afternoon and all the following day were spent in preparations for the grand event. Randy and Jessica practically barricaded themselves in the barn kitchen, his answer to my question about how many guests an enigmatic grin. Greta wasn't sure, he said chuckling. Okay, I thought, we aren't going to stress. Let the kids do their thing. I knew we had offloaded another big batch of stuff from the motor home into the barn from our field trip and they had taken the pickup into town at least once the next day.

Bubba and I were on exterior clean up, a game that might have more accurately been described as 'hide the junk'. We crammed everything we could carry into first one, then a second out building and were well involved with a third before we had the grounds looking more or less ship shape.

Mandy and Gloria, Billie I mean, worked on beautification, weeding, whacking and sweeping, raking, pruning, then finally towing a Ford tractor out of a shed and after an hour of jumping and bleeding and priming, got the thing running, Bubba the mechanic–I think it was steam driven it was so old–and then they all took turns pulling a five gang mower back and forth across the lawns and meadows, cutting all the way down to the back tree line.

Greta had the good duty. She and Celina did all the quality control inspecting, the two of them marching from one work gang to the other, circling the house, barn and grounds time after time, making sure everyone was working to Celina's specifications. It was real clear who the boss was.

About noon on Friday, twenty-four hours and counting, a big, really big, box truck pulled into the driveway, parking between the house and the barn. I was close by and the driver jumped down and said hey, where you want 'em set up? I said, what set up, the two-headed idiot sign apparently igniting over my head. All of it, he said, exasperated. I'll have to check, I told him, I only work here. 'All of it' turned out to be a forty by ninety-foot tent, twenty, eight foot tables and two hundred chairs. Greta told him where to go and in short order he and the six guys in the back of the truck set everything up under four of the humongous oak trees seemingly planted three hundred years ago with this exact occasion in mind.

An hour later he handed Greta a couple sheets of paper which she barely glanced at before pointing at me. I don't think they even spoke. I headed for the moneybag as soon as I saw her gesture. Seven hundred and change. For fifteen to twenty people? I didn't even ask.

Late that afternoon we all went to the beach and had a picnic, a combined culinary event, Greta's leftover ham on thick, grainy bread with lots of produce piled high, little pots of noodle and vegetable salads from the barn kitchen, a case of iced beer in a rusty tub, then another half way through. I wouldn't have thought eight people could eat or drink that much but we'd worked like field hands all day and the beach was wonderful, the waves big enough to play in but not daunting, the sky cloudless, eighty something degrees both air and ocean. It doesn't get any more perfect, one of the best days I had ever had, exactly what I'd fantasized about, me and my family.

Chapter Sixteen

Wedding day. Weather? Perfect again, the same as Friday, eighty something and cloudless, the slightest breeze, just enough to get the oak leaves dancing a slow waltz, the big pines keeping time.

Attitude? I was calm, wanting to sleep in again. Everyone else made up for it though. With two pillows on my head, I still couldn't close out the sounds. Voices, dozens it seemed, feet in the hall and up and down the stairs, hundreds. Doors slamming, water running and toilets flushing, a stadium full of bathrooms all going like halftime. I said fuck it in my mind and stuck on some gym shorts and went outside to pee. It's a country thing.

I think I saw all of them on my way out but I couldn't swear to any of their identities, either they were moving too fast or me too slowly, with my eyes half closed and my thoughts on my bladder. Greta was a definite on the way back in, no question it was her stoking up a coffee pot that had to have been a part of Clyde's failed enterprise in its youth. Too big for a domestic kitchen. Too big for an AA meeting. She snapped off some comment as I filled a mug from the regular pot but until I digested the contents, my ears were on strike.

Mandy touched me while I was leaning on the counter sipping and looking out the window, mildly aware that there were great clouds of white smoke billowing out of the far end of the barn. It had to be Mandy. Neither Greta nor my children would have grabbed my ass and crooned tonight, tonight in a lusty whisper. And Celina could neither reach it nor talk.

I was starting to come around, about seventy percent, still gazing out the window, clearly the first one to see the limo turn into the yard, thirty five feet of polished white steel and sparkling chrome. I was awake enough to wonder but not enough to care, life with Greta starting to really numb me to the unexpected. The liveried driver popped out and ran, really ran, to the rear door nearest the house and my window. He opened it quickly and stuck in his head, addressing what I could not tell for the darkened glass.

The 'what' kicked in the last thirty percent. In an adrenalized millisecond the slackness left my face, my eyes snapped open all the way and I imagine all my color drained right down to my feet. *Something* was draining into my guts and my balls didn't like it, climbing up toward my ass like they had a ladder. Clara was climbing out! Trying to. Mobility is an issue at her size and the driver was finding it difficult to gain purchase anywhere on her upper body to lend a hand. She made it, finally. I could almost hear her grunting through the closed kitchen window. Well, that made sense. Mandy had never been married, her mom ought to see it happen. Even if it was to be a short lived affair.

My mom, sliding out right behind her, didn't. Make sense. *I* hadn't called her. *Mandy*, I yelled over my shoulder into the house.

"Hush, boy," Greta said from her spot over to my left. "Mothers need to be at these things," me thinking, how the hell do you know who just arrived, you can't see them from where you're standing. Weird.

It was a big limo, at least an eight seater. Kathy and her husband Kile climbed out right behind Mom as Marsha and her husband Tom were getting out the far side. Sharon and her son Fred were right behind them. I didn't know whether to run out the back and try to swim to Bermuda or bite down hard on my lower lip and go on outside. The choice was taken from me when Mandy grabbed my right arm and dragged me through the porch, down the steps and into the yard, practically throwing me at my mother as we got close.

"Hi, everybody. What a surprise," I said.

"Well it shouldn't have been," from Mom. "Not if you would have done what your fiancée did."

"Call you?" I asked.

"Invite us! I did *not* raise such a dumb bastard! Are you taking stupid pills?"

"Not since last week, Mom," I said, giving her a careful hug. "I'm sorry. You're right but there's been a lot going on. I'll explain later."

"You don't need to. Mandy did. I love you, Chance."

"I love you too, Mom. Thanks for coming."

"You paid for my ticket," she said.

"I am a good son, aren't I," I said. I handed her off to Greta after a brief intro, like I had to introduce anybody to Miss Know-it-All, then I went to glad hand with the rest of the kin. We milled around for a couple minutes, then Greta took charge, herding everyone into the house and telling me to get dressed. I felt like a five-year-old, always being ordered about and always the last to find anything out.

I came back down in my uniform, feeling like a bit of an idiot, a clown maybe, in front of my older sisters, dressed like one anyway. People were hanging around all over the place, not just the limo crowd and the kids but another guy in costume, a reverse collar on an old time, black crow's tail suit and I guess his wife, in an 1860's original Dixie Chick's dress. He introduced himself, Reverend Something, the minister friend of Greta's who was going to do the deed. He and I walked outside to review the ceremony, me thinking, man, you could have talked to anybody in the place including Celina and gotten more information then you're going to get out of me. I was a mushroom as far as what was about to take place was concerned.

Mandy and I had spent about ten minutes total on our vows, at least together. We were each going to express our feeling in our own words at the appropriate time, her only direction was to keep it short. That was easy. I had no fucking idea what was going to come out of my mouth when the time came. I told him as much as I knew—he spoke, we spoke, he spoke, we were married. Keep it short, I added then asked, what do I owe you? Oh, it's on the house, he said. The reception should be payment enough. I figured he meant the food, maybe a couple of beers. Either that or even the damn minister knew more than I did.

Our next visitor was here for the whole afternoon, not just a couple cold ones after the service. It was another box van, smaller then the circus truck that had brought the tent but still pretty good sized. And it had 'BUDWIESER' in four foot red letters emblazoned on the side with 'The King of Beers' in slightly more humble script below. And below that a dozen taps sticking through the sheet metal side. The truck stopped opposite me and the preacher and a bearded head leaned down toward us.

"Hey, General," the man said. "Is this Greta's place?"

I just nodded and pointed down toward the motor home figuring he'd been to more of these then I had, he'd find his own place to set up. He did, parking in the shade of an oak tree with the taps facing the tent, ready for a broad side of beer as soon as somebody blew the charge.

I didn't have long to wait. I thought I was hallucinating, the bugle call a fair ways off. But I wasn't and as the reveille notes drew closer, I could clearly hear the sound of hoof beats then the sound of marching men. Our other hundred and eighty guests were here, turning into the drive, a Confederate Company or brigade. It could have been a whole fucking division for all I knew. They were led by General Lee, my best man's couple of friends right behind and also on horseback, ten of them. Then *their* couple of friends, a four abreast column of infantry, all with muskets and rucksacks and bedrolls. It was going to be a hell of a party, I thought, especially when the caissons, horse drawn two wheeled wagons, four of them, two pulling cannons, turned in behind the infantry.

As each member of the cavalry, starting with Robert E. himself, drew along side me, they did an eyes left and snapped off a precise military salute, my body, reacting from some primitive vein of instinct, going rigid and my hand of its own accord returning the salutation.

The break between the horses and the humans gave me a chance to glance over toward the house, all its occupants on the lawn, on every face a delighted smile, Mandy with Greta at her side in the front row, both in fluffy cotton robes, caught in mid dressing ritual, Mandy's hands clasped like a supplicant at her chest but her eyes just on fire with the spectacle, laughing, the sound echoing between the house and barn making me smile as the tears began to trickle down my cheeks. The preacher put his hand on my arm and squeezed it hard. It's your day, son. Laugh, cry, do it all. Live it up, he said and I said thank you out of the side of my mouth then laughed openly as I saw Kile and Sharon photographing the spectacle from both ends, Kile running after General Lee's entourage video taping the aft end of the cavalry.

The infantry did the eyes left thing but didn't salute but I held mine until the last of the wagons had passed by. Unbelievable, I thought. The relatives were starting to head back in until I heard Greta say wait, clearly, then heard another bugle calling from the road.

A minute later more marching feet, then the vanguard of the next regiment made the turn. My allies had arrived, the blue coats. All infantry except their leader, not as many and not as resplendent but as militarily shipshape a group of men as ever graced a parade field, again fully fitted out for a long campaign, bedrolls and shelter halves belted tight.

And led by Sergeant Hines who apparently held a much higher rank on the weekends, full colonel at least, maybe even a general officer. His command was a multi racial group but their uniforms were all the same, a unified replication of the North with its superior plant and equipment, better able to outfit and systematize its forces. The rebels had more on-the-face-of-it authenticity with their varied garb and mismatched arms but I was willing to bet that a re-enactor arbitrator would find the Yankees had less twentieth century in their arsenal. They were both a grand sight and the mostly pro-federalist crowd on the other side of the driveway was clapping wildly as the last trooper filed past, my arm and back by now sore from saluting at attention.

The ceremony was held under yet another monster oak, this one at the far end of the tent farthest from the house. And the beer. The minister was up against the massive trunk with us a few feet out followed by a semicircle of civilians in folding chairs then the two armies on opposite sides of fifty feet of fresh mowed grass. General Lee was on my right, Greta in a period gown with hooped skirt and bustle on Mandy's left. Sergeant Hines had delivered Amanda to my side. The minister gave a short invocation, blessing our union and thanking us all for coming then launching into maybe five minutes of rhetoric of the standard wedding variety. Then it was my turn.

Mandy was so fresh faced and beautiful, so absolutely perfect as a woman and a bride that I knew I looked like a big blue over dressed guppy as I gazed at her and fumbled for words. It was a patient crowd. Finally, to me it seemed like a month later, I started to tell her all she meant to me, how much I loved her and how long I had looked forward to our marriage. I think I spoke for maybe thirty seconds, an eternity to be described, and I cannot tell you precisely anything I said but it must have been pretty good. And loud enough.

When I was done, first the Union forces and a second later the Confederate, burst into loud and lusty cheers, applauding for at least as long as I spoke. The generals had to quiet them. Mandy's words made me cry, I couldn't help it and I didn't care. She loved me, that's all I heard and all that mattered. I don't know how long she spoke or what she said, my tears making me stupid and deaf, but when she was done, her ovation was as resounding as mine had been, probably louder. I was the lucky one. They were thanking her for taking me.

The minister spoke again, we ringed each other and I kissed her, vaguely aware that we were now legal, then the heavens came crashing down as first one side then the other let go, two hundred and fifty powder charges fired from right shoulders capped by two eight pound cannons going off together. The field, the tent, hell, half the county, was instantly engulfed in acrid white smoke, my ears ringing like they'd done it in a great gothic cathedral, the Rebel yells and Yankee cheers not registering in my numb head for at least a minute.

We were swamped in humanity then, hugged, kissed and man-handled for ten minutes, the two generals finally breaking up the mad scrum by announcing that the drinking lamp was *lit*! I thought the Bud van was going to be knocked on its side the charge was so enthusiastic. Picket should have had beer. Or Mead's men on Little Round Top.

Chapter Seventeen

The reception was a blast and not just because at irregular intervals skirmishers would fire their black powder weapons across the field at the opposing camp. After their men had had a generous taste of Mr. Budweiser's wares, the generals ordered their men to establish their bivouacs. I didn't know any of them were spending the night and I was surprised at the degree of order and discipline that was inherent in the re-enactor's role. Both sides marched back to the firing field and began to unload the wagons, apparently a shared resource as both blue and gray pulled out tents, iron cook pots and tripods, period folding chairs and tables, and quickly established an encampment, the only thing obviously marking it as not exactly civil war era was the small margin of open space between the two sides.

It was wonderfully authentic, some of the men telling us that they were nineteenth century to their under wear, me thinking I hope you're twenty first in your personal hygiene. They didn't smell bad but this was only the first day.

Before long there were a hundred plus two man tents set up in two long lines, weapons stacked in pods at regular intervals, the horses tied under the back tree line on the Confederate side, quietly munching lawn grass. The generals had tents set up closest to our really big tent, theirs complete with carpet and cot. When I teased Robert about it he grinned and shrugged saying authenticity is everything.

Randy and Jessica did a great job with the food and when it was ready, a mixed bag of teamsters brought two of the wagons around to the kitchen door and loaded them with stretchers of grilled chicken, cauldrons of beans and vats of salads, an immense pot of shrimp gumbo and another of jambalaya, cases of rolls and a hill of butter. All was served off the backs of the wagons, brought around between barn back and tent side and after the horses were unhitched, the food line stretched half way around the yard.

By four things had settled down and a group of troopers assembled at the head of the big tent by the wedding tree and began to pick guitars and banjos, an accordion man and three drummers joining in. There were a dozen vocalists including Sergeant Hines. Six of his people must have worked together professionally because they had a repertoire of high energy, gospel spirituals that had a hundred men dancing in the grass. Thigh slapping, boot stomping, down home music.

We partied till almost midnight by which time I was ready for some quiet time with my bride. My family had straggled off by age, Mom first, then Kile, Sharon, Kathy. My girls were still going pretty strong and so were a few squads of soldiers. I went into the house to find Mandy. Greta, Clara and Marsha were talking in the parlor. She went up stairs a while ago, Greta said. Try my room.

I climbed the steps, weary, wanting to just get my Baby and go down to our house and go to sleep. I knocked gently on Greta's massive walnut door and heard Amanda say come in.

"I thought you were never coming," she said. Even with all the candles, she was indistinct, the canopy of gauzy lace enveloping the entire bed. I drew aside the cloth and looked down at the silk

sheathed form of my supine wife. The coverlet was drawn back and she was stretched across the sheets on an angle in a provocative pose. She didn't need to. My equipment was already in motion and so was I, fighting with the buttons that were keeping me from jumping on her. There were hundred of them it seemed. I didn't remember having this much trouble getting into the damn costume but there hadn't been this kind of reward waiting for me then either. God bless the guy that invented the zipper.

After twenty minutes of frustrated clawing, it felt like that long anyway, I finally sprang free of my confines and got a chance to run my hands over her body, lock my lips onto hers.

"So, Mrs. Barkley," I panted in her ear. "You want to fool around?"

"I thought you'd never ask," she smiled, taking me in her arms.

We slept late, I did, Mandy with me when the sun came up but not much longer. I heard her splashing around in the bathroom at one point then she was back in bed with me for some tranquil morning loving then she was gone again and I slept. Bugle calls got me up for good. I pulled back the drapes and looked down at our wedding guests. There were a score of cooking fires going and as many circles of men with metal plates eating what looked like stew, some kind of gloppy brown stuff anyway. I hoped somebody had something better going down stairs. I was hungry.

I climbed into my uniform pants and pulled on my J. C. Penny non-authentic under shirt and went down to find out what was happening. Lots. There were people banging away in the kitchen, lounging in the parlor, hanging out on the porch. I saw most everybody but Mandy and Greta. They went to church, Billie said. You're kidding. Nope. Okay, she went to church, I thought. That wasn't too unusual. I went twice a year, Easter and Christmas, Mandy more often then that. But not so often that to have missed a week would have been a big sin or something. Her mom and

Grandmom went too, Billie clarified. And the generals and a bunch of the soldiers. They're going to sing. Ah, I thought, the gospel group. That explains it.

Billie said the church was just up the road and that they had just left. Could be fun. I ran down to the motor home and slapped on some deodorant and jeans and a golf shirt and trotted back up to the house. I asked Bubba if I could borrow his truck and he said do you ride? Ride? Motorcycles. Oh, I said, yeah I used to. Take the hog, he said, it's by the kitchen.

It had been a while but like they say, you never forget. I cranked it over, electric start, that was good, played with the gears while I sat there revving the engine then toed it into first and eased on out, coasting onto the road and then roaring away. Hot damn! I had forgotten what a rush it is, all that power right under your balls. I cruised into the parking lot of the first church I came to, not sure I was in the right spot till I saw the horses. The cavalry was there with two wagons. I parked by them and jogged up the steps, opening the doors from the vestibule to the sacristy quietly, trying to slip in unnoticed. It didn't work. My minister of record from yesterday was in the pulpit and he stopped preaching in mid-sentence to welcome me, pointing out into the crowd to his right, directing me to my bride. I grinned, embarrassed, and thanked him, working my way down the pew till I got to her side. She was blushing, how appropriate.

He uplifted our spirits for a while then the 'special guest singers' came up out of the crowd and the place started to rock, six soul men wailing accappella, then the organist getting with it and finally the regular choir adding some back ground. They did five or six numbers, the entire congregation clapping in rhythm, the preacher doing a holy jig off to the side and when they were done, he called out 'one more song, please' and led us all in 'May the Circle be Unbroken,' real up tempo, then said 'go with God, my friends' and cut us loose. It was the best church service I'd ever been to and I walked out of there feeling better than I had when I went in which, to me, should be the measure of any religion event.

When Mandy saw my transportation I thought she was going to balk at coming back with me but she climbed on anyway, having to hitch her skirt all the way to her panties which got an appreciative Rebel yell from the teamsters, she blushing crimson, me laughing out loud. We made it back safely, Mandy wrapped so tightly around me I could barely breath but it was only a mile or so. I pulled up by the porch and Bubba yelled over, let it run, we're going for a ride and a couple seconds later he and Billie tore out of the driveway, her hair flying straight back from under the helmet. At least she was wearing one. Mandy and I hadn't been. Fine example we were.

We spent the day lounging outside until Randy served up about forty racks of spare ribs. That got the beer flowing again. I was surprised to see the truck still there that morning but I didn't see the driver till we got back from church. I was having too much fun to go home he told me. I slept on the beach. Then he added, today's on me, my time and the truck. The beer's yours anyway, then he handed me the invoice. I paid him in twenties, a goodly stack. It was worth every damn one of them.

Around four the bugles rang out again and the men stared to break camp. By five they were formed up and, with another short blare of horns, they were marching, Mandy and I on the porch steps with most of the others close by. I said thank you about a hundred times, shook as many hands and got two high ranking hugs, the generals. Mandy got a lot of hugs, winks and whistles. She was wearing short shorts and a halter top, thinking about a beach moment and was a lot sexier then me. She also got a couple good kisses and was crying/laughing when the generals rode off.

"Pretty good wedding?" I asked as we watched them gallop away.

She wiped her eyes and stood tip toed up to me for a kiss. "Yeah," she said. "Pretty good. Thank you."

"Oh no. Thank you, Sunshine. You are my beautiful, perfect Baby and I love you more then anything in this world."

We went for a swim, just the two of us.

Chapter Eighteen

onday was reality again. The tent guys came and hauled off their stuff. For fifty in cash they took all the bagged trash. The troopers had left the grounds spotless, matted grass and a few clumps of fertilizer the only signs of the encampment. The limo came back around eleven and took the relatives away. The kids weren't leaving till the next morning so I had that afternoon to pin them down, one way or the other. I thought it best for us to do it in a group so I called a 'family meeting', laughing to myself at the irony. Getting more like my mother as I aged? We gathered around the plank feast table on the back porch, Greta at one end at my insistence, me at the other.

"Well kids, did you all have a good time?" They had, it was rhetorical. "And did you have time to talk about all this," I said, waving my arm in a sweeping gesture. They looked at each other and nodded. "Okay. Billie, you go first. What are you going to do?"

"Go home," she said. My heart sank. "Settle up with Paul," she continued. "We're going to sell the house and split the money. He agreed. He has a girl friend," she explained. "She wants her own house so now Paul has an incentive to end the fighting. My attorney will handle the sale," she said. "Then we're coming back to live with you!" laughing now cause she'd had me going there for a minute.

"Excellent!" I said, Mandy clapping by my side.

"You aren't going to regret it, Billie. I promise," Greta said as she stood and wrapped the girl in her arms.

"Jessica and Randy? I know you guys are conflicted on this. What did you come up with?"

"We aren't sure, Dad," Jessica answered.

"But we'd like to…" Randy was struggling for words. "Try it maybe?"

"How so?"

"We need to go back. I can't just not show up at work. Mr. Klein is a good guy, you know him, I can't screw him over, you know?"

"Yes. He is a good man and no you can not screw him over. What are you thinking, a sabbatical?

"Yeah. See if we can take a month off, come back. We can at least help you out around here for a while even if it doesn't work out. Jess' school doesn't start till after Labor Day no matter where she goes so we'd have the time."

"That would be great," Mandy said. "We'll have a most excellent summer, dude."

"Sounds like a plan," I added. "I'm very excited about this. Thank you guys, I love you all."

We spent the rest of the day hanging out, mostly together, some beach time in there for some of us, lots of eating although there wasn't nearly as much food left over as I would have thought. I realized that the bottled beer that we had chilled in the refrigerator, that I thought was all we'd need for the reception, had been planned for before and after so we dipped into it eventually.

Around three Greta suggested some fishing, me thinking where is there a pond, her saying surfcasting. Ah, sounds good,

I said. She led us to one of the sheds and pulled out four heavy fiberglass rods, a couple spackle buckets and some angle cut plastic tubes. What about bait, I asked and she sent Bubba to the barn fridge for a box of frozen shrimp, if Randy didn't cook them all, she laughed. He hadn't and we marched single file down to the water and she showed us how to rig and cast, leaving the actual hurling of the baited hooks to Bubba. Go out as far as you can and really let 'em rip, boy, she directed from the edge of the waves. He waded out waist high four times and soon we were 'fishing', sitting on the beach looking at poles stuck in pipe stuck in the sand. Like watching the grass grow.

"How do you know when you get one?" I asked.

"You either see the rod tip bending if it's a big 'un or you reel in every once in a while. You have to anyway to check your bait."

"And what's out there to get got?" I said.

"Supper, I hope. Whiting, blues, flounder maybe. Depends on the time a the year."

"I could go for some blackened swordfish," Mandy said giggling. "Catch one for me, Last."

"You better start swimmin'," Greta chuckled. "They're out there about, oh, fifty miles?"

"Not a problem," I said, peeling off my tee shirt and flexing my muscles. "I'll be right back." I went out as far as my kneecaps, splashed water on my face and walked back in. "No luck," I said as I flopped back down beside Mandy. "Sorry, Babe. Hamburger Helper again."

"Without the hamburger," she laughed.

Five minutes later Greta got off her over turned bucket and when up to one of the poles, its tip bending and flexing the same as the others as the current tossed the weighted hooks around on the ocean floor sixty or seventy yards from shore. She took the line in her hand and pulled on it then hoisted the pole out of its holder and gave it a hard jerk then started to reel, looking back at me and smirking. A couple minutes more and I saw a fish being drug though the water and onto the sand.

"Son of a bitch," I said. "How'd you know he was on there? And what is it?"

"It's a whiting. And years of experience. Stick it in the bucket," she directed, then said, "put some water in it first, you dummy!"

Salt-water fishing was not my forte'. Living in Pennsylvania doesn't afford one that many opportunities. Especially if you hate New Jersey. Greta's catch, though, got us motivated and pretty soon we were working the rods, at her direction seated on the other bucket. Now I knew why we'd brought two. And we were catching fish. About every ten minutes one rod or another would yield a foot long trout looking thing that Greta promised would be as sweet as candy once we'd filleted them and sautéed them in some garlic butter. They sure would be fresh.

When we had twelve she said that ought to do us for dinner, if we want to keep at it, we can freeze 'em. I declined and we all agreed to pack it up and go do the dirty work. I knew more about that part of the business. We cleaned them on a rough plank nailed to brackets on the side of one of the sheds above a spigot, the fish-cleaning place she called it, reminding us to bury the guts or toss them back in the ocean. Skunks, she admonished. Or coons.

When Randy and Bubba and I got back to the house, the post-catch or kill always man's work it seems, the ladies were well involved in both food prep and Greta's toddys. Should be a fun evening, I thought, all five females already laughing and carrying on, rock music coming from a stereo in the parlor. We handed off the fish slabs, helped ourselves to the contents of a big porcelain pitcher and retired to the screened porch to talk about manly things. And stay out from under foot.

Greta was right about the fish. They were excellent, salty sweet, drizzled with buttery lemon juice, a hint of garlic for some kick.

We ate all of them and spinach with more of the big ham diced in and the last of Randy's salads. And two more pitchers of toddys. I meant to ask what was in them but kept forgetting. Some of the applejack and maybe bourbon? Sugar for sure, they were sweet. And too damn good. I restrained myself but no one else did. Celina maybe but she got tucked in before the second round so she didn't count.

Greta told us war stories after she got loosened up, after the dishes were done and the candles lit on the feast table, the wind blowing in from the sea keeping us cool. She had been around the world in chunks, over thirty years, England the first leg, Bangkok to Bombay to Rome and back to England the last. She had been in combat zones on two continents, had R and R on a third, visited dozens of countries, spoke four languages that I knew of before the evening began, and interrogated thousands of people without harming any of them. Amazing.

"I bet your uniform was mighty colorful," I said, drawing my fingers down my left chest where all the campaign ribbons would have been attached.

"Oh, it was a grand thing," she laughed. "Weighed a bloody ton with all that crap pinned on there. Gave me neck aches when I had to wear the medals too."

"Medals?" Billie asked, topping off Greta's mug.

"Yeah, quite a few," she said.

"Come on, Greta," Mandy teased. "Give it up. What did you get?"

The old lady was off somewhere in her memories, maybe all of them weren't that good, but she came back in a minute, looking at Mandy but not really seeing her I thought.

"Greta," Mandy asked, hand on hers. "You okay?"

"Fine, baby girl. Just reminiscing. My medals? Okay, lets see. Legion of Merit, that's French. Order of Parliament, with second cluster, that's English, a Canadian Royal Commendation, and a

Silver Star. World War II. Another Silver Star and a South Korean Metal of Valor, Korea. Oh, and a Purple Heart there. A Bronze Star, a Purple Heart and a Medal of Honor for Vietnam. There's some little ones, meritorious this and that that I don't remember but those are the big ones.

No one said a word for two days or so after she was done, we were all just staring. Finally Mandy said 'wow' and that got my mind unstuck enough to say 'holy shit' and then 'how?' She turned to look at me, still sort of out of it, then her eyes focused and she smiled.

"Intelligence. Gatherin' it, sortin' through it, talkin' to people about it. A lot of stuff with captured pilots in England. And a couple parachute drops into France. Before D-Day. There were questions of loyalty in the Resistance. Those Frogs," she said wagging her head. "A devious bunch, ness pa?"

"Let me guess," I said. "Vous parley Francais."

"Oh, oui. Et tu, Last?"

"Not hardly. Three years in high school and I just said everything I remember." Make that five.

"And toward the end, as we closed in on Berlin, there was some work on the Holocaust. Course we didn't call it that back then, didn't know the scope of it, what all those cursed Nazis had done. But we began to get the gist of it after a while. It was a harsh time, I'll tell ya. We were all giddy from kicking their asses, the war almost over. Then we began to realize that all those stories about the Jews might be true." She stopped, looking away and I swear I saw the light just go out of her eyes.

"Greta," I called to her. "Come on back, girl. It was a long time ago." She seemed to hear me with a time delay but after a few seconds her eyes ratcheted back over to mine.

"You never forget," she said.

"Don't," I said. "But don't let it eat you up either."

"Do I look eaten, boy," she said, her bluster coming back.

"Don't make me answer that," I laughed. "Tell us more about your illustrious career. You have to be the most decorated female ever to serve in the army."

"I might be, Chance. I don't know. Don't care truthfully. Almost all of my commendations were issued in, ah, private, so to speak. I was in private my whole career. Usually, after I'd been home from overseas, a couple years sometimes, I'd get an official lookin' envelope. A lot of them were hand delivered by some fresh-faced junior officer. After a while I just tossed 'em in a drawer. One time I opened three or four of them the same afternoon. The oldest had been in there three years. There was always a letter, thank you for serving your country with such valor, blah, blah, then a couple sentences I've heard a hundred times, about the need for secrecy in our endeavors, same old shit. It's okay. I knew goin' in I wasn't in it for the glory," she said chuckling

"Sounds like you got your fair share of it though," I said, "even if they couldn't brag on you openly."

"Yeah, I was a superstar for a while. It kinda goes to your head no matter how down to Earth you think you might be. I liked it. I won't lie to ya. It was a thrill. But it was also a real long time ago and I'm over it now."

"Do you ever feel like putting on your old uniform," Mandy asked, "and marching in the Veteran's Day Parade?" all of us laughing along with Greta once she had digested the comment.

"Wouldn't that be a spectacle," Greta chuckled. "I'll tell you what, baby girl. You can do my funeral for me. You want a dress me up all the way, you be my guest. I'll be sittin' up on my cloud just laughin' away."

She told us how she had gotten most of the medals then, not always a hundred percent sure what action had led to which commendation, the combat information general, the wounds slight in context to the battles raging in those theaters at the time. The Medal of Honor, the big one from Vietnam, was related to Tet, her warning of something extraordinary in the offing going generally unheeded, only the division commander of the brigade she was actually working with at the time finally hearing her. She had practically tackled him as he made a perfunctory inspection of their fire base, he flying in on a slick for a twenty minute stop and go look at his forward positions, she there because of the unusual number and quality of the enemy contacts they were encountering.

Please, sir, listen to me. *Something* is going down. Something big! He did, putting her base and all his commands on full alert, ordering up the artillery and air support wings of his protectorate to full emergency status. When the offensive began a scant twelve hours later, his people, although skeptical to a man, were far better prepared then those of just about all of his brothers in arms. He looked like a genius and although he never gave her actual credit, he never denied that superior intelligence, from people within his own command, was the reason for his exceptional state of readiness. She got the Medal of Honor six years later, after she had been retired for three, the whole Tet debacle the subject of meaningless debates that had been beaten to death by almost every military and civilian historian who had ever studied the war.

"Greta," I asked. "Do you mind a question?" When she said no with a feral smile that should have been sufficient warning for me to keep my mouth closed, I said, where were you when the assault began?

"Sittin' behind a fifty caliber machine gun," she answered, the predatory look still on her face, scary enough to chill me to the bone. "I offered to give the whole gun crew a blow job if they'd stop drinkin' and pay attention till midnight. They was all gettin' ready to collect when the gooks hit the wire." After a long pause she added almost as an after thought, "We cut 'em down by the hundred lot." Then after a longer pause, "I didn't have to pay up a course. Half of 'em didn't see the dawn anyway."

That put an end to war stories for the evening.

Chapter Nineteen

We were all up early Tuesday, Mandy the impetus for that. I don't know if she woke me first and I dozed back off or if I was the last and she sat on my chest till I kept my eyes open but either way we were all scarfing up a big southern breakfast, eggs, sausage, grits and biscuits, by eight. The kids were packed and saying their good-byes by nine and by ten I was melancholy, missing them, their vitality and happiness.

By eleven Mandy was tired of watching me mope, me thinking I was concealing it, an open and pathetic book to my darling. She grabbed me by my left forearm and dragged me to my feet, until then sequestered in a porch chair staring out across the lawn toward the beach, bothering no one but not interacting except by single syllables with Greta or Mandy.

"Come on, Last, we're going swimming," she said to me, her little devil's grin making a promise. I hoped.

She led me down to the motor home in case I wanted fresh clothes and when I said I was okay, we marched straight through the dunes and onto the sand. She looked north and south, no one in sight either way. Amazing. Our own private beach this close to all that tourist clutter. I remember sitting on the sand watching her strip naked, I remember the wicked grin on her face as she backed into the water, like she was shouting at me from the darkened triangle between her thighs and I remember ripping my clothing off and charging into the waves after her.

The rest is more of a sweet dream. I know she swam away from me for a hundred yards. I know I caught her cause I can still feel her nubby tongue lashing my neck and chest, my hands locking on her butt as I hoisted her up and then down on my cock. I know we let the tidal surge do most of the work as the swells kept us locked in perfect motion. And I damn sure know that when I came, I howled like the alpha wolf on midsummer's eve, the moon full and all my enemies in retreat. The best sex I ever had. In forty years? Here I had to think, giving myself credit for the thought if not the act when I was thirteen. Good God it was great!

She had to have done it for me. Not that she wasn't howling at the same imaginary moon but what a man's fantasy! Beautiful woman lures you to the beach, shows you the target then lets you catch her and fire your missile. While she's clamping you in place with her talons, toes and teeth.

We floated in the waves for another twenty minutes, my softness never preventing me from staying where I longed to be until I wasn't so soft anymore and the staying became easier. The repetition caused no diminishing of the fun and I might have easily morphed into a merman if Mandy hadn't pulled away from me then and swam for shore. I wanted her still and I was swimming full tilt with that in mind but she made the sand well before me and stopped only to check that I was still far enough behind, laughing as she scooped up our clothing, giving me a great, lecherous view of her behind, then running naked up through the dunes leaving me to emerge from the surf alone, at least metaphorically as I had my cock in my right fist and as such had at least one stalwart ally in hand.

The cause was lost unless she had scampered into the motor home for a replay. She had not. Damn. I hosed off quickly in the airplane bathroom sized stall and slid into gym shorts and a clean tee shirt. She'd get hers, I thought. As soon as I recovered. When I got back to Greta's, the two of them were ensconced in the parlor as if me not being there with them had never been an issue, certainly not something to fret over.

That afternoon we went to Wilmington to visit a lawyer friend of Greta's to execute the sales paperwork. She was in essence holding the paper on the property so there were no income statements required, no old tax returns, just a few signatures and a pile of cash and we were the proud new owners of a house, barn and junkyard. We went from there to Greta's bank and then back to the house. The next morning we took her to the airport and sat drinking coffee with her till her flight was boarded. She had been consistently vague about her plans saying, wait for the post cards, it will make it fun for you like 'Where in the World is Greta' I laughed. We'll get a big map and push pins, Mandy said. All we knew for sure was that she was on a commuter flight to Charlotte.

We hugged and kissed her and went on home. Well, my love, I said as we sat in Greta's Jeep in the driveway, where do you want to start?

"We should probably organize the shop and get open for business," she said without a lot of enthusiasm.

"Yeah, I agree. But not today. I'm tired."

"And a little blue," she added.

"Yep." Profound.

I needed to call my realtor, my banker up north, have our mail forwarded, all kinds of stuff. It could wait till tomorrow. I took a pill and dozed in a porch chair till bedtime, Mandy curled up on a couch near by.

The next morning was a lot better. We got up at six and took a quick dip then, still in our damp swim wear, got after the barn, starting at the 'sales' counter and working our way out from there. Mandy sorted and tagged and cleared out the small stuff in front of her. We had a rough sketch of the lower floor that I had whipped up on notebook paper and an equally rough idea of how to lay out the place. Greta had some old carpentry tools, new enough to require electricity thank God, and I ripped and cut and spiked together shelves and a couple counter tops, Mandy stacking and displaying as fast as I crafted the spaces. By late afternoon, we had an island of organization in a sea of clutter. By the end of the second day, we were working on a continent, a small one but definitely a landmass. By the middle of the third day, I thought we could probably open the doors.

I had mail ordered some red, white and blue sales office style flags from my old pal Steve at National Flag and Banner in Philadelphia and they came UPS COD ASAP the morning of the third day. Mandy had driven into a quick sign place in Hampstead the day before and tomorrow our lettered signs would be done.

"Should we grand open the joint, Sunshine?" I asked her. "Tomorrow's Saturday."

She looked up at me from behind the counter, sweat running down the side of her face, dirt caked up to her elbows. "Ask me again after I've had a shower," she said.

Saturday I was at the sign store by eight and back by nine. By ten I had the barn draped with twenty feet of heavy plastic four feet wide. 'Greta's Antiques and Collectibles.' Simple. To the point. By eleven I had staked out six assorted 'open' and 'welcome' signs along the road frontage and six more along the barn. By noon Mandy had her first customer and by two the place was fairly packed. I had to stop raking gravel in the parking lot, there were too many cars in it to make any progress anyway, and go help her in the store.

We locked up at six thirty as the last shopper was pulling out, both of us a little shell shocked, never anticipating anything like this. I took down the flags in a hurry, afraid someone else might pull in and keep us open another hour. I was actually wobbly with fatigue and didn't want to sell another damn thing. Come on, I said. Lets get out of here, which meant walking a hundred feet and climbing on to the porch but the separation was symbolic as much as anything.

"Phew," she said as we flopped down at the table. "Where did all those people come from?" She laughed when I made a face.

"I'm getting a beer. How much was the take there, Mrs. Macy?"

"Vanderbilt, please. It has to be a few thousand. You fetch, I'll count."

I came back with two beers, an ancient manual adding machine that probably should be for sale in the shop along with the water heater and a tablet. We were under prepared for such entrepreneurial success. Greta's cut was to be deposited into her old business account. We had opened our own at the same bank but we hadn't gotten our permanent checkbook yet. We also had no accounting system at all other than a different notebook which Mandy had been manually recording all our transactions in. At this rate, we would run out of receipt slips some time tomorrow, Greta's inventory not too deep in that regard. We didn't have a brochure for the shop. Hell, we didn't even have business cards.

"We need a plan I think, Sunshine," I said.

"Duh," she said, not even looking up. "Three thousand, nine hundred and fifty four dollars," she said finally. "I need my computer."

"And a twenty four hour printer," I laughed. "One of us ought to go home and get some stuff. The other one needs to get with a printer Monday morning, first thing. And an accountant."

"You go," she said. "I'll stay, okay?"

I worked the shop with her till five on Sunday, then pulled down the flags and headed north in the motor home. I figured I could be back Tuesday afternoon. When I called her from I-95 a few hours later, she said we'd done over four thousand but she hadn't totaled it to the penny. Too tired, she said. She hadn't gotten the last couple out of there till almost seven.

Monday morning I drove my old Chevy down to the used car dealer and walked out with a check for eight hundred. I'd have given them three just to get rid of it. They drove me home. I took Mandy's car to get a tow bar and then went back to pack. We'd have to come back at some point to get the balance of our stuff but right now I needed tools, good ones, hammers and saws, computers, fax machines. I even had a desktop copier. Greta was going modern.

I called my banker. I love having 'a banker.' They're such impersonal institutions but when I bought our house from Jack's estate, I met the woman who had been 'his banker,' a young, pretty woman with a wicked sense of humor and a healthy disdain for most of the bureaucracy that surrounded her. She was a rule bender, the first I'd ever met in the banking business. I adopted her immediately as my banker.

"Lizzie," I said. "It's Chance Barkley. You have a minute?"

"I have two nice building lots out your way. You need a hobby, don't you?" She was always bugging one or the other of us to take properties off her hands, fix them up and sell them. She'd say, it'll give Mandy something to do on the weekends.

"I wish I could help you, Liz," I laughed, "but we just bought a business in North Carolina. I need your advice."

"Why would you leave beautiful Lancaster County," she said, sounding serious but I knew she was grinning on her end. We used to joke about the horse shit on the highways from all the Amish buggies.

"Opportunity done knocked and I answered the door." Then I explained my personal situation which brought the banter to a stop.

"I'm so sorry, Last. How's your little Darlin' taking it?" She and Mandy had been friends for a couple years and they joked about all my pet names for Amanda because after I met Liz, she always inquired after her by using one of them.

"She's okay. We got married Saturday. Kind of spur of the moment. The time constraint, you know? That's why we bought the property, so she would have a...future, I guess. Roots or something. My oldest kid is going to help her with it." I told her about the shop and house, about the incredible old woman we had met and then I explained my financial dilemma.

"If I don't sell the house, Mandy will get full value for it after..... later. But I might need the equity in it now to fix up the Carolina place. So my question is, can I get a loan on the future value if you will? I know I can't get mortgage insurance now, on a second position loan, now that my condition has been diagnosed, but can I borrow on the present equity even though I don't have a job? Is that confusing enough for you? If not I could say it again and really garble up my thoughts."

"No, that's alright. I think I'm sufficiently befuddled. Let's see. Are you asking to borrow more than eighty percent of your current equity?"

"I don't think so. Maybe. I've got a realtor doing comps to let me know what it's worth. Would that be a problem, if I did want to?"

"Yeah, probably. I can do some funky stuff on my own but that would be hard. Not impossible necessarily but difficult. And it wouldn't happen in a hurry."

"I can imagine. Time is an issue, obviously."

"What are you trying to accomplish exactly?"

"I need liquidity I think and probably, ah, seed money I guess. I assumed that the shop would generate some income and it has.

Jesus, we did almost eight grand in two days but we can't sustain that. We'll need new inventory, we already need business stuff, accounting systems, the usual. This lady used stone tablets, I swear. And I might want to open a restaurant. I definitely need to spend some money fixing the place up."

"Can you borrow against the business? Down there?"

"No. Our benefactor holds the note. Almost a no money down deal but even if I wanted to encumber the property, I'd need her permission. And I don't want to. And she's off traveling somewhere anyway."

"How about your 401K? I assume you have one."

"Yeah and I want to talk to you about that too. I want to have you administer it for me. That's pretty simple isn't it?"

"A piece of paper. I'll send it to you."

"Good." I gave her the new address. "But I don't want to lose the twenty percent for early withdrawal. Mandy will get that at full value soon enough. See what I mean?"

"Sure. It sucks but it's obvious. You're a business with good receivables, you just have a short term cash flow problem."

"Exactly. And an indeterminate date for receipt of the receivables," I laughed. She asked how long that might be, easier for both of us to discuss in the abstract. "A year plus or minus. No one will say for sure. Or knows. I can't imagine it could be much more than that."

"So," she mused. "How about this. We do a second mortgage on the house, put it in a money market account that you can draw on at your convenience. We make it a thirty-year term to hold your payments down. You can get a six months no payback clause in it, you could even make the payments from the loan proceeds cause you know it's for a limited time. I'll dig around on the over equity loan but we can start with this. Sound good?"

"Good as it's likely to get. You're sure you can get it approved, with my job status?"

"There's no one to ask. This one's on me," she said.

We talked about the details for a while, the appraisals and fees involved. She said she would take care of all of it and forward the results FedEx within a week. I thanked her profusely and promised to give Mandy the biggest hug I had.

I called Mandy's cousin at work to see if she wanted to live in the house full time. If not I needed to forward the electric bill and cancel most of the rest. She said she couldn't afford to. I said the rent is zero, pay your own utilities. She said sure. I said no roommates, no parties and no animals. Deal. I called the utility companies and put them in her name. I could have put them in Elvis' name as long as the billing address didn't change.

I let myself into Clara's house with Mandy's key and grabbed up our mail pile from a basket by her desk. I left her a note, thanking God she wasn't there. I wrote out all the current bills and put a note in with each to forward the final to North Carolina. I paid six months on the mortgage. I went to the post office and filled out address change cards for Mandy and me. I stuffed the motor home from back to front with everything I could think of that we might need. Then I stuffed her car with more and hooked it up to the tow bar. I called Mandy, took a leak and headed south. I was back by midnight, waking my Baby with licentious intent. She kissed me once and said go fuck yourself, I'm sleeping.

I had a little over twenty grand left from my severance package and about ten more that I'd run over to my checking account before we'd left Pennsylvania the first time. I wasn't sure what to expect from the equity loan, maybe fifty. Conservatively, that was our working capital. I could cash in mutual funds any time and maybe I'd do that rather then going into the house loan but at least it was there if we needed it. There was plenty to just live on, live high if we wanted, even if the shop never made another dime. But it wasn't all that much considering everything I wanted to do. And I didn't really want to draw down our take from the shop beyond business expenses, utilities and such. I wanted that to be Mandy's money. We had plenty of existing inventory, enough for a couple months I figured even if we did keep selling like beer at a football game. Raise your prices, I told Mandy. Supply and demand.

We kept the shop closed Tuesday so we could start an inventory and make some plans. I wish Gloria was here, I said. We need the help. She called, Mandy told me. By next weekend. That was a lot sooner than I expected. Good news. We made a list, then prioritized it. Landscaping was first, then painting. We should paint first, I said after I'd thought about it some more. That way we won't slop paint all over the new plants. Good idea.

We went to the Home Depot in Wilmington and bought five gallon buckets of exterior latex for Mandy's color scheme that I thought was going to look great but be a hell of a lot more work then white on white. We started on the barn, agreeing to leave the board siding alone but paint the eaves and trim. High ladder work for me. Fortunately I had one and had brought it back, tied to the top of the motor home. We stayed closed Wednesday so I could walk the ladder across the parking area, four or five feet at a time, all I could reach with a six inch brush, leaning in and reaching up to get under the soffit, switching hands to get a couple feet more on the other side, then leaning out precariously, one foot dangling for balance as I hit the spot where the ladder had rested at its last stop. Mandy worked the low windows and the barn doors, as far away from where I rained paint down as she could get. By the end of that day, I was too tired to put the banner back up, too tired to take the damn ladder down, my shoulders screaming, my wrists and biceps, even my thighs from climbing up and down, up and down. Tomorrow morning early I would hit the barn side above the shop door, then put the flags out and plant some flowers. I needed a paint break already.

That's how I spent the next four days, painting till I couldn't bring myself to climb another rung, then farting around with flowers and mulch and gravel till we closed. Mandy worked the shop like an antiques maestro, her natural gift of conversation a huge benefit. Half the time she knew more about her customers than their next door neighbors by the time they left the shop, usually with their arms or trunks or both loaded down with Greta's wares. We raise prices again Sunday morning, both of us running around the shop like hamsters in a wheel, a pen in our teeth and a fist full of tags, ripping off the old ones and adding ten or fifteen percent to everything. You can always knock it back off if somebody wants to bargain. And if you like them, I told her. But you can't tell the prick on the other side of the counter that for him, it's fifty bucks more.

Monday we started moving upstairs stuff down, that area to be a future sales floor but for now too full of *stuff*, unpriced stuff, to be navigable by the shoppers. And we needed the inventory. We cleaned and glued and clamped, scraped paint, applied stain and wax and finally price tags. We were moving into bigger items, furniture, farm tables and dressers, headboards and cabinets. Not that there wasn't still a ton of mason jars and milk boxes, Greta just seemed to have piled lots of bigger items in the old hay loft. It made sense when I thought about it. She could drive right up there from the far end of the barn and when she started her collection, there most have been plenty of room. Some of the stuff had a couple of inches of fossilized pigeon shit on it. Nothing recent so the new roof must have solved that problem.

Most of Tuesday was spent upstairs too, by me, with a lot of rearranging going on below. I never realized how much work was involved in antiques. Late in the afternoon I drove down to the bank and put most of the cash receipts in Greta's account—close to ten thousand. I put the checks in ours. We didn't take credit cards yet. Greta wouldn't even take *checks* unless she knew the people. And her friends didn't shop there much.

On Wednesday I put out the flags and drove into Wilmington. I needed more paint and I wanted to check into restaurant licensing. Paint was easy. Bureaucracies are not. I started at the county courthouse, looking for a Bureau of Inspections or a Health Department. They sent me to an annex across town where the building inspectors were. They sent me to Hampstead to see the local version. They told me how to apply for a permit to *build* a restaurant but didn't know what to do with someone who might already have one. Or part of one anyway. They suggested the Health Department. Back in Wilmington where I'd started the day. I decided tomorrow was another day and I'd try again then.

I painted for a few hours in the afternoon, climbing the ladder a relief after ramming my head against a wall all morning. The barn was nearly done and looking snazzy as hell I thought, with its red roof, weathered red siding and cobalt exterior trim. I was looking forward to moving on to the house, getting my painting legs so to speak. My body didn't ache like an accident victim at night now and I was trimming some body fat from all the exercise. My thighs felt like I could leg press an elephant, the muscles tighter, more toned then they had been in years. And I had a beach boy tan. Why not? What's a little melanoma on top of what's already cooking on the inside? I felt pretty good there too, some days going an hour or more without 'death' leaping into my mind unbidden. I'd had an occasional chest twinge but nothing in days like the searing sword thrusts that I'd had the previous couple weeks. Exercise must be good for everyone, I thought. Even the terminal.

Mandy was starting to get repeat customers plus friends of the earliest explorers. I'd hear her call out someone's name as they entered the shop, me dragging shit around at her direction or slapping varnish on some old thing in the corner and I had to just shake my head in awe. My own mother could have walked in and called me by name and it would have taken me a minute to place her face. Mandy was going to be a superstar, everybody loved her. And she seemed to know everything she had in the shop including upstairs, even the crap I hadn't swept the shit off of yet. Oh, you're looking for an oak credenza with a carved bust of Napoleon's pecker on it? I don't have that but I do have one with Grover Cleveland's left leg on it. Will that do? And she'd march them over to some wooden thing that I'd oiled up the day before and forgotten instantly. It was a good thing that I painted and she sold. I would have stood silently behind the counter all day waiting for people to bring me what they'd selected, no clue at all what we had to sell.

I tried the bureaucrats again Friday, thinking they might be more helpful at the end of the week. They were or I got lucky. I found an old guy in the Health Department that not only told me what I had to do to resuscitate Clyde's Folly, he remembered the original and its owner.

"Ol' Clyde was a character, yes sir he surely was," the man chortled, "but a damn fine barbecue man. When he bothered."

"Yeah," I said. "I heard he kept some uneasy hours," which got the guy laughing.

"A hell of an understatement that 'un is," he told me. "Now here's what you do," giving me the forms and explaining the process. It was easy, the paperwork simplistic and the inspections not overly rigorous. As long as you didn't have indoor seating.

"You wanna move the show inside, that's a whole nother ball game. My advice, sell take out. Let 'em sit at a picnic table. Hell, boy, it's warm most a the time round here anyway," he informed me with a wack on the shoulder, my Yankee coming through clearly I gathered, him not needing to ask where I was from.

I thanked him as I was about to leave, then asked him how long it took to process the stuff once I'd brought it back. You could be open next weekend he said laughing, like that was a fine inside joke. I'll do the inspectin' my own self, he told me, if you got that boy I heard about doin' the cookin'. Randy. From the re-enactors I assumed. The boys liked his food I guess, I said. You bet they did. And congratulations. You must be the general that got hitched. I thanked him again and got out of there. This was too big a town to be so small I thought. But as long as they liked us, I liked all of them. So far anyway.

Sunday afternoon Billie and Bubba pulled in the yard in a U Haul truck towing her car. I told them to park in the back where the tent had been till the place calmed down and we could sort things out. We were mobbed, like we were giving the stuff away. We had raised prices again that morning in another fit of economic theory meets reality but the people just surged through the shop, buyers, not lookers. I asked Billie to get behind the counter, please, and give me a break, even fifteen minutes, just let me sit down for a second. She handed me Celina with a big grin and said sure. A fair trade. Bubba and I went to the porch and had a beer while Celina toddled around inside. The parking lot would have been instant death. *I* didn't even like to walk around out there.

"Looks like you've got it going," Bubba said with a smile. "I like the paint job."

"I can't fucking believe all the traffic. It's been like this since the day we opened. I'm ready to retire," I said.

"We talked to Jess this morning. They're coming. Are you sure you're up to it? Not that you don't look it," he added. "You look good in fact. Lost some weight?"

"Yeah," I said. "The good way. From exercise. But I *am* tired. I don't have Mandy's energy, never have. Hell, nobody does."

"Making money?"

"Hand over fist. We keep raising prices and they keep coming in. Tomorrow we'll bump them again I guess. It's like a feeding frenzy."

"Can't bitch about that. What do you need me to do?"

We sort of dawdled around, us boys and baby, for the balance of the afternoon, me showing him the new set up and explaining our plans. I told him we would start by organizing the rest of the upstairs, running some new lights, getting some additional sales space for the big stuff. Then paint the house. We went back over around five as the crowds thinned out and helped the girls close up, then we all trooped back to the porch and caught up while I cooked dinner.

Paul was being good, had signed off on everything and there was a 'for sale' sign on the house but some of her stuff was still in there. Bubba was going back up mid week–his Harley was in the rental truck along with Billie's necessities–to look after the house, mow the grass, keep it looking presentable for the realtor. And to keep Paul from moving back in. He also had some work left, a project under way that he had promised his boss he would stick with. Billie had given her boss two weeks notice. He told her to work one, take one as vacation and go with God, she had been a good employee and he was sorry to see her go but it sounded like a great opportunity. A nice guy, she told us. Sounded like it. We ate a hasty stir fry then went for a swim then yacked it up some more and went to bed.

Monday, with four of us working and taking turns keeping Celina out of trouble, we got the upstairs cleaned and sorted, moving all the 'to be worked on' items to one side and roping off the area, making it a fix it shop. Mandy thought all the tools and clamps and saw horses, the smell of Howard's Orange Oil and polyurethane scenting the air, would make a great sales point for the shoppers. I was going to feel like a circus bear working in there but as long as they didn't try to talk to me all day or start throwing peanuts or half eaten hotdogs at me, I figured I could handle it. Bubba said the furniture repair looked like fun and I said have at it, I'll paint.

Tuesday the girls spent all day on marketing presentation, setting up displays, arraigning furniture groupings, hanging old stuff on the walls and off the ceiling beams. By the afternoon, it looked so nice I felt like moving in. Too bad it wouldn't last more than a few hours after we opened up Wednesday morning. Bubba and I finished the planting beds, weeded and edged, raked and swept. The barn was ship shape.

I took Celina into town with me to drop off the restaurant papers and do some shopping. If I was on the make, I'd find a cute little kid to rent then go to a grocery store and just wander up and down the aisles looking helpless, waiting for women to come to me! It was ridiculous. I guess they all assume you're hopelessly inept at child rearing and stop to offer advice. I probably am but is it that obvious? We got out of there as soon as I'd grabbed enough food for dinner.

I wanted to have a real dinner together, something grand and leisurely, a family affair, so we could relax and communicate. I wanted the luxury of having my family surrounding me. I had to practically drag the girls out of the shop when the roast was done, slipping past medium rare and about to hit loafer sole before I finally got them to quit working and come have a toddy. It wasn't ruined but I was a little grumpy at their failure to recognize what I wanted, till then I think believing that having them all here would make me some kind of patriarch, if not commanding and receiving worshipful obedience, at least getting the respect my lofty if short lived position seemed to warrant. It was not going to be like that at *all*. I might be the oldest male but my females were not going to grant me any kind of special status as a result. We were all equal in their eyes and what they wanted was going to drive their actions a lot more than what I wanted just because it was me doing the wanting. At least they liked my dinner even if I didn't think it was all that great.

We were all about sated, talk general and inconsequential, when Billie turned and addressed Mandy. "I sure liked your doctor," she said.

"What doctor?" Mandy asked, me getting a premonition and not a good one.

"Dr. Hardy, the gynecologist. I saw him last Friday."

"Why?" she asked. "Are you okay?" Amanda thinking Billie saw him for her needs, not ours, me pretty sure what was coming next.

"Yeah, I'm fine. He thinks there's a real good chance it will take. Better than fifty fifty, he said. I was just right in my cycle," she grinned.

Mandy looked at me, puzzled, then maybe from my expression, started to catch on, moving quickly into shock and on to anger.

"The implant," she said finally. "You got, what, implanted? Is that what we're talking about?"

"Yeah. Dad gave me his number. Was I not supposed to? Whoops," she said then started to giggle. "What now?"

"You *knew* about this?" Mandy demanded of me.

"I….I guess. I mean, sort of," I said. "We all talked about it but I…I didn't know we had given the, ah, green light. I thought it was on hold."

"Daddy," spoken to me as if I was a recalcitrant child, "you gave me his number and told me he had all the information, all I had to do was go and see him. You did *not* say 'when you tell me to go.' I went. You're pregnant. Probably."

I couldn't help but smile. It reminded me so much of a teenage girl's lament, in reverse, this time the daughter explaining the facts of life to the father. 'Now I told you what could happen if you weren't careful.' Whoops indeed. Big whoops.

"Well." That was as profound as I got.

"Deep subject," Mandy said, sarcasm thick. "Now what, genius? Are you going to orchestrate a second hand abortion? You asshole!" she screamed.

"It was an accident," I said, then started laughing as I thought about the role reversal again. "I'm sorry," I said, trying to stop. I explained what I'd been thinking, how ironic it was, finally getting a grin out of Mandy. Billie had been smirking the whole time, Bubba too polite to let his opinion of our lunacy show.

"Come on, Sunshine, what are you thinking?"

"That you are an *idiot*," she said.

"Besides that. We knew I was an idiot."

"Just what we talked about. This child will be a demon," she said, then added, "and you won't be here to raise it with me," one tear getting loose and trickling down her cheek.

"I'm sorry, Sweetheart. You're right. It was a stupid, selfish idea. We can take care of it, the problem."

"Yeah," she said quietly. "It was stupid. But he'll be *our* devil child. A blond haired, green eyed brat, just like his father," then she came around the table and climbed onto my lap and kissed me. "Congratulations," she whispered to me. "You're going to be a daddy. Again."

"Shouldn't you be lying down?" I said to Billie. She just rolled her eyes and laughed.

Chapter Twenty

If Bubba hadn't had to go back, our routine would have been established—the girls selling, Bubba fixing and helping them and me painting, baby sitting, cooking and running errands. I could live with that if they could and it seemed, as the days passed, that Mandy and Billie were going to make an excellent team, both of them so happy and energetic that they made me feel ancient half the time. Celina did her part to keep me young though, always ready for a playmate.

I built her a big sandbox against the house on the barn side, strung a canvas tarp over it, piled all her outside toys in the corner, then fenced in the whole area with 2x4's and wood slats I'd found in one of the sheds. She couldn't get out and we could get and see in. I spent as much time in there with her as she did alone and she didn't much mind being the only one running the Tonka trucks and back hoes around in our personal quarry slash construction site. We had a hose bib right there so we built golf course communities with water hazards and farms with stock tanks, even our own beach resort with private ocean. I don't know how the girls felt about my priorities but I was pretty happy with them.

Bubba was back in ten days at the wheel of another truck, this one a small step van with the logo of the previous owner painted out. He backed it up the earthen ramp to the hayloft and I helped him unload the balance of Billie's possessions and some of his own, the Harley first. You travel light, I quipped. I left a lot of junk at my parents, he said. It was mostly that, junk, he laughed. I traded my pickup for this, he said, indicating the step van. What do you think? I think it will come in real handy for hauling antiques, I said to which he replied, exactly.

We subdivided a section of the upper level with more 2x4's and a pile of dusty, wooden doors to create a secure storage area for their things. The doors made nice walls, no two the same and there were several dozen more in the pile. We kept going, bisecting the barn completely with another door wall then creating a room that I thought would make a good office once we cut in a window. The next day we put in six, one in the office and five in the future sales area over the existing shop. Greta had at least fifteen of them, salvaged from some old castle, huge double hung units with eight individual panes of wavy glass in each sash. Once the sun cleared the eaves each afternoon, the new shop was as bright and comfortable as a living room, columns of dappled light flooding almost every corner of the space.

Like most timber barns, this one had an intermediate layer of horizontal structure between the floor of the former hayloft and the rafters far above. Someone, I suspect even before Greta's possession, had spanned lumber from timber to timber across the shop end as if in preparation for enclosing the area below. We had done the walls and they had done the hardest part of getting ready for a ceiling. And we had the ceiling material now that the barn had its ten years new roof, a big pile of twelve-foot long, once galvanized sheets of steel.

We slid them up the timber posts and across the ceiling joists and dropped them into place, two sheets end to end covering the width of our new display area. We repeated the motion thirty times and then tacked a few pieces above our door wall and we had a twenty four by sixty, twelve foot tall wood and tin brightly lit shoe box of funky grandeur, already full of cleaned and tagged antiquities ready for sale.

After that I pretty much retired from the antique business, the sales end anyway. The three of them could handle it and I found myself getting in the way of their operation more than I helped out. I was okay with it. I moved on to the house. And the restaurant business.

My Health Department buddy had come out on schedule and spent ten minutes writing up a list of deficiencies that had to be corrected before he could approve my take out license. The most serious and expensive was a new fire extinguisher. And a couple for that shop he suggested. Good advise. He then spent two hours sitting on an old kitchen chair in the shade of an oak tree drinking left over wedding beer and telling me tall tales about coastal Carolina and the inhabitants of this richly historic land, my benefactor and her family in particular.

I learned more about Uncle Clyde, about the young wife that had left him for a dentist while he was in the Ardennes Forest losing the lower third of his right leg, returning bewildered, turning embittered. About Greta's father who had tried to help his older brother heal, tending him for years, hauling him out of drunk tanks all over three counties, setting him up in business more than once, even making him the beneficiary of his life insurance above his own daughter, that money the seed for Clyde's Folly. Fortunately, Arnie didn't leave the homestead to Clyde too, my gossipy friend chuckled. Other wise you wouldn't be standin' here, he said. Ol' Clyde, he'd a sold this here piece a prime real estate in about five minutes.

"Now Greta," he said, "she's more like her daddy then Uncle Clyde. He was a decent man, Arnold was, always around if you needed a hand. Clyde, he was always around too but he always had his hand out! Greta, she's a rough old cob on the outside but she got a heart a gold. She just don't want you to know it," he laughed.

"What about the second sight business," I asked. "You believe in that stuff?"

"No sir, I do not," he said, slapping his spindly leg so hard I thought he might break it. "'Cept with Greta. She got it alright. But we ain't gonna talk about that today. Give me another beer, boy. I got to get home!" said like I'd been holding him there at gun point all day forcing stories out of him with thumb screws and truth serum. One for the road. I hadn't seen adult drinking and driving since they changed the laws in Texas. What a character. He was probably Greta's lover, I thought, making myself chortle with the image of their bony coupling.

I called him at his office two days later and said, I got your list done, when can you come back? When yer makin' barbecue out there, he shouted in my ear. I'll send you a license, you send me an invite to the grand openin'. Good deal, I said.

I took the boards that we had cut out of the barn to install the windows and spiked them together into six rustic picnic tables and placed them in a shady spot off the end of the parking area near the sliding kitchen doors. Even if we didn't open the take out operation, it made a quiet spot for our exhausted antiquers to take a break. We got some gypsy picnickers that didn't even pretend to look at our merchandise but other than an extra bag of trash once in a while, they didn't bother me and I left them alone. It made us look homey, down to Earth, and even more successful than we already were.

The second afternoon of picnic work, I was nearly done, outside in front with a tool belt and a Skill saw, I got a visitor, a black man in an Oldsmobile station wagon older than Jessica. He parked up by me and climbed out slowly, a handsome old gentleman with white hair and a distinctly military carriage. Where's Greta, he asked me. What's she doing to the place? I told him that Greta was off adventuring somewhere, reminded that she hadn't written as promised, and I told him that we were watching the shop in her absence, not entirely accurate but not a lie either. I hoped the old broad came back soon and lived with us. I missed her.

He seemed crest fallen at my news and I asked if there was anything I could do for him. Well, he said reluctantly, Greta likes the old stuff. Whenever I come across something, I bring it over and we haggle over it for a while. You mean she'd buy it off you, I asked, really not clear what he meant, Greta as mentor or Greta as purchaser. That offended him, the implication that he was a purveyor of junk or looking for a hand out. I apologized, saying I misunderstood, could I see what he had? He wasn't mollified so I added, she told us to look out for any of her friends that might come by, make sure we treated them good.

He led me around to the back of the station wagon, lowered the tailgate and began to slide boxes out onto the edge. He had old books, some assorted bottles and jars, a couple heavy ceramic crocks and two beautiful, glass front, pine kitchen cupboards, in their original stain, no layers of crappy paint to scrape off before hanging these babies on a wall.

"I'm Last," I said, extending my hand. "My wife Amanda runs the shop with my daughter Billie." His name was Augustus Johnson, Gus, and I told him the truth. Two truths. "I don't haggle well, Mr. Johnson. I don't have the knack for it. And I don't have a real good idea what your things are worth. Do you know what you want for them?" He gave me the two-headed idiot look, my reputation spreading, and I was pretty sure I knew what he was thinking. You're in the antique business and one, you don't haggle and two, you don't know shit about antiques? He was right if I was right about his thoughts. I tried another tact.

"What would Greta have done, sir? Can you educate me?" That struck a cord because he gave me a big smile, now thinking, I imagined, that I was a fish on the line. "Run me through the process," I added, hoping the guy liked to teach the young or the dumb.

"How long you been here?" he asked. "I saw Miss Greta just last month." I told him. "Looks like you're making a go of the place." We're trying, I said. Then he explained the system. He'd bring in his merchandise. So would a lot of other people. Greta would make coffee, or toddys he grinned, if it was late enough, and they would shoot the shit for a while, catch up, how's the family, Cousin Sam, Aunt Ruth. Then they would wander over and go through the lot. Greta would say five bucks for all of it. He'd say fifty. Ten. Forty-five. Twenty tops, not a penny more. Twenty-five and I'll carry it upstairs. Done but you're killing me here, Gus.

I got us each a beer and we sat at one of my new tables. "So how's Uncle Buck, Gus? That arthritis still bothering him?" I asked with as straight a face as I could manage.

"Now you're getting it, boy," he said, his grin wide, his teeth perfect. We talked for an hour plus or minus, had another beer, then I told him I wanted to buy his wares, meaning help him out but knowing not to phrase it that way, but I really didn't know where to start. Those cabinets are worth a few dollars for sure, I added. Help me out, Gus, I'm still learning.

"Okay," he said. "Just this once, then you have to follow the rules. Deal?" I agreed and he said a hundred and fifty for the lot. I was stunned, thinking he'd say a thousand and guessing we could get four hundred for each of the pine pieces. As is, no work on Bubba's end.

"Gus. Mr. Johnson. I know I'm not good at this but, well, that isn't enough for what you have there. They're worth more." I expected to get my 'look' again but he just stared. After maybe ten seconds he reached into the back pocket of his pants and pulled out a post card, glanced at the front and handed it to me without a word.

Gus, it said. There's some new folks running my place. Go over and see if the boy's honest. Don't ask the girl, she'll pay you *too* much. It was signed Greta. I flipped it over and studied the Eiffel Tower for a second then handed it back.

"A test?" I asked. He nodded. "Why? I thought she was a mind reader."

"I think it was horse shit," he said. "She can read your mind for sure but she may not be just right all the time is a possibility. That or she just wanted us to meet and the post card is her inside joke. That would be just like Greta."

"You are a damn fine actor, Mr. Johnson. And I am not a mind reader but I guess I passed."

"Yes you did, Mr. Barkley. I'm glad. I'd hate to think Greta was losing her touch," he said. "Besides, I like you. I'm glad you're not greedy." I thanked him and suggested he meet Mandy. He said, let's conclude our business first.

I countered him with six hundred. He said four and we settled on five, two hundred a piece for the cabinets and a hundred for the rest. He told me 'that crap ain't worth a hundred' and I said call it a bonus for the lesson. We shook and I walked him into the shop, introducing him as our new buyer. All three of them looked at me like I was nuts till I explained. Mr. Johnson could be our purchasing agent, I said. We need someone to go to auctions and garage sales and he has the knowledge. Are you interested, I asked him? We can talk, yes sir, we can surely talk about it. I had assumed I'd have to do most of the re-inventory work as long as I was able and I wasn't looking forward to it. We'd probably make more money paying him to negotiate for us than if I'd have gone out there. For me it would have been yeah, I'll buy it, no it's too much. He'd say, are you crazy? I'll give you half. And he knew lots of people with lots of stuff.

Chapter Twenty-one

Jessica and Randy arrived on Saturday, amazed, I think, at the number of cars in the lot, the people hanging out at the picnic tables admiring their purchases and the changes to the place. Wow, Jess said when I saw them from my perch on the ladder and climbed down. I was about two thirds done the front of the house, this a much more time consuming affair, lots of scraping and sanding and a three color Colonial Williamsburg paint scheme on Greta's ginger bread Victorian. There were times I felt like ripping off all the ornate moldings and slapping up aluminum siding.

Then Jessica got a good look at me and said double wow, you look awesome! I posed like a cat walk model and did a slow spin so she could admire my twenty pounds thinner body and my surfer tan. Pretty cool, eh, I grinned, then I hugged her and shook Randy's hand and said I'm really glad you're here. Thank you.

We unloaded their stuff, parking their car down by our vehicles in the back and had a big reunion with the antiques crew and Celina who made a serious attempt to bust out of Alcatraz as soon as she saw Aunt Jess. I left them all in the shop, wrapped up my painting for the day and went in to cook what I hoped was the first of hundreds of full-blown family dinners.

Jessica and Randy came in and offered to help but I declined, wanting conversation more. I told them about the take out license, saying if you want to give it a go, you could open tomorrow. He said sure, let's do it and I walked them out to the kitchen and unfurled a banner I'd had made that week. Not as big as Greta's but designed to wrap the corner of the barn to catch the eyes of travelers going both north and south. 'Clyde's Famous Barbecue' in red letters at the top with 'Featuring Chef Randle' below in smaller script. I wanted to maintain the historical connection, I said, but get you some credit too and make it clear that we were under new management. Is it okay, I asked? You can change it if you want, I won't be offended. It's great, he said. How are we going to work this? It's your show, I said, you run it. Let me know what you need. If I can swing it, you can have it. Go shopping now if you want, there's time till dinner.

We had a pre-Thanksgiving turkey and all the goodies, a boisterous meal with lots of laughter. Perfect. That day we had gotten our first correspondence from Greta and I was saving it for desert. It went well with a batch of applejack coffee. It was addressed 'To My Family.' 'I'm back in England with some old fart friends of mine from the war. There aren't too many of us left, I'm afraid. I did Paris and spent some time in Germany. Tomorrow I'm off to Rome. More later, love Greta'. When is she coming back, Billie asked and I said, you know as much as I do.

The next morning I helped Randy and Jessica set up for their opening day, putting out some more banners and moving the picnic tables closer to the source of the food, trying to make it clear that they went with the barbecue now, not with the antiques although stopping for both would be welcome.

I had called my Health Department curmudgeon at home Saturday and told him the grand opening was tomorrow, come on out, the meal's on me. He said he'd see me after church, adding it's right up the road. About twelve thirty, as I was standing in the yard admiring all that I had wrought, feeling like a conductor just before he brings up his baton for the opening night concert, all the weeks of practice behind, what looked like a funeral procession came slowly down the highway, fifteen vehicles all with their left turn signals on. I thought, what the fuck is this, then recognized my health inspector at the wheel of the first car, this one his, not the counties, a vintage Lincoln, undertaker black.

Our parking constraints became immediately evident, room for six not sixteen. I should have had a flag but I made do with my arms, waving the last ten cars over onto the grass on the other side of the picnic area. More gravel and some railroad ties, a mental note for Monday. It was a well dressed crowd at least, almost all the women heading directly into the shop and most of the men gathering by the slate black board that we had found in the kitchen and fastened to the barn side with strips of lath. If you looked closely, you could still see the last menu that Clyde had proffered up. Our prices were a bit higher but if a chalkboard was good enough for him, it would work for us.

Randy had decided to start slowly, chicken or ribs with sides of salad or beans, or sandwiches carved out of the same animals the entire bill of fare but the selection seemed to satisfy and within fifteen minutes, he had dished up thirty meals, Jessica handling the ordering and taking in the cash. I tried to pick up the inspector's tab but he gave me a ferocious frown and told me he didn't take 'no bribes', slapping a twenty on the slab of wood we had nailed to a couple of saw horses as a rudimentary serving counter, telling Jessica to keep the change.

I watched the food operation off and on all afternoon, chatting occasionally with the customers and making mental notes of areas that needed work. Like an ice and soda machine maybe although nobody bitched about the aluminum cans. They were cold, that's what mattered most. A real service counter and a cash register were going to be a must if the kids really made a go of it although I thought the cigar box was a nice touch, sort of retro Bohemian. More parking definitely. And some kind of sheltered seating. Otherwise we were talking a strictly seasonal operation and then only when it wasn't raining.

After the inspector had finished eating, I sat down across from him and said, what do you think? Is it good enough to sell, meaning be successful, appealing to the locals. Hell yes, he answered. That boy can flat cook. You ain't gunna have no problems. As long as you open regular, he added with a grin. Hypothetically, I said, what makes inside seating different then outside? You wanna know how to bend the rules, is that it? I said no but that's exactly what I meant. He said, if you go to convert part of that old barn into a dinning room, you need bathrooms and heat and a fire suppression system and exit lights and all kinds of bells and whistles that I'd installed in a hundred new buildings and that would both cost a fortune and ruin the character of Greta's charming, dusty structure. It ain't worth it, boy, he concluded. All you need is a little protection from the elements, an awning maybe.

How about this, I suggested? We build a shed off the side of the barn and screen it in. Would that work? He told me I was a devious Yankee for even thinking like that, then added that next I'd want to pull out the screens and nail up a few windows. I said he was as good a mind reader as Greta. He told me as long as I didn't put in a permanent structure, he thought I could get away with it. Permanent like what, I asked? How do you draw the line? Don't build a big Goddamn heated addition and be calling it a Goddamn porch, he told me. I got the idea.

The kids served almost a hundred meals before they ran completely out of food, stripping my larder bare as well as their own. Toward the end they were grilling Celina's hot dogs and selling left over turkey sandwiches. At four, Celina and I went into town and bought a family pack of T-bones, a bag of potatoes and salad greens so we'd have *something* for Sunday dinner. There weren't any leftovers left.

We closed up both operations at five on the dot, me yanking out flags as quickly as I could, hoping no one tried to turn in before I was done. I made another mental note—we needed a heavy rope to string across the driveway so people got the idea when we wanted to be left alone. It had been a hell of a day, the kids grossing over a thousand and the girls nearly six, their best single day sales total ever.

Mr. Johnson had come in about two, just to say hello, and was pressed into service immediately. He had a wonderful understated manner with the customers and a knowledge of antiques superior even to Amanda's, quietly guiding people through the shop, explaining what things were, when and sometimes where they had been made and how they might be utilized in a contemporary home. The older folks just loved him, thanking him repeatedly for his time and the history lesson. Billie was in awe, following him around the shop like he was a tour guide.

When I was done yanking the flags, I asked Gus to come in and have a drink with me. A toddy, he asked with a mischievous grin? Yeah, I said. I need your expertise with the formula. Randy was cooking tonight, the last of the coals raked into a corner of the barbecue pit when I got back with the steaks, so Gus and I had time to fiddle with the toddys till we were both satisfied that they were as close to Greta's as we were likely to get them to be, then we retired to the screened porch and watched the ocean for a while from a couple of creaky rocking chairs, the pitcher and a bucket of ice between us on an upended nail keg.

"Do you have family, Mr. Johnson?" I asked after refilling our glasses.

"I'd prefer if you'd call me Gus," he said, then added, "Some. Cousins mostly. My wife passed in '85." I said I was sorry and he said it's been a long time.

"No kids?" I asked. He shook his head and I wished I hadn't asked. "I'm sorry. That is surely none of my business." He made a hand gesture but then surprised me with his comment.

"You're a lucky man to have yours with you. They're fine young ladies. With good men, too. And Amanda, she's just....special."

"Yes she is," I grinned. "Thank you."

"You don't get the credit for her, son," he laughed. "She was special before you ever came along." I had to agree with him on that.

"There's something I want to ask you," I said after we were done chuckling. "It concerns her and this," waving my arm toward the shop and grounds. I told him about my condition, the time line, his face never registering the pitying look I so loathed. "I was hoping you might, oh, stay on, help her out, after I'm gone. I'm not sure how to express it. I'm not even sure what I mean, I just feel I can trust you, that maybe you might like working with her, if you had the time."

"Time," he said, looking away from me now, back out toward the pines and the dunes. "Yes, I have time. Nothing but time." He turned back to me then and he stared, really boring in to me, brows wrinkled up, frowning almost as ferociously as my health inspector. "Did Greta put you up you this," he demanded. "Is this one of her damn charities?"

"No, sir," I said, really surprised at his reaction. "I thought of this one all by myself. Why? What did Greta do to you?" He wasn't completely convinced it was obvious but after a good pull on his tumbler he answered me.

"She's always trying to get me to do some damn fool thing for her, wanting to pay me to work around here or help her in the shop. I don't need her money and she doesn't have it to give. That woman's got a hard head, I'll tell you."

"Well, the way things are going, we do have the money and I think it's pretty clear we need the help. Today was busier than most with the food, I guess, but not that much busier. And you know your shit. And I'm not going to be much help soon enough. I'm worried about being a burden to her. To them. I'm planning ahead, you see?"

"Yes I do and I'm sorry, son. For your troubles. I'd like to help y'all. I think I'd enjoy it."

"I think you might. We're a fun bunch," I said laughing as I raised my glass and clinked it with his. "To the antiques business. May we all get rich."

"And die happy," he added winking at me.

"I'm working on it, Gus. Thank you."

We made a fresh pitcher and carried it out to the picnic grove. Jessica came to tell us the steaks were almost ready. The rest of the family was already there and we passed the pitcher around and then I said I'd like to make a toast. A short one, I added when they groaned. We had a great day, I started. I hope all of you enjoyed it as much as I did. Here's to many more and to the newest member of our family, tipping my imaginary hat toward Gus.

I told Mandy about our conversation as we ate and Gus confirmed his willingness to help. I'd never seen a black man blush before but when Mandy jumped up from her bench and planted a kiss on his cheek, I swear he turned red, smiling like a school boy.

We need to talk details, I said, figure out how to pay everybody. This is going to be more than a hippie commune now, we have food, antiques, buyers, suppliers. This is a real business. I think we need to treat it that way. As long as it's still fun, Mandy giggled. And we're all still family, she added, putting her little pink hand on top of Mr. Johnson's big, callused brown one.

I suggested we have an actual business meeting in the morning, take notes, toss around ideas, figure out how to manage the enterprise. Everyone agreed and we spent the rest of the evening in jovial well being, Gus heading home around eight when Billie took Celina up to bed. A great day indeed. There was nothing more I could have asked for out of life except more time to live it.

Chapter Twenty-two

I was first up the next day, beating even Mandy and Celina, a rare event and I attributed it to the pain that brought me up out of a sound sleep around five. I tried to gasp quietly but I knew that if I stayed in bed, I'd have Mandy awake in a minute so I slipped out, bent half over with my left hand squeezing as much of my right chest as hard as I possibly could. I made it to the bathroom, took a pill and a piss and inched my way down the stairs to the kitchen. I knew I had at least ten minutes to get through till the pill did anything unless the pistol shot of fiery lead eased up on its own.

I made coffee, filling a mug as soon as that much accumulated in the pot and began to hobble toward the porch. Another round hit me, this one a magnum fired point blank, the first one feeling like a cap gun in comparison. I lurched back to the counter and sank to my knees, placing my mug on the floor. I opened the base cabinet and tilted the big jug of applejack over, spilling some but topping off my Texas sized container with four or five ounces of the potent liquor. I left the mess, barely making it back to my feet with out spilling the rest and again went for the porch, my target the closest rocking chair.

I made it, just, groaning like an old dog under a wood stove, lapping at the laced coffee between moans. Ten minutes can be a long time. I was done my mug, thinking about another, this one with less caffeine and more alcohol, when the curtain of semi-delirium finally lifted, whether on its own or from the booze enhanced narcotics I'm not sure. Nor did I care. I was literally panting, more than the shallowest breath till then a screaming addition to the gun shots in my breast.

I remember thinking I didn't want to be found like that, especially not by one of the kids, not this morning, not ever. I got up and rinsed my mug, cleaned up the floor and went outside into the shrouded, predawn mist laying like cumulous formations across the yard. Slowly, older than the oldest living man, I baby stepped toward the ocean. It took me twenty minutes I think and I had to lie down on the sand as soon as I cleared the dunes. The surf was up. Maybe a tropical depression was out there riding the Gulf Steam north. We didn't watch enough TV to stay current on even the weather and in this local, in late summer, I thought vaguely that that probably wasn't such a good idea.

After a while, I may have even dozed, I got to my feet by way of my hands and knees and stepped slowly toward the waves. They looked so ethereal in the half-light, beckoning me to join them, their rhythm continuous and uncaring, womb of Mother Earth. Come back to me, she called. It's safe, it's warm, join us. And I might have, right then just waded out and gone away, peacefully floating out to sea. I shambled a few steps closer and the next rushing breaker, bigger than the rest, slapped me nearly to my chin.

The fucking bitch was lying! Christ, it was fucking cold!

I bounced backward, my eyes snapping open and all thoughts of a cozy final swim disappearing in a flash of shivering misery. Whatever was out there churning up the waters had driven away our eighty-degree tidal bath tub and replaced it with a polar bear's delight.

I *ran* away, making it to the motor home door intent on grabbing a towel or a blanket, anything that might still be on board before I remembered that Jess and Randy were camping in there. They'd probably shoot me if I barged in at six, naked, smelling of apple brandy and looking like a wet, rabid dog. Shit!

I wrapped my arms around myself and trotted back to the house, thinking about our bed and Mandy's hot little body tucked there in.

I got one leg up against her before she shot up and smacked me on the top of my head with a wind milled open palm. Get away from me, she shrieked! You're freezing! No shit, I thought, why do you think I'm after your heat, but I kept my mouth shut and rolled up in the blankets in a quivering, fetal ball.

"Last? Are you okay? Are you sick?" she said a second later. "You're wet. What have you been *doing*?" I told her about the pain, the pill and the walk to the beach. I left out the booze and the Siren's song that nearly lured me in. I thought maybe a swim would make me feel better, I said, but it was too cold.

She concluded that I was an idiot, then asked if I had made the coffee. When I nodded she slipped on a robe and went downstairs, returning in a few minutes with two normal sized mugs, the one she handed me smelling of sweet apple brandy. Just a little, she said, to take off the chill. It did. I felt almost normal again in a couple minutes. Except that I was moderately buzzed from the pill and my self-medicating coffee of before. I went back to sleep.

When I got up the second time, I had a headache and was nauseated. When I awoke the third time, I felt pretty good, took a shower, dressed and made it downstairs, a food-seeking missile, the smell of eggs and ham and home fries heavy in the air. Unfortunately, the things that made the smells were almost all heavy in my family's bellies, a scrap of ham and one limp slice of toast all that remained. I was not happy and Billie taunting me with 'you snooze, you lose,' didn't help my mood. I wrapped the scrap, poured the dregs of the coffee and wandered miserably out to the porch where all the noise had been coming from. And realized almost immediately how unnecessary I'd become.

The meeting was over, Gus policing the breakfast dishes and the girls preparing to go fart around in the shop. Jess and Randy were making a food list and Bubba was already gone to put a second coat of varnish on a hutch he was refinishing. How'd everything go, I asked? Fine, fine, Gus said, grinning at me. A big happy family. Great, I muttered, feeling like going back to bed. I didn't find out till that evening who was getting paid what and how and then all Mandy would tell me was that they all had shares in the business, would keep track of and be paid by the hours they worked and get bonuses at the end of the year. Sounds like socialism to me I said but then concluded that maybe that wasn't so bad. I spent the rest of the day painting, what I could reach from a six-foot stepladder. No high work again today.

Late in the afternoon, I got Jessica alone for a few minutes and asked her straight up what she thought about staying. She smiled at me and said they were discussing it. How's motor home life I asked and she said good, we skinny-dip a lot, at night. I was glad they didn't do it early in the morning. It might have made an awkward meeting on the dune path, all of us naked in the dark. I'm not trying to push you, Angel, but if you do decide to stay, we need to hook you up over at UNCW soon, for the fall semester. She smiled again and said she knew that. I wanted to keep going, ask more questions, what are you discussing, push her to my way of thinking regardless of what I had just said but I knew it would probably be counter productive. What I wanted was what I had, all of them here, and I wanted it to stay that way. And maybe I just wanted someone to listen to me, heed my advice, do what I said instead of ignoring, humoring or protecting me. I'd need all that and a lot more before too long but I didn't think I needed it yet. I cleaned my brushes and myself and climbed in with Celina and we built an elaborate sand castle complete with mote and then demolished it from both sides with a tiny John Deere front end loader and a Cat bull dozer. She laughed like Attila at the gates of Rome when we started our siege and we made motor noises while we crashed into the walls again and again.

Not a bad day after all, I thought, as we ran our heavy equipment over the last of the castle, the devastation complete, just backfilling the carnage now. You want to help Grandpop make dinner, Darlin', I asked her with a tickle. I got the appropriate giggle and we marched off to clean up and cook. She wanted hot dogs and I thought good, that's what those greedy breakfast hogs deserve, a fatty tube steak. I broiled four, I ate three with onions and mustard and left the remainder of the package out on the counter. There's dinner, help yourselves. I don't know what they ate. Celina and I went fishing. We didn't catch a thing and I didn't care, it was nice just to sit on the beach and watch a child play, racing against the waves, back and forth a hundred times, naked and laughing like a maniac midget.

Chapter Twenty-three

It was mid August before I had the house painted completely. Greta's big Victorian sparkled like an Easter egg, rose and teal and burgundy, the doors bright as glossy lemons, Mandy's color choices nearly causing fender benders as people braked to gawk, the change so dramatic it snapped your head around. I was going to move inside next. I wanted to strip all of the old style flowered wallpaper, patch and paint every room, then refinish all the wide plank pine floors. I was planning to do one room at a time complete even though it would have been more efficient to move all of us out, strip everything, patch all of it, paint en mass. But I wanted to localize my mess as best I could, I told Mandy, not adding that I was afraid I wouldn't be capable of finishing the entire house once I started. But I needed a project. I was out of the antique business and had never even been in the restaurant operation other than paying for the crushed stone and treated wood ties that Bubba had used to put in the parking lot expansion.

They were serving up barbecue five days a week, most days selling out by the time the shop closed even though they were progressively more aggressive with both the quantity and variety of their menu. I had been unable to get an answer out of Jessica about their long-range plans and it was starting to piss me off. I wasn't going to build the fucking dining shed if they weren't going to be here. I didn't want to run the food operation, I wanted to work on the house and play with Celina, fish and swim, rock on my porch, read a book, enjoy the good life while I still could.

Randy finally gave me the information accidentally. He asked if I could go back to Pennsylvania for them and get the rest of their stuff, he didn't want to send Jess by herself and he figured they couldn't do it all and get back in the two days they were closed each week. I gave him what must have been my dumbest look because he said we're staying, didn't Jess tell you? I said no she hadn't and he said she's waiting till she has her class schedule I bet, to surprise you.

It turned out that her food shopping trips to the restaurant supply house that we'd opened an account with were also covering for her negotiations with the admissions office at UNCW. They had been reluctant to accept some of the credits from her community college in Pennsylvania and had wanted her to repeat the courses at the local version down here. She said no and had entered into a protracted battle with the dean. I was so proud of her for standing up to them and for doing it on her own. And as much as I hated to admit it even to myself, I had to give her mother credit for that hard headedness gene. I probably would have bitched out the dean but then given up. She had stood up to him and won according to Randy. They wanted her to retake a freshman level English requirement that she thought she had already fulfilled but that was it, they would accept all the rest and she could take the lit class at UNCW. She was signed up and starting in two weeks. They were staying. I told him I'd be happy to go north for them, had to for myself anyway, thinking wait till I get my hands on her.

Which I did an hour later when she got back from town, Bubba's van loaded to the roof with cases of ribs and chicken, fresh hams and produce. So, I said with a nasty smirk, how do you like owning your own business? Randy told you didn't he, she responded. Yes. You didn't seem to be in any hurry to. She gave me one of her terrific smiles and a kiss on the cheek and I swung her around like she was five, a taxing chore at her size. I am so glad, I said. Thank you. Thank *you*, she responded. Do you know how much money we're making? I laughed and said no but you guys can provide dinner if you're so wealthy. Celina and I are going to the beach.

I thought about taking Celina north with me but figured it would take me twice as long to pack and move everything with her helping so I settled on just me. On Bubba's Harley. I had a U Haul reserved for a one-way back. I left Monday morning at five hoping to get back Tuesday late. I had to get their stuff from the apartment and a whole shopping list of things from our house. Our bulk possessions were a dilemma. I didn't want to empty the house, make it look totally abandoned and Mandy's cousin hadn't wanted to move out of her house, knowing eventually we were going to sell ours, but I also didn't want to leave it for Mandy to do after I was gone. Plus we didn't really have room for our furniture at Greta's. Not in the house anyway. Not unless we started selling off her stuff and we hadn't had either the need or the desire to do that. Plus most of her furniture was more desirable than most of ours. Maybe we should put our things in the shop, future antiques.

I took three heavy duty construction clean up garbage bags of my clothing to the Salvation Army, left our living room furniture, bedroom stuff and a couple floor lamps and packed everything else. The cousin was okay with it. Her only needs were the bed and a TV. I was too tired by the time I was done to even drive the hour east to the kid's apartment so I took the bike to a take out joint and got a Philly cheese steak and a six pack and collapsed on the couch. I thought about going to visit Clara but didn't have the energy either physically or mentally. Tuesday morning I loaded the bike in the rental truck, drove to the kid's place and drug their stuff down to the van. It was pretty clear they were even money on moving down when they came back before their 'sabbatical' because almost everything they owned was already boxed and bagged. It took me longer to clean up then it had to load. I was back at Greta's by seven and they had saved dinner for me, Jess massaging my shoulders while Randy got me a plate of grilled chicken and a Caesar salad. Now they were here all the way. No going back. I ate, had a couple toddys, took a pill and slept till almost noon. No place like home and damn glad to be there. My end game was all that was left.

Chapter Twenty-four

Jessica started school Wednesday after Labor Day, fifteen credit hours on a Monday, Wednesday and Friday schedule. I thought that was plenty for a transition from part time community college to full time four-year program and she thought it would give her time to help Randy. School comes first, I told her, so we hired Gus' cousin's kid to help out at the barbecue pit. He had a talent it seemed and a family history of back yard slow cooking. Within a week, Randy's sauce gave way to Otis' Sauce Supreme and a week after that we gave him credit via a newly printed banner add on tacked to the barn below the two sided original. The day Jess started school, we started the shed addition, Bubba and Otis doing the grunt-work, me the brains of the operation.

They dug a bunch of postholes and set cedar 6x6's on Sacrete footers then lagged horizontal 2x4's across them to stabilize the assembly. We bolted a ledger to the barn and spanned front to back with 2x12 rafters, sheathed in the roof with old pine planks and tacked more of the old galvanized barn roofing panels to that. By the end of the third day—it wouldn't have taken that long if I'd have had the stamina to work more than an hour or so between rest breaks—we had a good looking enclosure and I let them put in the stone patio themselves, offering advice only on how much sand to tamp into place and how to start the layout of the random slabs of local sandstone. When you're done, I told them, I'll help you set the windows. Despite my inspector friend's admonitions, we were going to skip the screened in stage and go right to used, wood double hung windows that Gus had found. And a wood stove for heat. Hell, it looked temporary to me.

It was around this time, as my strength was obviously starting to ebb, that I began to do some research on my condition—the condition of dying. Lots of people had been there before me I figured, some of them must have done some writing on the subject before hand. I wasn't sure what I was after when I first wandered through the Barns and Noble outside of Wilmington, not a scholarly text on the disease that was killing me certainly, I already knew everything relevant on that score, the oncologist who wanted me for another experimental subject more than willing to provide all the biomedical information I asked for but less than forthcoming regarding the ancillary affects of his wonderkind treatment regime. I was more interested in the philosophical musings on the subject, the wisdom of the elders, if you will. Surely there had to be a whole hell of a lot of it because what other topic was so universal, crossing without prejudice all boundaries geographic and cultural, unfazed by race or creed, even species, genera and phylum irrelevant.

I was a little disappointed. There were books, of course, but no section of shelves dedicated to the subject, no aisle denoting plaque, certainly no wall mounted advertisement that guided the curious shopper like those prominently displayed above the mystery, science fiction and romance stacks. Death didn't rate a section despite its omnipresence, the ubiquitous nature of the topic apparently irrelevant in the minds of the book store's executives.

Did mankind simply ignore our common future or was the idea so mordantly abhorred that even here in this bastion of collected thought it was shunned, whatever slim body of work available on the subject camouflaged amongst the religious or philosophical texts dedicated to a more general study of mankind and his ultimate destiny.

I did find, on that first trip, a headline that summed it all up succinctly, no words spared on the title here, all three of them fairly screaming out the reality—'*How We Die*,' by a Connecticut doctor and surgeon. Half science, half reflection and all fascinating, I read the chapter on cancer standing in front of the carol that held his and a dozen other roughly similar dissertations, all displayed in a back corner of the book mart under the general and innocuous heading of human health. There was an oxymoron. I guess death, in its most polite form, could be described as an absence of health. I wanted to buy it, the book, but I didn't want Mandy to have such a smack-you-in-the-face reminder of what was going on but as I read past cancer and on to the doctor's conclusions, I realized that much of what he was saying was exemplified by my unwillingness to openly display his thesis. The very act of not discussing the inevitable, whether it be a premature demise such as my own or the elongated decline of someone like Tex, robbed both the dying and the living of a chance to understand this most basic lesson of life. I bought the book, carrying it out of the store and into my home unbagged, then with highlighter in hand, rocked on my porch while I studied the man's thoughts.

What are you reading, Last, Mandy asked when she banged through the screen door on her way to the bathroom. I looked up at her smiling face, the life force so great in this effervescent child-woman, her happiness with our new situation so complete, the morbid reflections on her father's death and her mother's greed almost gone, and I said, oh, a novel I picked up in town. It's pretty good. She said great and scampered on to her destination. Sorry, doc, I thought. There's a time for everything and this ain't it for discussing a permanent sundering from my beloved Baby. Maybe some rainy November evening when the sun's gone down and I'm holding her in my arms under the covers. I have that much time left and she has more than that amount of need to be happy. And much more than that amount of right to get it while she can. I put away the death book and gathered up some fishing stuff and Celina and we went down to the ocean. I wasn't in denial, just postponement.

Chapter Twenty-five

I had never experienced autumn or winter in the south, except Texas during hunting season and this was a whole different animal. It didn't get cold like the north, just cooler then wetter and we didn't have the dramatic deciduous color changes that marked the passage from too hot and too humid to too cold and colorless like Pennsylvania did. It was more like a slow decline from hot to damp. It wasn't unpleasant, we swam till November and could have surf cast, without the chest deep wading that July had encouraged, probably all winter most days without seriously freezing our asses off. It was a seasonal progression remarkably similar to my overall condition, a slow if inexorable change, from a preponderance of great days with a few not so good ones thrown in, to a glut of not so good ones with a few not too bad interjected to leaven the mix. I was fixed on short-term goals now—the house room by room and the holidays, one by one.

We had a Halloween party, inviting all our wedding guests and everyone we had met and liked through the business. It was a monstrous affair, a costumed extravaganza, all the guests encouraged to spend the night either in the Tent City that arose on the military encampment or in the barbecue pavilion or up stairs in the barn. The house was full enough with just us although a dozen extra souls who hadn't planned sufficiently for their own enjoyment slept on couches and floors. Randy and Otis made breakfast for a hundred the next morning and we ate it all. It was the best two-day stint I'd had in weeks. We all missed Greta in both our thoughts and speech. She was in Japan per her last communiqué and headed for Hawaii there after. I desperately wanted her here for Thanksgiving, my favorite holiday overall.

The holidays were my next big thing to plan after the costume ball. I had three bedrooms done in the house and wanted to complete the last two by Thanksgiving and hopefully a couple downstairs spaces by Christmas. I wasn't sure what I'd fixate on in the new year. Dead President's Day didn't inspire me much and Easter was a good ways off. Valentine's and Saint Patrick? Maybe. Right now I was busy with the two biggies.

I called my mother the afternoon of the second day of the Halloween bash, after we had cleaned up and said our good-byes to the last guest, and I asked her how she would feel about coming north for an extended stay. How extended, she asked and I said late November till early January. She told me politely that she could not, too many obligations to the church, the ranch and her own friends. I understood. The offer was heart felt but not tendered with any hope of success or real conviction that it was even a good idea, more a semi-melancholy lament, an 'if some family was good than more family was better' rational. We settled on Christmas week and I told her I'd invite Kathy and her brood to join us, again without any expectation of acceptance. I didn't get one. Kathy was already committed to Kile's kids, especially the oldest one, his new wife and their newborn son. That was okay. Mom would do.

But one mom begets another and Clara was not so reluctant to join us. She was coming for Christmas too. I did not outright object to inviting her for Thanksgiving but I was secretly ecstatic that she couldn't make it.

I worked as long each day for the first three weeks of November as I possibly could, scraping and painting beyond the threshold of pain, well past any desire to play, fish or swim. Celina missed me, taking little pleasure in her indoor toys, admonishing me hourly to take a break with a pant leg tug and an imploring or accusatory countenance. I tried to balance our needs but mostly told her, in a bit, Sweetheart, Grandpop's busy now. It didn't make a lot of difference to her. I got the last bedrooms, ours last of the last, steamed, patched and painted but didn't have the energy to battle the voracious drum sander across either floor and couldn't begin to face the clean up required from all the dust if I had. Next year. There's still plenty of time. Maybe Bubba can sand, I'll stain and poly.

I moved on to food prep for Thanksgiving the Tuesday before, Celina and I doing a couple hours in the Food Lion, now not so much the object of helpful female attention, either because most of them were used to seeing us or I was looking less like a potential mate and more like an ambulatory leftover from someone's ghouls and goblins event. I didn't think I looked that bad but I knew I wasn't looking my all time best either. We got the biggest turkey, spuds and onions, celery, bread, corn, even a small ham for variety. I got the oysters because I didn't feel like going back again the next day. They'd keep.

I set Celina up at the little kitchen table with crayons and coloring books and got to work peeling and slicing. I loved this holiday half for the food prep and half for the camaraderie, especially if I had it at my house with my family but not much was lost by having friends in their stead. It was a day meant to be spent with people you loved, not at some obscure in-law's musty barracks with a bunch of 'relatives,' most of whose names you couldn't for sure remember. I'd spent a lot of those during my indenture to the

Hell Bitch. This year it was us, including Gus and Otis and Otis' parents and younger sister. We'd invited Robert E. and Sergeant Hines and his family but they already had plans. I worked hard on Robert because he was alone and his holiday involved a ten-hour drive to Tampa for a three-day stay with his first cousin and his wife and kids, finally leaving it at, if you change your mind, just come.

By six on Thursday morning the turkey was in and the coffee made in Randy's commercial brewer, dragged onto the porch for the duration of the weekend. I pulled a half mug, listened up the stairs for sounds of other awakenings, then topped it off with applejack. There had been two more jugs of it in the basement I had discovered when the first one went belly up but I was going to have to find another option for the bad days and real soon. We were about two big batches of toddys from being completely out.

My family came down singly over the next several hours and as each one wandered into the kitchen, I offered breakfast. By the time Jessica arrived in her flannel footie jammies, where she found them in her size I can not imagine, I was down to a cup of diced potatoes and two eggs. We split them, my second serving but who knew that but me? By one they were all dressed and starting to clamber for dinner, every burner on the stove keeping cadence with their demands, hissing and plopping sounds issuing from every pot.

I made a weak batch of toddys and told them to go watch football, give me an hour. I had the turkey out, gravy in progress when the sound of tires on gravel got me to glance out the window. Robert E. Cool. With a date it looked like. I went back to work, figuring he'd find me eventually. Then I heard the squeals, screams and laughter, then Greta's commanding voice then more laughter. I turned off the gravy, wiped my hands on a towel and charged the porch. Robert had barely cleared the porch door and wasn't going to get any further till the joyous huddle surrounding the old lady either broke up or fell back. It didn't. She had to bust out, striding through their midst and over to me, wrapping her arms around my waist without a word, tears running down my cheeks as I embraced her.

"Glad you could make it, Gret. You two have this planned?" I said, pointing at Robert.

"Would I do somethin' that low down?" she said, looking up at me with a wicked grin.

"Every chance you get, I'll wager," then I picked her up and kissed her but I couldn't hold her long and she caught the wince as I set her down.

"We'll talk later, boy," she whispered in my ear. "You go fix us a drink! Better yet, I'll fix it myself. Come on, show me how you're ruinin' dinner."

Mandy and the girls crowded around her at the kitchen table while she sloshed together a batch, commenting that mine had no damn *spirits* in 'em, hadn't she taught me anything? I told her we were almost out and no she *hadn't* taught me the secret of her damn toddys. She called out, Augustus Johnson! How could you let these people run out of applejack and he trotted out to his car and in a minute returned with an ancient two-gallon crock stopped with a new cork. Give me that empty one, Last. I'll refill it for you. I should have known, he said, winking at me.

It was the best Thanksgiving ever, the food perfect—and I'm my own worst critic—my family all together, new friends on hand and everyone in high spirits. Greta was the icing, the whole desert for that matter. I wasn't all that surprised to see her because if she was ever coming back, it would surely be for Thanksgiving. At least that was what I'd been telling myself for the last month. She'll come back for me, for all of us on this most special of family days, our patron, the one who had made it all possible. I started crying while I was washing the pots, the dishes already stacked and drying. I don't know why, I wasn't in some depressed funk before hand, just the opposite in fact. I guess I was giving thanks, mentally saying to whomever was responsible for such a perfect day, I appreciate it, I really do and then I was sobbing, silently shaking with the force of my emotions. I mopped at my face with a dishtowel, pivoting toward the stairs, unwilling to be discovered so denuded, running away. No luck. Greta caught me by the arm before I made the third tread, now you see her, now you don't in reverse, appearing like a genie and dragging me back as if I was a forty pound child.

"Let it out, boy. It won't hurt you none, unless you don't". Then she sat me down on the stairs and held me in her arms while I cried and cried. At one point she shoed someone off, one of the kids I think. Mandy wouldn't have listened to her on that one. She talked quietly to me the whole time although I don't remember anything she said. Finally I was through. I wiped my eyes again and trumpeted my nose into the now about ruined dishrag then gave her a wan smile. Tears of joy, I said. I'm so glad you're back, then we were both crying, which is how Mandy found us, wrapping us both in her embrace and joining in the sobfest. That got me straightened out. I can't bear to see her cry. Alright girls, I said, that's enough for now, I've got a kitchen to finish but by the time I had cleaned myself up yet again, it was done, Robert, Otis and Gus taking charge.

We watched a little football, drank a toddy or two, got a detailed travelogue of Greta's adventures, had some pumpkin and pecan pie that Otis' mom had made and then our guests departed. Except Robert. He and I talked till almost eleven, both of us about half in the bag by then. We talked about me, then about him, his divorce, the Bureau, cases he had worked, then his aspirations and regrets. I was surprised to learn that he was only forty-six, way younger than me. The white hair, I said, it makes you look older. The price you pay for fame, he laughed, even if it's only faking someone else's identity.

Finally I got around to what had been skittering about in my mind as we talked. What do you think of Mandy, I asked as nonchalantly as I could. She's great, he told me. A real little darling. You're a lucky man. Then he reddened and gave me a chagrinned smile adding, sorry, that was tactless. Luck runs both ways, Robert, I said. If I could trade her for a longer life, I wouldn't. Yeah, I am lucky. What I'm getting at was all I managed before he held up his hand and said don't. Not now, not ever. Just a thought, I said. I know, he answered and I understand your motives. I'll tell you what, he said as he poured from the pitcher, saying last call. If it makes you happy, after you're in your grave for a year and that beautiful woman has had a chance to mourn, I'll invite her out to dinner and we'll talk about you for a couple hours. I'll tell her about this conversation, about how you were trying to fix us up before you even took to your deathbed. That ought to get me off on the right foot don't you think, then we clinked our glasses and laughed like a couple schoolboys.

I walked him part way down to the motor home where he was going to hole up. It isn't good for the FBI to be flaunting the local DUI laws. Then I went back to the house and sought out the arms of my most beautiful darling. I was happy, blessed and dying.

Chapter Twenty-six

Toward the very end of November there was a rough time. I had a three day spell of feeling like home made shit, too tired to get out of bed for two days, making it down stairs for a couple hours on the third. Greta spoon fed me turkey soup and told me stories the whole time, not leaving me even when I begged her to. Just let me sleep, I whined. She'd give way to Mandy after dinner but then be there again in the morning with a mug of coffee and a big, malevolent smile. On the fourth day I got up just to get away from her. I couldn't take any more mothering. And as soon as I got moving, I felt better. I wondered if she knew that I would and purposely set about driving me out with her devious obsequiousness.

The one thing my debilitation allowed was thought, when I could tune Greta out or when Mandy fell asleep. She had been hardly less talkative then Greta during her shifts. And what I thought about was Christmas, presents I wanted to buy, the work I wanted to complete in the house, even the menu I wanted to prepare. And about how, without any doubt, this was my last one. Not my last good one, not more than likely my last one, this was it. The finale'. That may have had as much to do with getting up as escaping from Greta did. And maybe I just needed a good rest because by the afternoon of the fourth day, I was back, as much as I ever expected to be.

I started with the porch, our biggest space and the home of the feast table where we had every meal. By Thanksgiving night, it had been almost cold in there. I drafted Bubba and we ripped out the screening and framed openings to receive the rest of the big old windows that were stored in the barn. Where did you get these things, I asked Greta while I was prepping the holes. An abandoned plantation house over that way, she said, motioning up the road. Gus thought they were too good to crunch up so we got 'em out just ahead of the Fire Company. They burned the house down for practice.

We hung all ten of them, then put in a real door behind the screen one and wired up some electric baseboard heat strips. By December first we had a cozy room with a terrific view. The next day I painted all the windows and the new trim I'd cased them in. What do you think of the place, Greta, I asked, not making the connection till then between all we'd done and her time away, like she had never left now that she was back. It's beautiful, she said, just like I knew it would be. I'm real proud of you, boy, she added, laying her hand on my arm. For some reason this made me blush furiously. I was proud of me too and maybe that was it. You're not going to leave us again are you, I asked, out of my mouth and out of the blue, no conscious thought preceding my question. No, Chance, she said, I'm not and I smiled and said good, thank you. And then, I love you, you old goat, again without thinking about it, which made her laugh out loud. I love you too, boy. I love all of you.

From then on I had more time to work without having to baby sit. That was Greta's job of choice, but now, whenever I went into town, it was the three of us by mutual consent. Greta was rarely out of earshot and I found that immensely comforting.

I got the parlor painted, touched up the stain on the wood trim in the library and then, in a burst of energy and some coordinated room isolation and sleeping rearranging, sanded all four floors over two days, vacuumed up my mess, and in two more days, stained and applied three coats of poly to all of it. Then I spent a day in my rocker recuperating and Christmas shopping in my mind. I thought about normal presents like bicycles and clothing, compiling a list of what to get each of them but eventually realized that individually they would be okay presents but they were going to be reciprocated in kind and honestly, the last thing I needed was another flannel shirt or pair of Levi's. What use would I get out of them? A waste of money. Then I thought, what does my family need as a whole? What will make life better for them in the future? Jess and Randy needed better living quarters, that was obvious. Even with Greta back, we still technically had a free bedroom but they were young and in love and wanted some separation. There was still a lot of unused barn space on both levels but converting some of it into a house would require all the mechanical trades, plumbing, heat and electric, and more energy than I had available.

Billie and Bubba had taken the second biggest bedroom and the one that adjoined it and created an apartment within the house and they were comfortable with what they had although they could use some more closet space and their bathroom was a little cramped for the three of them. We could breach a couple walls, close up a door and make the space more user friendly.

Mandy, my beloved, needed what? A healthy husband. Maybe next time. About the best thing I could think of to do for her was to prepare for my on going decline and immanent fall. I knew that I was going to go through a period of decreasing strength and then declining mobility, it had already started, and that eventually I would not be able to climb the stairs. Or make it to the toilet. And we didn't have a bathroom downstairs. Should I even bother to rig up a death chamber, I pondered, or was the inception of incontinence the indicator that it was time to pull my own plug, time to get out with whatever personal dignity I had left, before my Baby had to swab my ass like I was her baby, a two hundred pound producer of stinking diarrhea and not much else.

Holy shit! The baby! My mental juxtaposition of infants and their offerings suddenly reminded me that I hadn't given *one* thought to Billie's pregnancy, or if she was actually having one, since we had first discovered she had been implanted. What was I thinking to not be thinking about that? About myself obviously, wrapped up in my own needs, anguishing over my own anguish. Selfish by omission. I got up out of my chair and went looking for someone to ask. I found Mandy first, rearranging in the shop.

"Is Billie pregnant?" I demanded.

"Am I Billie?" she said.

"No. Do you know? I can't believe I just forgot about it! What was I *thinking*?"

"About other things, Last," she said, finally stopping what she was doing and coming over to me. "It's okay, we understand."

"It's *not* okay. It didn't take, did it? That's probably a good thing. You have enough to do, more than enough to do soon enough. And we need to talk about that, all of us. We've been acting like nothing's wrong, you know? We aren't facing reality." She put her fingers on my lips then backed away a step and looked at me.

"Last. It did take. She's five months pregnant, you jerk. Haven't you noticed? No, obviously not," she continued. "You've been doing your thing and we've been doing ours. You wouldn't know. We haven't let her do any lifting, we make her lie down, get off her feet every hour or so. Bubba and I kept an eye on her so she didn't dislodge the fetus. She's been under prenatal care with a woman in Wilmington. You *have* been in your own little world, haven't you."

"Nobody tells me shit," I said. "What's the due date?"

"April first!" she giggled. "I hope she delivers right on schedule, too. I love the irony."

"Me too. April Fools for everybody!" Now I knew what Mandy's Christmas project would be—a nursery. That only left Greta. Maybe she'd like a downstairs suite, after I was done with it. She was still as spry as a teenager most days, only occasionally did she complained about soreness in her joints and that was mostly weather related. I'd tried to get her to move back into the walnut bedroom but she'd refused, saying it was ours now, not hers and it was too damn big anyway. Maybe she'd get a regular gift.

"There's a whole bunch of stuff we need to talk about," I said to Amanda. "Not just me." After work, she told me. Now go away, I'm busy.

Gus was more sympathetic and I grabbed him as he was pulling in with a load of goodies he'd picked up somewhere. I explained the spatial issues and he said, I know just the boys to help you out, three handy men brothers who between them could do almost anything except organize a business that paid them what they could probably command if one of them had the ability to market their talents. In exchange for a plate of Randy's food, he told me, he could get them to come talk to me. He made the call and I spent the afternoon with a tape measure and a tablet and by the time they arrived at five thirty, I had enough rough sketches to give them the idea.

We all ate ribs and chicken and drank beer at the picnic tables, then I toured them through my thoughts. We talked about plumbing runs and trunk lines, breakers, partitions, soffits and sheetrock till I was pretty sure they had the picture, then we negotiated an hourly rate and a start date. I was part of the deal. As long as I was able each day, I would be there to layout and direct their operations, me thinking I would be a pain in their ass and resented, in the way, they apparently more than happy to have someone to direct their attack. Gus told me later that they tended to get into long, and loud, arguments on the job and had scared off or otherwise alienated an awful lot of customers. Repeat business was nonexistent. That explained why they could start in two days. Great. It would take me that long to do the material list and get the stuff sent out. I had another project. I was happy.

That evening I took Mandy for a walk, for privacy. I told her what my Christmas presents were going to be for the kids and made her promise not to let them buy me durable goods. I don't think I could stand to open a bunch of normal presents, I said, everybody pretending nothing was wrong. Tell them to get me a case of good German beer and a box of pretzels, something we can all enjoy, I said.

Then I told her about denial, how we were all guilty of ignoring my condition and the problems with that approach to imminent death. Death is part of life, I said, quoting from my research. If we pretend that nothing is going on, we all lose the opportunity to learn from this, to better understand ourselves, each other, and life in general. I knew I wasn't making a lot of sense. I knew what I meant and even to me it sounded garbled. I tried again. I'm going to die. Soon. Six months say. That needs to be out in the open. It's part of our everyday lives. We need to talk about it, laugh about it, make sick jokes, I don't care but we can't just ignore it. Do you see, I said? I'm okay with it. Really. I need you guys to be okay with it too. And the best way to do that, for y'all to be okay, is to talk about it. Get it?

She said she did but it was obvious that it was easier for her, for all of them, to pretend. That's denial. She looked at me for a long time then said, Last? Can we wait till after Christmas? I held her then and said sure, Sunshine, there's no hurry. As long as you don't let them buy me a bunch of crap I'll never be able to use. I don't think I could stand that. Have them buy me Depends and plastic sheets, baby food. That would be funny. She didn't see the humor and I guess from her point of view, it wasn't very funny. Okay, I said. No death gifts. I'll settle for food and drink.

The Slocumb brothers arrived on schedule and we began in the barn, on the second floor over the kitchen. They worked like demons and it was all I could do to keep ahead of them with chalk line, speed square and pencil. On day one, we laid out and they framed up all the partitions and ceiling joists for a big cathedral living room, a bedroom, bath and study, enclosing two thirds of the remaining upstairs space. On day two, I marked locations for an hour or so and they cut, chased and drilled everything for the HVAC system, a giant, high efficiency heat pump unit that would also condition the second floor sales area, Bubba's shop and blow some cold air down into the first floor. I took the afternoon off while they ran wires and glued PVC pipe for the electric and plumbing. They were good to work mostly unsupervised for the next couple days, insulating and drywalling and I was thankful for the respite. They made me feel absolutely ancient. I spent the time shopping for light fixtures, paint and bathroom tile. And for Mandy and Greta.

By the fifteenth we were ready to wrap a ribbon around the door we'd installed on the far side with a note that said 'Don't Open till Christmas.' Obviously the kids knew something was going on over their heads but I would not allow them inside to see it till it was done which was days earlier than I'd expected. We'd had time to do custom colors on the paint, Mandy's choices after she made some discreet inquiries on preferences from Jess and Randy, sand and refinish the wide plank floor boards, even cut in a spiral stair from the living area to the kitchen below, done on the last day, a Monday, so I could lock them out of their own business.

On the evening of the day we were done, I marched the entire household around to the new door and said merry Christmas kids and handed them the keys. I think they liked it, Jessica's tears giving it away. Their stuff was all inside, clothing hanging in the closets, posters and twinkle lights installed, a bed and dresser from the shop, end tables and nick knacks, candles and lamps. Obviously, I said, it being your home and all, you can rearrange but we wanted you to get the idea right off. I think Jess liked the study best of all, brand new Dell computer on a rustic farm table, barn wood shelves floor to ceiling. Randy, I'm pretty sure, was more into the living room with the built in bar, big screen TV and the leather furniture, Gus' discoveries but looking almost new. Feel free to raid the shop, I added. Within reason.

That night Mandy and I moved back into the motor home, Billie's crew into the walnut room and the next morning the Slocumbs moved into the house—to renovate the bedroom apartment. I had already repainted and refinished all those rooms so there were some decidedly mixed emotions on my part watching those guys ripping into my work even if it was at my direction. I'd given Billie and Bubba design input on this 'surprise' so I didn't lock them out of the progress and it was a lot less work. By the twentieth they had a new bathroom with soaking tub and shower, a walk-in closet, sitting room and access from there to Celina's bedroom. And two operable skylights, one over the tub and another over the bed. They loved it, as did I. Mandy and Greta just shook their heads, giving each other knowing female looks, the crazed male in their midst too bizarre for rational explanation.

The kids moved back in but Mandy and I stayed in the motor home. A small surprise, I told her, nothing too elaborate. I think she was afraid I'd do something that would irrevocably fuck up our magnificent bedroom. The Slocumbs only needed a day in that room. Bubba had done most of the work in his shop, following my hand-drawn schematic for the crib, changing station and panel screen, all walnut which had cost me a bloody fortune, kiln dried and shipped from a cabinet shop in New Bern. All the brothers had to do was a little cutting and patching, install a couple lights and place Bubba's furniture, then put a tarp over it all to maintain the secrecy.

I hung the mobiles and pictures, put in the mattress, sheets and toys, and stocked the changing area with diapers, wet wipes and baby powder.

On Christmas Eve, I cajoled all of them into coming with Mandy, Greta, Mom and I to the candle light church service, the carrot a promise of a great meal to follow, the stick the promise that those who did not attend would not eat. Or drink or be merry. Our marriage minister greeted all of us by name. I assume Greta had a hand in that. No one's memory could be that good. He hadn't seen the kids since July and I don't think he spoke to them then. Maybe he was a mind reader too.

The sextet of gospel singers was there to perform, along with about ten of their friends and the forty member regular choir. The gospel guys must have brought scores of their non-singing friends and relatives because it was the most salt and pepper church congregation I'd ever seen, much better integrated then most Presbyterian gatherings, that's for sure. The organist had some back up as well, two white guys on guitars and a black guy on bass and another behind a set of drums. Christmas rocked, high-energy gospel, sweet, beautiful blues and old fashion carols sung with the best, most complex mix of vocals I'd ever heard, live or recorded.

The minister was basically an MC, leading a couple short prayers and asking us all to live the true spirit of the holidays in his five-minute sermon. Other wise it was a concert and a damn fine one. Aren't you glad you came, I teased Jessica as we walked out, the crowd smiling around us, all of us greeting neighbors and friends like they had been away for years. Yes, Daddy, she grinned. It was cool, from Randy, those guy's can wail. You bet, I said, I wouldn't steer you wrong. Hell, I had no idea it was going to be like that. I was expecting your typical church service, with candles and a few less dreadful, more Christmasy hymns. But I smirked like the producer of the whole event, very self-satisfied with my success.

Then we went home to party, all of us gazing in silent wonder at the virtuoso Christmas display I had whipped up in the weeks before the big event as we pulled into the driveway. Tonight was the first time I'd plugged it in. Mandy had two decorated trees inside but I was in charge of the outside. Every tree along the road frontage was wrapped from ground level to the very top of my reach from the next to last rung on a twenty-six foot extension ladder. We had floodlights on the barn illuminating wreaths made from pine bough wrapped wagon wheels with bed sheet bows. The house was twinkling from chimney top to shrubbery, red, white and green strands running up every corner, around every window, door, bush and porch post. Nothing understated around here. I wanted to shout it from the rooftop.

I also wanted to roof mount a damn near life sized Santa, sleigh and reindeer, glowing with incandescent splendor, that Gus had discovered at a yard sale but Mandy would only allow it to be plugged in behind the barn so we could see it from the feast table but no one could see it from the road. She nixed the giant plastic candles and six-foot toy soldiers completely so we were reduced to a 'tasteful' display. If you can describe twenty thousand Christmas light as tasteful in any configuration.

This was the grand opening, all of them on together for the first time and if we didn't blow any breakers, we were going to cause some rubber necking, at least from our fellow worshipers as they began to stream by leaving the service. We had only been home a minute, Mandy working on hors d'oeuvres, Greta on toddy patrol, me firing up the main courses, when I heard cars in the drive and then voices. I looked out just as the last of the re-enactor gospel singers and all of their friends mustered up by the porch door and broke into an acappella medley of Christmas songs so good, so pure of harmony, they gave me chills.

Greta, I shouted, more toddys, quick! Mandy, more cups, lots of them. Kids, come with me, and I led my family out side to great our guests. Either the singers were traveling with an inter-racial entourage or more of the congregation thought this was a prearranged and open to the public concert event because first two, then two more, then a whole slew of vehicles—I lost track in there somewhere—pulled in behind and the occupants gathered around to see the show. Bubba and Mandy, a service team, began to dispense plastic cups of toddys to all takers, then Jessica and Billie were serving canopies from pewter platters, the singers never missing a note, sipping and chewing I guess between breaths. Greta came bustling out with a second pitcher, shouted a few hellos, then scooted back inside with the empty first one. Dad, Billie yelled as she sped past, tray held high on an upraised palm, more food. I must have given her my best two-headed idiot stare because she stopped and stared back at me for a second. Hurry up, she ordered.

More food, I thought. Of course. I knew this was going to happen, had planned for it. Not! Randy was already in the kitchen dismembering king crab legs that were still steaming in the pot. The main event, going to the rabble! Not rabble, neighbors. And friends. On Christmas Eve. Oh, what the fuck, it's only food. Randy carried out a couple dozen toast points with cream cheese and crab chunks and I sprinkled oregano and Parmesan over the clams that were going to be served raw and ran them under the broiler. The scallops went into a few pats of sizzling butter and were forked onto Triscuits with a round of black olive sliced on top. Billie got those, handing off her empty platter in return. I glanced out the window as two more cars and three old pickups parked in the barbecue lot. Gus, Otis and family and the Slocumbs. With dates! Shit! Our dinner guests better get in on the hors d'oeuvre or they weren't going to eat at all. At least Gus had a jug with him.

We improvised for another hour until my seven course Christmas feast was empty shells and a few raw vegetables. I was rooting through the freezer for something I could transmogrify quickly when Mandy came to get me. Come on, Last, she smiled, tugging on my sleeve, some of our guests have to go and you aren't being very sociable. My gums were slapping together for practice, in case my mind ever came up with an appropriate response to this statement, when she just grabbed me and said come on! She pulled me to the porch door and then shoved me on out. Coincidence or someone's prior planning, I never found out but as soon as I immerged, the whole crowd, seventy or better by now, started singing Old Lang Sine, all the way through, loud as hell, then they were cheering and back slapping and Merry Christmasing everybody, mostly me it felt like.

I was hand shook forty times, kissed about as much and by the time they all filed back to their cars and trucks, everyone laughing, some still singing snippets of their own design, I was half laughing, half crying and wholly bewildered. Greta got one arm and Gus the other and they were leading me back inside when I said, what the fuck just happened here to neither of them and Gus said Christmas did, Last, then Mandy had her arms around me, her face bursting with radiance, more internal light then that old back yard Santa ever generated no matter what sized flood light was stuck in his gullet and she kissed me hard on the lips and said I love you so much you wonderful man and then I laughed right through the tears that were running down my face and I said I love you too my Beautiful Baby.

Chapter Twenty-seven

C hristmas day was quiet, family time, Celina the only bit of rambunctiousness and, after the night before, almost anything short of a brass band or a house fire would have been a let down. A relief was how I looked at it. I don't think anyone but Mom got completely dressed, pajamas or sweat pants more the order of the day. We ate a caloric monster of a southern style breakfast, eggs, grits, sausage, home fries. I was about starved before we went to bed and only hungrier the next morning. We opened presents, lots of baby stuff for Mandy and I, a good choice of gifts I thought, wondering who had steered the kids in that direction, guessing Greta.

In my exploration of the house, I had discovered a picture of Greta in her dress uniform with the Medal of Honor draped around her neck. She was posed on a parade ground with a flag on her left snapping in a pretty good breeze. It was a great shot except she was scowling like a Mother Superior. I had Jessica cut and paste a happy Greta face from somebody's wedding onto the younger, meaner soldier then add me in my general suit on her right. Computers. A photo lab in town blew it up and I framed it myself with an ornate, gold inlayed, wooden thing I found in the shop. That was for Mandy along with a Civil War era gold locket I'd found in a second hand jewelry store. I put her Dad's picture in there.

Greta got a blown up composite shot of all of us, our faces overlaid onto a mixed bag of re-enactors, male and female. Even Gus and Otis were there. I framed this one too in an even older black, leather-clad rectangle, the sepia washed photograph looking authentic enough to pass a cursory inspection from a curator. She also got a locket, this one silver with Mandy and I on either side when you snapped it open.

Celina got toys, sand box stuff from me, as much for my own play time as hers, my presents to myself. The kids got stuff from Mandy, Greta, Mom and each other and Mom and Greta got stuff from everybody. Gus showed up about noon with his arms full, a second trip to his car required to off load all the gaily-wrapped packages. I asked him what he was doing and he said I haven't had anybody to shop for in a long time so shut the fuck up, a huge smile on his face. The first time I'd heard him curse. It got a belly laugh out of me. My present was a hand painted, glazed ceramic jug with a moist tan cork sticking out an inch. Pop that thing and give it a pull, he whispered to me. I did and when I looked over at him, we were wearing matching smiles. Would you like to try a taste of this, I asked politely. It's mighty fine. Don't mine if I do, he said. It was some derivative of the applejack I guessed, smooth as Mandy's thigh and just as good to put your lips on. We took little nips for an hour, nobody seeming to notice till Greta caught us and demanded a taste. Then she passed it around the room. Hey, I yelled, that's my present but Gus whispered, I've got a shit pot more. Bought five gallons of it! After that bit of news, I let my jug circle without complaint. It eventually came home.

We ate prime rib, slow cooked over night in the barn stove and tender enough to cut with the side of a plastic fork. Not that we were eating Christmas dinner off of paper plates, it was just that good. And acorn squash with brown sugar, restuffed potatoes, green beans with ham hocks, Caesar salad and an apple cobbler that Gus made, bubbling in brandy syrup and topped with whipped cream. It made up for the seven fish feast that we hadn't eaten the night before in spades. And then some. Gus said, the best Christmas ever. He was right. If only it could last forever.

It lasted a week anyway. We closed the shop and restaurant for the holidays, advertising our intent well in advance, and spent the down time relaxing. Randy's living room became a sports bar, the males rarely missing a football game. They had hung all my mounted Texas deer plus assorted hides, horns and heads that I'd accumulated over the years for the country western bar that I had always intended to construct in my basement but had never gotten around to actually completing. There was an eight foot flag of Texas, buffalo and deer skulls, hubcaps and saddles, old advertisements for guns, whiskey and chewing tobacco, cowboy hats and baseball caps, potted cactus, old rifles and shotguns, antique crocks and jugs, even a stuffed armadillo. It was exactly the room I'd envisioned only bigger, with a high, beamed ceiling and better furnishings. They called it the Last Chance Saloon and Randy dealt out the beer and applejack from the working side of the barn plank bar top that Bubba had constructed along one entire side wall, even cutting down a couple mammoth, gothic columns to frame the bar back mirror.

The five of us guys, Gus and Otis seldom went home except to change clothes and shower I guess—they didn't stink—and sometimes the girls, especially Billie who actually enjoyed football, lounged up there for days. The rest of the women did a lot of I'm-not-sure-what. They were gone frequently, sometimes all day. There were packages and bags piled up on their return so there must have been a considerable amount of shopping going on.

They did most of the cooking when they were home, dinner still our together time, no one exempt.

It was also a time of year that visitors seemed to prefer. Almost every evening, at least one or two and sometimes three or four cars or trucks would cruise into the lot, some of the occupants looking at the 'closed' sign on the shop and kitchen doors and then getting back in their vehicles and pulling right back out but most of the time they didn't even glance at the businesses, just walked over to the house and knocked on the door. To me they were almost all strangers. To Mandy and Greta they were Mrs. This or Mr. That, or Jean or Joan or John or God knows who all came by. And they all brought gifts! Cookies, a candle, a fruit cake. I thought they were *all* fruitcakes, especially the ones that lived with me.

We got dried flower bouquets, a hand made medieval look-ing Santa Clause, fruit baskets, all kinds of ....stuff. About half of them would come in, have coffee or a toddy and about half of those could be prevailed upon to stay for dinner. They all knew all of us by name but, as hard as I tried, I almost never knew who *they* were, invariably limiting my salutations to generics. They were uniformly kind and polite to me and enthusiastically exuberant with Greta and Billie and especially Mandy, everyone's favorite sur-rogate daughter or niece home for the holidays.

Mom leaned over to me as desert was being served one eve-ning, Mandy yacking it up with two seventyish couples who had 'just stopped by to wish us season's greetings' then stayed for Greta's fried chicken and mashed potatoes after demurely inhal-ing huge mugs of toddy. How does she do that, she whispered? Do what, I whispered back? Remember everything. She knows their *grand* children's names for God's sake! I have no idea, I told her, I can barely remember my own. It's a real talent, she said, an amazing gift. No shit, I thought. That's the Incredible Miss Amanda.

I was humbled by all the attention we were getting, happy for my Baby that it was directed towards her and thankful for the thoughtfulness, the kindness of these people who in reality were almost strangers to us. Despite Mandy's extraordinary social memory and incredible empathy, these were customers, people who had bought things from us, and were now stopping by to *thank* us for being storekeepers! Go figure, I thought. I wasn't sure if we had, by sheerest chance, moved in amongst some bastion of pure Christian humanity, some secret society of niceness or if Mandy really *was* that gifted an individual. Or if it was Greta.

I still wasn't completely convinced that she wasn't the manipulator behind all of our good fortune, the puppet master that tugged and jerked all of our strings in some syncopated opera, the music for which only she could hear. But if that was the reality, so what? There was no evil intent as far as I could tell. Quite the opposite. And she'd made all of my dreams come true, a united family in a better circumstance then any I could ever have imagined. It was as close to perfect as anyone had any right to expect. I only wished it could last longer. For me. But that was never part of the bargain, never the expectation. If the trade off for this home place, this united front in a disjointed world, was my demise, then it was a small price to pay. For them. And for me. I could retire, permanently so to speak, without fear for their future. I could go peacefully after a job well done. What a rare gift *that* was, not mine to them but life's gift to me, to be able to die with a clear conscience. Without realizing what I was doing, I offered up a prayer of thanks, to God I guess, to whomever or whatever had orchestrated my existence.

I have never been a religious man, never accepted the need for organization in one's spirituality, never really was spiritual in any traditional sense. But I always believed in something greater than me. I believed in something more than random chance, that more than trillions upon trillions of aimless cell combinations were responsible for life as we know it. Maybe the Earth is just a petri dish sprinkled once with a smattering of amino acids a few billion years ago and God is a bored lab tech with millions of similar experiments in progress simultaneously. Maybe he doesn't give a fiddler's fuck about any of us, any of this, he's just glancing down every couple hundred thousand years to see who's killing whom at the moment. But he's still up there. Something is.

And maybe the Christians or Jews or Arabs are correct, that God is a much more personal and hands on deity, maybe our own little, regional omnipotent being. That would be better, that would allow for some one on one. The only thing I was positive about in that scenario was that all the big, single God religions were wrong about their own infallibility, and conversely, the wrong headedness of their rivals. If there was only one God, even one God for just man and Earth, maybe not the God of the Martians or the rest of the galaxy, and surely no one God could be hands on with a billion billion Earths full of needy, whining civilizations, then that God was the God of *all* of us, not just the Catholics or the Buddhists. He may even have sent down a few Christ's or Mohammed's to help us get it right but our religious differences of opinion were just that—our failure to interpret universally enough the teachings of those prophets and not an elitist, one-tribe-over-another preference by God. That is so self-evident that I cannot believe I'm the only person on Earth that understands it. But I may be and I know I'm right. And I fully expect that if there is a Heaven and if I get to go hang out there, I'll be meeting an awful lot of Taoists, Baptists and Hindus, Aztecs, Eskimos and Zulus.

On New Year's Eve we had a party, to my knowledge a spontaneous get together for maybe a hundred people who all decided it would be great fun to go visit the crazy Yankees that lived out at Greta's. I had no hand in the planning and if the girls did, they did a lousy job of estimating the provisions required for a gathering of that magnitude. Fortunately, all our guests seemed to be of a like mind because they all came baring gifts of snack food or casseroles, beer, wine or liqueur. We were spread out from parlor to patio, saloon to ocean.

Robert E. brought cases of fire works that he said he'd been much happier confiscating then the cocaine or heroin they were looking for at the usual bust. He also brought a dozen of his FBI pals and their families to witness the destruction of the illegal goods, Chinese mortars, star shells and exploding rockets of a size far too big to be sold legally even in North Carolina. They were way too powerful to be ignited in some suburban back yard but perfect for a magnificent bombardment over our dunes.

On New Year's day my plans to watch nine or ten hours of football, quietly, were disrupted by a hangover of last night's guests who, although ostensibly of like mind, were more interested in a raucous, dollar limit poker game that Gus instigated, the players rotating in shifts all afternoon and into the evening. They might have gone home if Gus had left the jug of smooth brandy in his car or if we'd have run out of beer or if Randy had stopped feeding them. But it seemed as if we had God's own stash of junk food and a brewery in the basement along with a restaurant. I played enough to miss the Orange and Rose Bowls completely and most of the Fiesta. And lost two hundred bucks. By kick off of the Cotton Bowl, Texas and Oklahoma with a shot at the national championship for the winner if Florida State lost the next night, I insisted that we concentrate on the important things and shut down the distractions.

Gus had to borrow a grocery bag to hold all the crumpled bills and stacks of change he had accumulated. Robert E. said he broke even, Sergeant Hines, a late re-arrival, wouldn't say and Otis was almost in tears. I know better than to play with that man, he said, pointing at Gus. He gets me every damn time. Two of the Slocumbs were in about the same shape and the third probably worse off.

Bubba said, I'm down a bit. Randy was smart enough not to have played at all. I bet Gus cleared a thousand dollars between all of us and the five or six others who had donated during the course of the day. Texas won, barely. I went to bed as Gus began to agitate for a resumption of play.

We had one more day of 'rest' before we reopened for business and I took full advantage. The most exhausting thing I attempted was a little fishing, just Greta and me. We caught a couple of decent flounder but not enough for a meal so when we were ready to give it up and they were still breathing in a bucket of ocean water, we tossed them back in. We'll get 'em another time, she said with a grin. Damn right, I said. Plenty of good fishing left for me but in truth, I wasn't so sure. Maybe I was just partied out, tired from all the guests and the socializing, or maybe it was post-holiday depression setting in. I don't know but I was shot, weary, achy and grumpy. And I didn't have a concrete short-term goal, a project to finish, an incentive to drag myself out of bed in the morning.

There were a lot of long term things to think about, things I'd do in the spring if I could, a garden, a fenced in yard for Celina and the dog I wanted to get her, a patio with a stone grill behind the porch, an improved walkway through the dunes, maybe even a gazebo thing by the ocean. But the house was done inside and out, at least as far as I was going to take it, the kids all had space with privacy, the businesses were self-sustaining and I was nonessential. I needed to fix my forward thinking on the baby. I didn't have anything else, at least at the moment.

Chapter Twenty-eight

Jessica made the Dean's list for the fall semester and signed up for eighteen hours for the spring. I convinced Mandy to take one class, Tuesday and Thursday mornings, a senior level history of Middle Eastern conflict seminar that I thought would rekindle her interest in all things academic. And give her the opportunity to make some new friends. And be a diversion for her when things disintegrated for me.

Billie was getting notably large by January and Bubba was in charge of tying her down, making her take it easy. He made her sit behind the counter, rigging a padded, adult sized high chair so she could work the register without standing. They hired Otis' sister Eugenia to help Mandy with decorating and restocking. She was a beautiful, boisterous teenager, a box of chocolates, sweet and out going and Amanda immediately adopted her into our extended family. Another mouth to feed, I kidded her. That child needs to go to college, she responded with a fiery glint in her eyes, and I intend to help her get there. And to help her succeed, I thought. I also thought she'd be a big help with the baby and with Celina who had adopted her almost as quickly as Mandy had.

Family's where you find it, I told her, repeating Tex's old adage, so let's help her anyway we can. That got me the hug I'd been hunting for, not that I didn't mean what I said, Eugenia was a good kid and I was happy to have her around. Mandy got her into a freshman level history course as a non-roster observer on her same Tuesday-Thursday schedule and they whizzed off to college together on the first day of classes. How did you manage that, I asked? Eugenia's high school transcript would have necessitated at least a year in community college normally but Mandy had managed to bypass that roadblock. I sweet-talked the Dean of admissions, she said, then added unabashedly, and promised him ten percent off at the shop. I just shook my head. All Eugenia had to do to gain regular admission was to pass her one course and Mandy would never allow her to do anything else. Hell, she'd get an A.

Bubba spent as much time as he could with Gus, going hunting they said or on an antique safari. They made an unlikely couple, a handsome, white haired black man teamed with a burly, tattooed redneck. But they made an excellent combination and found and purchased a nearly continuous stream of everything from fixer upper roadside treasure-in-waiting to certifiable, eighteenth century heirlooms. The shop was making money. Lots and lots of it.

Randy and Otis had their act together as well and were also doing splendidly. Their volume was down with the decline in beach traffic but, especially on nice days, they still sold out more often than not. And they had plans, to move inside eventually, when they had the cash to modernize, but in the mean time to branch out, do some catering, parties and weddings.

They were experimenting with menu options and I was their guinea pig because I'd tell them what I thought, what it lacked or had too much of. Most of the time, I could honestly say, it's damn good. Jessica cranked out a color flyer for them and we displayed

and distributed it anyway we could, Bubba and Gus always buying
and advertising simultaneously, Greta passing them out in grocery
stores or on street corners. Nothing shy about her. Even Robert E.
took a stack of them but whether to hand to his fellow agents or to
press into the palms of forgers and bank robbers we never knew.
They started to get calls in mid February, as soon as the weather
began to leaven a little and people started to think about spring
events.

Greta and I were the home guard, the bankers and baby sitters,
the food shoppers and cooks, mail openers and bill payers, the
domestic god and goddess of Chateau Barkley. It was good duty,
would have made a nice respite for a hard working, healthy man.
It was good for me in that I was increasingly not robust enough for
anything else. My wind was going, my right lung of less and less
assistance in converting the piney, ocean scented air into usable
combustion gasses. And the pain was growing along with the pro-
fusion of traitorous cells in my chest, a pill every day a given, the
bad days requiring one early and one late. My weight was holding.
Apparently the renegades hadn't escaped my upper body or if they
had, their parasitic overtures to my other organs, liver and bowels
particularly susceptible, had either been rebuffed or the enemy
beach heads too small as yet to interfere with the intake or pro-
cessing of food. So I still looked pretty good which I thought was a
blessing for my family. And my mind was alright.

Greta and I talked a lot, on the days that I felt like it, every
day for Greta whether I responded or not or was even pretending
interest. She kept after me though. The more she told me about
herself, the more I harassed her to write it down. It was a fascinating story. I'm just practicing on you, she told me. I'm gonna tell it
all again to Mandy, when the time's right. And she'll write it down,
I teased, and make you famous! She'll make us all famous, boy. I
got it all planned out. You are a devious woman, I laughed. She
told me I didn't know the half of it.

We planned the garden, laid it out on paper. She got me interested enough to go with her to the Agway and get starter boxes and soil, seeds, stakes and string, big bags of fertilizer and lime. Screw that organic crap, she chuckled. I'm too old and you're too feeble to be shoveling cow shit. I agreed with that. It took both of us to load the sixty-pound sacks into the back of her Jeep. I was still strong enough to swing an eight pound sledge and, I thought, walk behind a rototiller but the rental guy had to put it in the Wagoneer for us and Bubba had to unload it.

Otis wanted in on the garden, fresh herbs mostly but also peppers, lots of hot ones he said, so when it turned out that tilling a garden in soil that hadn't seen a plow in a decade was a lot harder than I thought, we let him make the first few passes, then I was okay to follow along as the churning tines broke up the clumps into smaller and smaller pieces. Plus Greta's old garden plot was too small. There were a dozen regular diners now and even if Celina didn't eat much and I wasn't going to be around to enjoy the harvest, the rest of them would be and Otis was gung ho to help Greta with the grunt work. So we planned big.

I tacked wide pieces of scrap wood to every window sill on the porch and by the end of the next day, we had a plant nursery going, tomatoes, broccoli, cabbage, beans, peas, lettuce, four kinds of peppers, all in their own trays in their own little green house.

Something to care for, she said. Something alive, I added. Yes. And something to look forward to, besides the baby. You ain't goin' to die till you give up, Chance and you ain't goin' to give up as long as you have something to live for. So keep it simple. You need to live for these little plants comin' up, then live to plant 'em. Then live to *eat* 'em, she finished with a laugh.

We talked about me a lot. She was the only one I could be completely honest with, no worries about hurting her feelings, no denial in that tough old broad. She said she was close enough to following me to know exactly what I was going through. The only difference, she grinned, was that she was old and I wasn't. I told her I'd meet her at the Pearly Gates. She said don't hold your breath, I might be headed south. I said bullshit, you're the softest hearted woman I've ever met. She said soft-headed maybe, then added, Mandy's the soft-hearted one.

I asked her what she thought about forcing my family to face the fact that I was dying, to confront it and deal with it. She asked what made me think they weren't and I said because we never talk about it. How often do you tell Jessica or Billie that you love them, she wanted to know? About, I don't know, every couple weeks? Do you think they forget you love them in between? No, I said, but.... I didn't have a but to add. Well, boy, they know you're dyin' and they ain't about to forget. They're all a them dealin' with it as best they can, mostly by just bein' here with you, watchin' over you every day, talkin' with you, havin' dinner with all of us together. You don't think those kids would like to go out at night, maybe go dancin' or to a club, go away for the weekend? I gave her my look but I was stating to get the idea. They stay here, I said, to be with me. To maximize our time together. That's about it, she said. Hell, they built a shrine to you in that barn. And Billie's here right under your own roof. They ain't doin' those things for themselves, you dumb shit. They're doin' 'em for you. They're copin' just fine, the best they can. There ain't no need to rub their damn faces in it every day, make it a soap opera. The best thing you can do for all of them is to just be happy, to tell them you are, with yourself and with them. You are a smart woman, I told her. And wise. Thank you, she said. Are you leavin' the 'ass' off smart and wise? It took me a second but then I laughed.

I was sitting in my rocker with a toddy after that, Greta and Celina out exploring or visiting, out being birds of a feather, and I thought, she's exactly right. What's to be gained by outing the whole death thing? Does anyone *not* know? Can it be far from all their thoughts, especially Mandy's? They may not dwell on it as much as I did, I hoped not anyway, but they all knew. And they were all making sacrifices to be with me, to make my last days comfortable. They were doing exactly what I wanted them to do—be together, with me. The best thing I could do for them was just what Greta said—be happy. Lead by example if you will. I was so worried about them not learning that which I had to teach, that I was being a lousy professor. I wasn't showing them the most important lesson of all—not to be afraid. Because surely that's what kept me in my bed or on this rocker, I thought, on those days when I simply could not bear to face a human being or was too tired to lift my hand in greeting. Fear. Self-pity to be sure as well but wasn't that just another manifestation? Fear of death is fear of life. Fuck that! I got up and started thinking about dinner, something special, I thought, that the kids will like. I made Philly cheese steaks, real French fries and onion rings.

The next day I got a dog. Gus, as always, knew where to send me, knew a man. The dog was ostensibly for Celina but it was really for me, a flop eared, sixty pound, six month old mutt with the most expressive eyes. The owner had two toddlers and two other dogs and wanted to keep this one just because he was so laid back with his kids. The children were piled on the dog's prostrate form in the backyard when Greta, Celina and I got there. But his wife had said enough, something's got to go, so he reluctantly kept the wife. He gave us the dog. I offered him a fifty but he said give him a good home, we'll call it square. Now I had to build the fence I'd been thinking about.

I needed help with the auger but I did the rest myself, dismantling the sandbox enclosure for some of the material, using the last of the wood in a shed for some more and buying a load of cedar one by six's for the balance. It took me a week but when I was done, Celina and Sartoris had an eighty by one hundred foot playpen off the back of the house. One leg ran along the garden and would double as a bean trellis and I figured to put the stone patio inside the fenced area too, where the enclosure met the back porch/dining room. There were two shade tree oaks inside the perimeter so we put the sand box between them and strung the tarp in one rear corner to cover all the heavy equipment, plastic cars, buckets and shovels. Eventually I would either move one of the out buildings inside the fence or build a storage shed that would double as a garden shack. One project at a time.

Sartoris was re-named after a Faulkner character. His previous owner had called him Bubba but I thought that night prove confusing around our home. He was part bloodhound, part shepherd and part lab I guessed with maybe a little milkman thrown in. A true American melting pot mutt. He took his new circumstances with aplomb, sniffing about for twenty minutes then flopping down in a corner by the old sand box enclosure, a living pillow that Celina took full advantage of. At night she returned the favor, his head now propped on her butt or belly, both of them snuggled in under the covers. Maybe it wasn't my dog after all.

By the first week of March we were planting outside, my little shoots carefully nurtured in their bedding trays now ready for the next step in their big adventure. Greta and I worked side by side with kid and dog as audience. Billie had been about banished from the shop by then so we put a padded rocker inside the fence and let her supervise all of us. The stone patio was done, ten days of back bent torture, each rock slab drug and tamped into place followed by a gasping period of rest.

By the end of the second week of March it was warm enough most mornings to sit out there and have coffee. Which is where the five of us were on a Tuesday when the house phone rang. Greta, at eighty something, was the least physically challenged by the task of going to answer it. She came out a minute later with the cordless and tossed it to me. It your mom, she mouthed.

I got the same sinking sensation I used to get when I'd be out shooting pool with my work friends and the bar phone would ring. It's the Hell Bitch, I always thought, trying to track me down, which she had an uncanny knack for doing and the conversations were never pleasant.

"Hi, Mom," I said. "What's up?"

"It's Dianna. She's in a coma."

"How long?" I asked.

"A couple days, maybe a week." She knew exactly what I meant.

"What do you want me to do?" I said. I really wasn't sure.

"I don't know," she answered. "For you it's complicated. If you weren't….sick yourself, I'd say come down."

"Dying, Mom. It's okay to say it. It's better if you do. No bullshit. You see what I mean?" We had talked about this, mostly on the way to the airport after Christmas and while I sat with her in the terminal. I was still in my 'no denial for anybody' period back then so the conversation had been frank, brutal almost. But even with my new insight, I still didn't want to dance around reality.

"Dying," she said eventually. "How do you feel? Are you in much pain?"

I told her I ached constantly, would probably be debilitated without the meds but that I looked and felt pretty good other wise. "I'm still doing a bunch of work," I chuckled, "it just takes a lot longer than it used to. And if you want me to, I could come down."

We talked about that for awhile, pros and cons, time line for services and internments, then she suggested I might want to call my cousin and see if he needed any help. He wanted to bury Dianna's ashes on the ranch, maybe build a little shrine and didn't have a clue about the where or how. Apparently they, Josh and Dianna, had all this planned before she lapsed into the coma. They'd had years to figure it out, not like her dying was some big surprise which reminded me that I needed to formalize my own arraignments pretty soon. Then Mom threw her knuckle curve at me, a guaranteed strike.

"Have you spoken to your sisters?" she said.

"Spoken like how?" The honest answer would have been a simple no. Except by phone at Christmas when Mom was with us.

"Have you said good-bye," she said with a bit of exasperation. Cut the crap, Mom, I thought. Say what you mean.

"No, not yet," I said. "I really haven't felt the need," I lied. I was just avoiding it.

"Well, this might be a good time to do that."

I chewed on that for a while, knowing she was right but not wanting to admit it and certainly not wanting to go through the hand wringing histrionics that were implicit, in my mind, in those encounters with my sisters. They knew I was sick of course but they did not know the extent of the problem or the exact prognosis. They certainly did not know that the end was in sight. I wanted to say, why do I have to but I knew the why—I wasn't a teenager any more, I could no longer simply avoid unpleasant or uncomfortable situations just because I was an emotional coward.

"Alright," I said. "You are correct. Let me talk it over with Mandy and I'll get back to you." Talking it over with Mandy took about nine seconds. We're going, she said. Convincing her that maybe her impulse wasn't the best course took hours. You have to run the shop, I told her. And you have classes. And Eugenia needs you. And Billie could drop our foal any time. My arguments were sound. The one I held back, the one about having already done her part for Dianna, already having been served her ration of death, with more to follow soon enough, ultimately wasn't necessary.

Mandy had spent several weeks helping Dianna with her kids after Dianna had gotten the death report when she'd been expecting a clean bill of health. Once she started the endless rounds of additional treatment, she'd rapidly become too sick to cope with two per-teens on a daily basis and Amanda the Stalwart had flown to Texas and pitched in. When Dianna recovered sufficiently, she politely asked Mandy to hit the pike. We both thought Dianna, sick as she was, wasn't too keen on the adoration her sons lavished on Mandy and there might even have been a touch of get away from my husband, I ain't dead yet jealousy. So Mandy had held back her tears and flown home.

Greta would go with me, I said. And Celina and the dog. We'd take the motor home, leave Friday morning. It shouldn't take me more than a day to drive it I figured, if Greta could spell me for a couple hours now and then. Mandy made a comment akin to the blind leading the blind and within another hour Gus was signed up, grinning with relish at the prospect of a cross-country antique expedition. Maybe on the way back, I told him, which didn't dampen his spirits even a little. He just wanted to go on the adventure.

We were packing and prepping when Mom called again. Dianna died an hour ago. Damn, I said, that was fast. There's a service Friday morning, she said. In Austin, for the neighbors mostly. They had been so supportive through the whole fucking ordeal that it made perfect sense to have a service just for them. The family would have plenty of time to mourn later.

Sheila and Marsha were going to the neighborhood affair. I said I doubted that we'd be there in time, then I thought, well, we could leave now and I told Mom we'd call from the road. She added that Josh needed my help with the ashes, could I stick around for a while? I said sure, then she told me all my sisters would be there for the internment at the ranch, like she wasn't going to reveal that tid bit until I promised that I'd stay.

We left at six PM, picked up I-20 where it begins in Florence, South Carolina and drove all night. The babies and one or more of us slept for twelve hours, the rhythm of the road a powerful sedative, the little ones, dog and child, not stirring once till we stopped for gas in Meridian, Mississippi. We ate a big, greasy, Waffle House breakfast, stretched, crapped and stocked up on sodas and snacks and hit the road again. We crossed into Texas about noon, Central Time now, and took the scenic route down U.S. 79, avoiding Dallas and its megalopolis of traffic nightmares. The last time I'd driven through there, I'd felt like a steer going to market, a hundred-mile cattle chute of highways under construction. I couldn't face that in a motor home and as good as the Texas Department of Transportation might be, I seriously doubted if they were done re-arranging all that roadbed.

It was slower going now and not just because of the two lane roads and all the little towns. Celina wanted to sit up front, she wanted to sit in the back, she wanted someone to play with and the dog wanted to sleep. Good dog. We stopped for lunch in Carthage, got ice-cream in Palestine, and gassed up again in Buffalo, all without seeing an elephant, an Arab or a bison. Still, we were ahead of whatever half-assed schedule I'd mentally out-lined which was just to get to Austin by ten Friday morning. We could either keep driving and get to Josh's house around nine or ten at night, a house I knew from my mother was crawling with other mothers, aunts, cousins and a sister, or stop somewhere and roll into west Austin an hour or so before the service.

We found a camp ground with hookups near Pflugerville, bought and grilled some steaks, tucked dog and kid in after roasting marshmallows, then passed Gus' jug around for an hour as we sat in lawn chairs by the camp fire. A good trip so far, I commented. Thanks for coming along, I really appreciate it. Never turn down a road trip, Gus chuckled. Life's too short, Greta said, I think in agreement with Gus although perhaps just as an overall philosophical statement.

We showered in the camp ground, changed into our best jeans— it was Texas after all so jeans were appropriate funeral attire—ate some snacky food on the road and pulled up near Josh's house, a block past there were so many cars out front, right at nine. Mom's minivan was there so my apprehension about introductions to all the people whose names I should know but knew I wouldn't was lessened but I warned my fellow travelers anyway that if I didn't make a formal presentation, it was because I couldn't, not because I didn't want to. They laughed. They'd seen me in action, fumbling with my memory as I stammered in front of someone I'd met three or four times but whose name alluded me. Mom had no such difficulty and shepherded Greta and Gus through the crowd, Celina in her arms. It was mostly a blur. I managed to not embarrass myself too much offering words of condolence to Josh and promising my help at the ranch. He said he'd come out Saturday.

I only had time to get a hug from Marsha and Sheila, both of whom asked how I was doing in a more than offhand inflection and I said good, pretty good, then we had to hustle off to the Catholic church at the end of the road, too far for me to walk but not for a lot of the young suburbanite neighbors in their jogging suits and sun dresses. We piled back in the motor home, Mom, Sheila and Marsha included, and drove the more ambulatory off the road and onto the sidewalk with our passage. This ain't a damn bicycle path, I thought as I blew the air horn to clear the way. Not very Christian of me but I wasn't in the most Christian of mind sets anyway.

The service was long, the priest long winded and a droner to make it worse. He deigned to allow a few lay people to say a few words but the speakers were mostly crying and that of course got everybody else in the huge, sterile cathedral crying as well. I didn't know any of the speakers but I recognized Dianna in their content and I thought all of them hit some part of her dead on.

We got out just before noon and I got turned around and back to the house a few minutes later, idling out front as I discharged my passengers. I'm beat, Mom, I said. We're going to head out to the ranch. She said she'd be along in a couple hours and I suggested I stop and get something for dinner. Silly me. She had casseroles made and in the fridge. We'd eat around six. Booze, I asked? Beer? Nope, she had it all. We took off, traveling north and west at high speed and crossed the cattle guard onto Barkley land at two on the dot. A long two days. All I wanted was a pain pill—I hadn't taken any during the trip for fear of falling asleep at the wheel—and a big, stiff cocktail. And a phone so I could call my Baby.

I showed Greta and Gus around, more like told them to go look around on their own, then got what I needed and retired to the deck. I was beat. I hadn't been exaggerating to Mom. Tired and hurting like crazy. I didn't really appreciate how much I needed the Percs till I stopped taking them. It would be Oxycoton before long I figured, a couple weeks at best. Thank God my friends had come along. I'd probably be in a rest stop in Alabama about now if they hadn't so when they joined me on the deck, Gus with a glass of something dark, Greta with a coke, I reiterated my thanks of the night before. I got the same general response although now there was a large component of awe mixed in and gratitude for bringing them to this beautiful spot. And it *was* nice, a perfect Hill Country spring day, seventy five, cloudless, wild flowers a carpet of color under the lime green mesquites. Just like the day of Tex's service. Sitting on that deck, looking out across thirty miles of rolling Texas hills had always been worth the trip to me.

Celina and Sartoris were still in the motor home. After an hour I made a move to get them up, afraid they wouldn't sleep that night or that she'd wake up alone and be afraid but when I went in the two of them were wide awake and rough housing on the bed. Want to see Grandmommy's big house, I asked her? She was an adventurous sole. She beat both me and the dog down the steps and into the courtyard. I was so glad we'd brought her along. I always got a smile on my face when I looked at her because she always had one on her's when she looked at me. Symbiotic happiness. I was going to need some of that when I talked to my sisters. I went inside and crashed on the couch.

I was snoring when Gus woke me with a gentle shove on the shoulder. Somebody's coming, he said. More than one car, I think. I was standing by the time Mom came through the door but I must have looked pretty out of it because she immediately asked if I was alright. Just sleeping, I told her. Sheila was next in, no box of her favorite wines but a body bag sized duffel on wheels dragging behind. She must be spending the night, I figured. She had enough room in there for two people to stay a week—or Sheila a few hours. Martha was right behind her with Tom in tow. That was a pleasant surprise. I was looking forward to seeing him but I lost him to Gus about eight seconds after the intro, the two of them on the deck laughing all evening.

Anybody else coming, I asked my mother? Not tonight, she said and without meaning to I said thank God, out loud. Sheila heard my comment and started to razz me about being a hermit then she caught herself and said I'm so sorry. I said about what? I am a hermit and I'm damn proud of it! That made her laugh and I figured, what the hell, she's smiling, her kids aren't here, no time like right now so I made a drink and said come on, we need to talk.

I think she was dreading the conversation more than I was. She met me on the back steps off the deck by the laundry room, the west side of the house where we'd sit to watch the sun go down. It was just setting but the day had been too clear to offer up one of those magnificent pink and orange and scarlet bomb blasts that I'd seen so many times from there. She had a big goblet in one hand, not the dainty ones from her normal at the ranch wine tastings, a bottle of French Bordeaux in the other. I kept it simple for her, the I'm dying and it's okay speech. She cried some and hugged me more in twenty minutes then she had in twenty years. I told her my conclusions from the experience to date, family came first, bullshit was out, death was part of life, don't be afraid. She asked a few questions, medical first, then how Mandy and the kids were coping, finally how I was coping, like my pretty speech had been so much fabrication. I said Sheila, I'm not kidding you. It really is okay! I put my family in a place where they have each other and have a chance to grow and thrive. The rest is just details. It took her a while but I think she finally got it. After the sun was all the way down, she asked two more questions. What's with that Greta woman? Where did you find her? I said I'm not sure who found who but I strongly suggest you go ask her. I added a warning: don't be fooled by that old lady's looks, she's incredible. I *didn't* tell her she can read your mind. Let her figure that one out on her own.

After dinner I built a small fire and Martha and I talked for a bit. Tom and Gus were still at it somewhere outside and Sheila was helping Greta put Celina down on a couch in the big back room. And getting her brain shop vac'ed I imagined. Mom was doing dishes and making phone calls so it was private as long as neither of us started shouting. We didn't, hadn't since I was the bratty baby and she was the oldest sister so she'd had a disproportionate share in my up bringing for a few years. Not that I remembered those times but Martha clearly did, her way of talking about my death apparently being to start at the very beginning of my life.

I steered her toward the present, bypassing about forty years of my history in the process. I don't know if she wanted to relive it so she could remember me after I was gone or if she was afraid of the present circumstances and this was her way of avoiding the topic but still focusing on me. I said Marsha, it's okay, so tired of using that trite expression that every time I said it, I felt like I was going to puke. Then I told her why it was okay. She listened politely, nodding in the appropriate places then said, I'm glad they're doing well, meaning Mandy and the kids. Then she asked me about an act of neighborhood mischief from when I was about twelve, everyone assuming I was involved but me never admitting it. Fine, I thought. Let's reminisce.

Josh was due out by mid morning on Saturday, bringing his mother, Mimi, Dianna's mother and her two sisters, Dianna's sister and the two boys. We had damn near enough relatives coming for a Thanksgiving and Mom treated the occasion in much the same way, bustling about in frenzied preparation. This event, however, had a more spontaneous quality to it because it had not been anticipated, couldn't be planned for weeks in advance. The result, I figured, was going to be a whirlwind of near neurotic commands from her to all of us. But just as she was starting to get her boiler fired up, the steam rising, all the gauges approaching red line, Greta took her by the arm and led her back into the kitchen and a few minutes after that, they were sitting on the deck sipping coffee as if there was no one else on site, no one coming, no guests at all for the foreseeable future. I have no idea what Greta said to her, never asked, but I've never seen my mother so serene in the face of an impending visitation. And she stayed that way all day, only once asking me to help her with a table, never snapping at anyone. Greta stuck pretty close to her, the two of them doing the food prep. I did see Greta slip a little vodka into a juice glass at one point but I'm not sure who the tonic was ear marked for.

Marsha took Josh's boys in to play with Celina while Josh and I walked slowly around the outside of the house. I want her close, he told me. I'm not sure why. So she isn't lonely, I said. He looked at me for a moment, then said yeah, that about explains it. I wanted him to find the spot that made him happy but after an hour it was pretty clear that none of the locations we had scouted were doing it so I suggested we walk around the back of the Locust wing. There's a place over there that I like, not mentioning my plans to maybe be planted there myself. First come, first served. I had options. He knew immediately that I was right, that this was home for his wife.

It's perfect, he said. Close by the house but private. Yep, I said and there's a nice view, down the fence line and all the way to

Bullhead, an aptly named mountain about five miles off. We got some shovels and a rock bar and some gloves and started clearing the spot. He wanted a pit big enough to keep her ashes safe from curious animals, an unlikely prospect but I didn't question him. I was not a lot of help with the rock bar, the up and down motion with twenty pounds of steel feeling like someone was chopping on *me* with the damn thing. I could pile rocks though so I built the low wall he wanted around the perimeter of the little grotto.

We worked all day albeit slowly on my part, Gus and Tom pitching in once they discovered what we were up to. Josh was going to spend the night, the rest of his clan going back after dinner. Marsha and Tom would take him home Sunday late, after he finished the path to the gravesite and some brush clearing. After dinner he made a point of seeking me out in private, following as I headed for an isolated piece of deck to take a leak. Can I talk to you, he asked and I said absolutely. We sat under the stars on the deck and he got right to it. I guess he had learned the life's-too-short-to-beat-around-the-bush lesson for himself.

"What made you decide not to do the chemo? The doctors must have hounded you to let them try." He didn't waste any time so I gave it back to him the same way.

"Dianna," I said. "I didn't want to go through what she did. I'm sorry, Josh, but she suffered way too much."

"Yes she did. And I blame the mother fucking doctors," he said, the first time I had ever heard him use that word or any like it. "They lied and lied, the bastards. They knew they couldn't save her. And they knew what she would go through."

"But they told you what they thought you'd want to hear," I said, "and completely down played the side affects. They need to experiment. They need rats and we're it. People like Dianna and me. I owe her a lot, Josh."

"Yeah," he said.

"Do you think they prolonged her life?" I asked.

"I don't know. Probably. But the cost, my God. She would have been so much better off having a couple good years."

"Not three or four dreadful ones. That was my conclusion although the time lines were a bit different."

"How long do you have?" he asked, right out there, no bullshit.

"I don't know," I said. "But it's nice to have someone ask. You're the only one who's had the balls. A few months yet I imagine. I feel fair to good half the time and poor to shitful the other half. But the balance is shifting toward shitful."

"It will. I hope the end isn't bad for you."

"Thank you. If it gets really nasty, I might just opt out. You know, when I can't hold my water so to speak," I said.

"Is it in your bowels?" he asked. "I thought it was in your lungs."

"It is. Breathing is the hard part."

"You should be okay then, incontinence wise. Dianna was. Even though her liver was shot. She finally just stopped eating. Then went into a coma. Then she was gone. The last few days were really quite peaceful for her." He was very earnest and it must have been hell for him to talk about.

"I'm truly sorry, Josh. She was the sweetest kid, it just doesn't seem fair. I'm sure you've heard that a thousand times."

"Yes, a few, although most people would prefer to avoid the topic entirely," he said, finally smiling thinly.

"Don't I know that syndrome. I'm trying to educate my family but it's slow going."

"Maybe they're better off with their illusions," he said then thanked me and excused himself.

Gus joined me after a while, the smallest earthen jug I'd ever seen clutched in one brown paw. Greta said you might need a shot he explained as he passed it over. I took a good swig and handed it back and said no, it was alright, but when I stuck out my hand for its return, he pulled it away laughing and said if you don't need it, you don't get it. After he relented, I told him what we had talked about.

Gus said what we all knew—it was the *fear* of death. Fear of the unknown. A man needs faith, he said, either that or the sure knowledge that he's going to a better place or that he's done all he can for those he's leaving behind. You've done all you can, Last. You can be happy with that. I damn near cried, he had so succinctly summed it all up. Thanks, Gus. You've had no small part in making it possible. Posh, boy, he said with a grin. I ain't done a damn thing. It's Greta you owe. Before I could answer, he amended his statement. Actually, you don't *owe* her. She's getting as much out of this as you are. A family, he added, seeing that I didn't understand. Some good folks to be with her when *her* time comes. Me too for that matter. Thank you, Last Chance Barkley, for bringing your kin to us.

"You are most welcome, my friend," I said. "To your health and long life," and I tipped that fine applejack to my lips and took a long pull.

On Sunday Josh finished his shrine without my physical help. I couldn't lift a golf ball let alone a boulder. Gus and Tom helped him though and they were done by the time Mom and I got back from church. My offer to accompany her I think nearly caused a faint, one hand going quickly to her chest, the other waving off to the side seeking purchase on something solid. I'm serious, I laughed. Mandy and I go almost every week. Mom drove. We sat together after I ran a gauntlet of Presbyterian humanity. The minister must not have gotten the word that I was there in person because, when he called out my name along with those of several others in the prayer chain for the ill and the infirm, I raised my hand and waved at him. Mom smacked my arm but most of the congregation, those behind us, laughed to the consternation of the preacher, especially when he looked down and saw me smiling up at him. I had to brave an even bigger crowd of back slapping well wishers to get out of there so by the time I was bunkered into the minivan, I was exhausted. Home James, I said. I need a pill.

She made me talk about my sisters, our conversations and the one I had with Josh. I told her Sheila seemed to understand but Marsha was blocking out reality, both reactions the opposite of my expectations. She said neither surprised her, that I didn't give Sheila enough credit and maybe I gave Marsha too much just because she was the oldest. You look at Sheila like a spoiled rich kid, she said. You forget she had to work hard for what she has. I thought, marrying money is that hard, but I kept my mouth shut. I'm glad you talked to them, she concluded. They've been so worried about you. I didn't say, with good reason. I did say, they don't need to, Mandy and the girls are going to be fine, knowing that's not what she meant but wanting her to see what was important without fighting with her about it. Or hitting her in the head with it. She got the message, telling me she would always be there for them. Good, I said. That's what I need.

We probably could have left on Monday. I'd spoken to two of my four sisters, they could pass my good-byes along to their families and Kathy was in Philadelphia anyway but I had promised Mom that I would stick around for Dianna's internment. And the rest of my crew were in no hurry to leave, especially once they found the cattle tanks, man made ponds, three of them, all just popping with large mouth bass, sunnies and perch. And despite my longing to be back in Mandy's arms, I did love that ranch. So we had a little vacation. I pulled out a road map and circled the surrounding towns, those that had some antique shops, and turned Gus and Greta loose with a credit card and a wad of cash. Make sure there's room left in there for us, I yelled as they pulled out in the motor home. They were gone for three days, making an adventure out of it I guess, even though they could have done the same thing in a series of day trips. Everybody else was gone by then too so Mom, Celina and I had three days of quality time. Gus and Greta had taken the dog.

We talked a lot, mostly Marshaesque reminiscing but also about Tex, the kids, the whole family. We took turns introducing topics and running them out to their conclusions, often venturing in to might-have-beens. She finally asked me about my burial plans and I told her I wasn't positive yet, gave her the scenarios I'd thought about and asked her opinion. Well, she said, is there still room over by Dianna? There's no reason you couldn't share. I laughed at that, thinking about Mandy's reaction to my spending eternity with another woman. I told her I would probably be split up, half coming here, half staying in North Carolina. She said she could live with that, then blushed at her word play, the combination making me laugh again. Maybe I'll dig myself a hole over there, I said. All you'd have to do is throw me in and kick the dirt back in place. She laughed and told me I was awful. I explained my proposed head stone remarks and the process I had used to reach my epitaph. She gave me a look appropriate to my status as a card carrying, two headed idiot but said if that's what I wanted, she'd see to it. Unless I think of anything else, I told her, we'll go with that.

I did dig myself a hole, flattening a spot twenty paces east of Josh's cemetery garden, then chopping out a pit sufficient to hold a quart of pebbly ashes. All my pallbearers would have to do was pile the stones on top. They could set the head stone with a bag of Sacrete. If anybody wanted to plant a couple barrel cactus or a yucca plant nearby, that would be okay too. Just transplant them from the ranch. It would be a good excuse to go for a walk.

I also had time to write down my formal instructions to my heir and executor, Amanda. I thought about splitting those duties, making Greta part of the team legally, but figured it was unnecessary, she'd be right there anyway and was not going to withhold her opinion whether Mandy asked for it or not. It took almost an entire day to hunt and peck out the letters on Mom's old Gateway but once I was done, I felt relieved, a burden lifted that I had not even realized had been pressing on me. I had Mom witness it and ran her a copy. I know it needs to be notarized and forwarded to my attorney, I said, but keep it just in case I get hit by a beer truck or something on the way home. You'll at least know what I had planned.

The antique commandos rolled in late Thursday, all fired up over the shopping coups they had engineered, dragging me out to inspect the bounty by flashlight. They had some good stuff but we were going to look like the Beverly Hillbillies on the way home. Friday midday the Locusts started returning, Sharon and her husband Ray first so while he was blah blahing to Mom, I took Sharon out side and gave her my 'I'm okay, good-bye' speech. She wasn't really prepared for it but that was a good thing from my point of view—it held down the time and the questions. I thought, that's a relief, I can do Kathy over the phone but as I was heading back inside, Sharon grabbed my arm and said, it's not going to be that easy for you, we'll talk later. Damn. I hadn't expected that kind of reaction. I thought she'd get all weepy and wave so long when we pulled out in the motor home.

By noon Saturday there were about forty mourners in the great room, half family, half friends and neighbors of Josh and Dianna. Mom's preacher said a few words, then just about everybody else said something. Then we marched single file out to the park Josh had created and everyone cried when he put her silver cased remains in the ground and started to slowly add dirt and stones. It didn't help that he was sobbing with each shovel full. Greta finally got the spade away from him and sat him on the low rock wall that semi-circled the grave. Gus and I took over the back filling, piling the larger stones all around the disturbed area. The minister spoke again and then we adjourned back to the living room for Mom's buffet. And cocktails. Lots of cocktails.

At around three, I had a chance to tell Josh about my potential addition to his cemetery. I thought he might be pissed about it but after a second of contemplation, he put his hand on my shoulder and smiled for the first time that day. Good, he said. You always made her laugh. I took that as a compliment although a more sensitive soul might have considered the possibility that Dianna might have thought I was a buffoon. Still a compliment to my way of thinking.

All the non-family and some of the blood went home shortly there after. I got a monster, almost painful hug from Tom. He had to be pried off of me eventually, tears pouring down his cheeks, coherent words refusing to come out. I soothed him like a wounded child as I walked him to his car, finally, after another long hug, getting him inside. Marsha drove as always. She gave me a squeeze and made me promise to call if I needed anything. Last time I'll see them I knew, waving goodbye as they drove off. One down, too many to go.

Sheila was next to leave, her son Simon in tow. Her husband John was away on business she had explained and their daughter Brooke was sailing off the coast of Ireland with some school chums. I wondered if their marriage was not doing so well but saw no up side in asking. Give them my regards, I said as I hugged her. We'll see you soon I hope, she told me. Huh? When, was all I could think. I said sure will then drive carefully and they were off. That was easy. Maybe she did that act on purpose to make it that way. Good. Thank you, Sheila. I knew Sharon wouldn't be as easy, but she wasn't going back before we left the next day so there was plenty of time for her to ambush me in some dark hallway. And of course she did.

After dinner, Celina tucked in, Gus and I looking for shooting stars off the east corner of the deck, Sharon came to find me. Let's talk she said, appearing at my elbow. With my head craned back, gazing straight up, I hadn't seen her approach and I jerked about six inches into thin air when she spoke which made Gus laugh like hell.

A little jumpy, Last, he said between snorts. Sharon always affects me that way, I replied, grinning at first him then her. I think I'll go freshen up, he said and held his chair for Sharon, smirking like a damn fool the whole time. He knew how much I was not looking forward to this conversation.

"So, little brother," she started. "Did you think you could blow me off with that practiced speech?"

"Yeah, pretty much. I was hoping anyway. It's not a topic that engenders a lot of dialogue usually."

"Maybe not but I want details. I want to know what it's like."

"You're kidding, right?"

"Not hardly, pilgrim," she grinned, her John Wayne fair to not too bad. For a woman.

"Okay. That's a new one anyway. What are you thinking, learn from the master?"

"Maybe. Sort of. You're going where all of us have to and you…. must have given it some thought. Because it's premature for you. Like Dianna only she refused to discuss it."

"She was always sure she could beat it," I said. "The doctors did that to her. False promises, unrealistic expectations. Selective information sharing. Josh called them mother fuckers. Have you ever heard him curse?" She didn't answer me.

"But you know better," she said.

"I'm not foolish enough to believe in miracles just for me. Call it playing the odds, statistical relevance, whatever. There are zero," I added with my hand making the symbol between our faces, "zero examples of people with my condition living five years." Five was the magic number for the medical community to count your treatment as a cure. If you made the big five, they were gods. "I don't think anyone's made two with my diagnosis. You understand the difference?" Dianna had started out with a lumpy breast. Lots of women get past that, reach their doctor's five-year goal. They may have been disfigured, bald and traumatized beyond any expectation of a normal future, but their doctor could put a check mark in the win column. Yeah, she understood.

"You're saying she had a chance and you do not."

"Sort of. I doubt that her doctors conspired to conceal the metastasis from her. It happened and they didn't pick it up till after all the breast stuff was done. But at that point, when it was already in her brain and liver, her limps, hell, they should have told her the truth."

"You're going to die," Sharon said.

"Yep. You can't win 'em all. Unless you're an omnipotent oncologist with a raging ego the size of Montana and you just aren't emotionally capable of recognizing your own humanness. They wouldn't let her go. It's like it would have been an admission of guilt, not just failure. They tortured her in my opinion. She was on massive doses of chemicals almost till the day she died. What was the point of that? How blind or arrogant could they have been? She was already *dead* for Christ's sake!

"I didn't get far enough along in their machinations to personally understand the mind set. I just knew it wasn't how I wanted to go. And that's the key–I don't regret it." She was silent for a long time.

"I think that's a very good thing," she said eventually. "No regrets."

"That's the key, Sharon. No regrets is as good as it gets. The rest is all just speculation."

"You're lucky, Last. Sounds weird doesn't it?" she added with a burst of laughter.

"Yeah it does but that's exactly right. I was lucky to have the opportunity to think about it, work it out. Plan for my family and have them help me with the plan. That's so much better than dropping dead on the back nine, I don't care if your caddy is a Victoria's Secret model. Even if you're ninety," I said laughing along with her. "I *am* lucky!"

My gang was up early the next day because I woke them. We moved enough old Texas crap up on to the roof so that some of us could sleep some of the time, said a bunch of good-byes, then climbed in and took off. I wanted to be home. My good-byes with my mother were really easy because she said I'm coming to watch my grand child be born and I said you better pack a bag and climb in here with us cause it's due any day. She said call me when the water breaks and I'll hop a plane. I think it was as much to post pone her good-bye to me as it was to watch Billie off load some scientific miracle that had a direct genetic tie to her but that was okay—I'd be happy to see her again. And I was damn happy to post pone that particular good-bye.

We drove straight through, all of us taking two or three hour shifts and half the time changing drivers without pulling over. We got home Tuesday just as they were putting out the open flags, not running over Mandy only because I started to blast the air horn about a quarter mile away, giving her ample notice to clear the way, the road trippers were home. We got lots of hugs, Billie's from long distance because it looked like she'd gained thirty pounds in a week and a half. Water weight, she explained. It happened with Celina too near the end. Maybe we ought to yank that kid out of there, I said to her, before you explode! She told me to go fuck myself but I had other ideas. Can you watch the shop for an hour or so, I whispered to her, leering at Mandy. Mandy said ten minutes ought to be plenty and we trotted off to the house.

I don't care how exhausted I might have been or how debilitated my condition might have rendered me, when I'm done rolling my beautiful Baby in my arms in ten minutes, please put me to sleep. Like an old dog that pees on the carpet, my time will have come. It took me longer then that to undress her and twice that long to kiss and touch and tongue every square inch of her silky flesh, especially those parts that hold the damp musk of her intimacy. Ten minutes my ass, I didn't let her up for my projected hour plus another to match and only then when she pleaded a biological need and caught a glimpse of the traffic below. Billie's swamped, she stated from the bedroom window, me admiring her butt as she parted the curtains and bent over to peruse the parking lot. She's fine, I said as my dick stiffened. Gus is down there with her. Come back here, just for a minute, I promise. She looked at me like she was a wise nine-year old and I was an unsavory stranger selling imaginary chocolate bars. Later, Chance, she said as she pranced bare-assed into the shower. Fuck! Well at least I could still get it up. And keep it there. And I had a possibility for that evening. Damn it was good to be home!

Chapter Twenty-nine

Mandy called my mother on April tenth and told her if she wanted to see Last Chance Junior's arrival in this world, she better get on a plane but quick. I was bed ridden at that point but upon hearing this recitation, I said there ain't no way she's going to make it. Billie looked like a cow about to give birth to a veal buffet for a hundred hungry Vikings and even if Mom got immediately in her van, drove two hours east or south to Austin or San Antonio and happened to get a flight out quickly, there was no way she could make it to Wilmington—or even Charlotte if we drove to pick her up—before Billie's alien stomach burst forth something!

Mom did her part and Billie held off on her's and fourteen hours later my son was born via my daughter's womb with my wife and mother, other daughter and assorted friends, boy friends and relatives to be named later in attendance. No up country, down holler, back woods, Hill Billy birth party was ever better attended. We'd had enough time to get Mom there so Greta and Gus had more than enough time to make it a low rent, tongue in cheek, trailer trash, father fathering festival, a costumed ball of the illiterate southern masses, at least as portrayed by our friends and neighbors.

All of them had name tags identifying their dubious relationship to the newborn. Mine said Father/Grandfather, Mandy's Mother/ Step Grandmother. Jessica was Sister/Niece and poor Billie, beaten down from twenty four hours of on again off again labor and bereft of much of her sense of humor as a result, was saved the humiliation of being tagged as Mother/Half Sister but that didn't stop someone from installing a poster board sign above her chair in the dining room that identified her as just that. Greta wore a Grand Dame/Great Grand Dame placard around her neck and Gus carried a three by three bill board pinned to his back that named him as the Great Grand Father Emeritus so it was pretty clear whose great minds had conceived the theme for this get together.

And it was way well attended despite the by definition last minute confirmation of the date. Bubba and Gus walked me down the stairs from the bedroom once sufficient numbers of guests had arrived to justify my insertion into the mix and it was right then, as they guided me out onto the porch and then down to my patio where the lights were strung over head and the revelers had reached critical mass, that I realized this was my goodbye more than it was my son's hello. He made a convenient and jovial excuse to congregate around our home but really they were here for me and my family, to see us once more as they wanted to remember us, all of us alive and smiling, celebrating something wonderful and remarkable.

It took all my reserves of strength to maintain a happy façade, not that I wasn't glad they were here, I was just too far gone to be much of a party animal. I wanted nothing more than to go back and climb in bed but I knew I would not see most of them ever again.

The day after our return from Texas I had taken a quick southern route toward the here after, going from moderately robust on occasion to nearly bed bound almost continuously. I told myself and all of them that all I needed was some rest, it was the post road trip, I'm exhausted, blues. But after three days of being nearly constantly horizontal, I wasn't fooling anyone, myself included. I made a mental list of things I still needed to accomplish or complete, between Greta's nonstop ministrations, and then with her help, saw most of them to fruition.

She mailed my last testament codicil to my Yankee attorney, sent little thank you/good-bye notes to my sisters, deposited the last of my mad money cash into an account we opened just in Mandy's name, called some friends of mine in the north to get their addresses so I could send them their own notes of farewell and then she dialed up Kathy for me one evening a couple days before Billie split apart at the seams, handing me the phone only after explaining to Kathy who was calling, third person, as it were.

"Yo, Kath," I exclaimed in my best imitation of boisterousness. "How are you guys doing up there?" It took her less then one second to realize my happy act was just that and then she began a fast paced question and answer session that lasted almost an hour—a record for any conversation between me and one of my sisters. By the time we signed off, I suspected that she'd be at our door within a few days and so she was, perhaps the coincidence of her arrival simultaneously with that of my mother partially the result of conversations that they had had independent of ours, before or after the fact. She was a welcome addition to our Appalachian Fest even though, with the exception of Sheila, no one was farther removed from ass scratching, toothless mountain society than Kathy.

Her hug was returned without any of the tentative qualities that were inherent on my part in any physical encounter between me and my other siblings and when she let go of me, she stepped back a pace and said, you look like shit to which I replied, it's the costume. That made her laugh because I wasn't wearing one. Most everyone else was, overalls or calico dresses, straw hats, no shoes or socks, hair plastered down or teased to impossible heights, teeth blackened out, corn cob pipes clenched between the openings. Otis and clan arrived in a mule drawn wagon looking exactly like a scene from *As I Lay Dying*, complete to the brother with the concrete cast and the hand made plank coffin, theirs with two stuffed buzzards nailed to the lid. Dibs on the casket, I yelled as Otis' father whoa'ed the mules to a halt by the patio. Half the guests thought that was hysterical and the other half were aghast. It takes both kinds I figured as I hobbled out to greet them.

I rallied sufficiently to make a good night of it but I paid like a bastard the next day. Between my now normal state of wheezing decrepitude and a hemisphere class hang over, I was too sick even to sip Greta's life sustaining chicken and vegetable broth. Mom and Kathy sat with me off and on all day but the extent of my conversational response was a series of ill timed grunts and an occasional burst of foul gas, the fumes thus released as bad from the upper end as they were from the lower. I had become a Listerine junky in an attempt to mask the noxiousness of my breath. Mandy swore it didn't stink and maybe it was just a psychological reaction on my part to what I knew was happening in my chest but I was convinced that the putrefaction had to include rotten, fetid breath as a byproduct and even if I couldn't suck the medicinal tasting juice into my lungs, at least the coating in my mouth should temper the stench as it passed by.

After dinner they brought my son to me but I wouldn't hold him until they brought me one of my masks from sanding the floors. I was convinced that the horror residing within me was fully capable of riding a hot current of stinky air out of me and into my child. I'd rather never hold him in my arms than put him at risk for that. Mandy joined us then and, after an eye rolling glance at my mock surgical attire, asked me whether I'd decided on a name for our offspring. We'd beaten this back and forth for a month and, as far as I could tell, were no closer to agreement then we had been at the beginning of the debate. Maybe my failure to seriously entertain anything other than Texas Jack Barkley had something to do with our lack of progress but then again, surely her failure to see the beauty of that moniker was partially to blame. She liked Lassiter Chance Junior and I absolutely refused to recycle a name that had caused its original owner such problems. And even if I was John Smith, I wouldn't have wanted to memorialize a life that, up until its last few months, was so bereft of social significance. This boy needed a fresh start, his own chance to do something, without any more baggage attached then our combined DNA and family histories were already going to heap upon him. Of course that was partially her argument against naming the kid Texas—too much stigmatism.

After some initial rehashing of our stalemate, I said alright, give me a couple minutes and I'll come down stairs. Gather up the crew, I added. This is a family decision. But I get final say. It took me an hour to get into and out of a hot bath that Mandy drew but I would not accept any other offers of assistance. Go away, I told them. I'll be down shortly. I shaved carefully, deodorized, flossed and gargled then crawled into a pair of Levi's and a flannel shirt. I couldn't manage socks, bending over that far was just too hard, too little air getting in with my one and only half dead lung crushed up against my knees. I *could* slip into my oldest, most slipper-like pair of Tony Lama's though. I even cinched on my best, most beat up and supple leather belt, the one with the fist sized silver buckle that said 'LAST' in raised letters, a humorous, to Mandy and I when she bought it for me, take off on the bull rider's trophies that were ubiquitous amongst the weekend cowboys from Dallas and Houston when they paraded through the small touristy towns that surrounded my parent's ranch land in the Texas Hill Country.

I thought I looked pretty damn good considering. Forty pounds lighter then my prime fat fighting weight but what the hell? I had fought a losing battle to be rid of those pounds for years and now they were gone. If you didn't know I was nearly dead, you'd think I looked better then I had since I was in college. I ought to write a diet book I thought as I headed down the stairs. Apparently everybody else thought I looked pretty good too cause I got a round of applause when I limped onto the porch.

It looked like we were going to have a séance rather than a naming party. There were a dozen candles lit, one on every windowsill and three hurricane lanterns swinging from the rafters above. My child was resting in a car seat, sitting in the middle of the feast table like a centerpiece, two ancient oil lamps casting a flickering glow across his face. The household was all accounted for, each of them in their favorite place around the table. My spot at the far end was vacant except for a steaming mug of something, a witch's brew most likely judging by the mystical atmosphere of the room.

I stood behind my chair and looked at my family one by one then bowed my head and said, bless this food which we are about to receive. Amen. Bubba, carve the kid.

My mug held an apple brandy toddy spiced with cinnamon and molasses. The level five Oxycoton I'd taken before my bath was on cruise control as it motored through me and the brandy added a mellow zing. I almost forgot about the bayonet in my chest. Okay, kids, I said. What are we going to call this guy, opening what I anticipated would be a round table discussion. It was. Round and round. Dozens of names were tossed out for review, me tossing away most of them with a well considered no, no way, fuck no or are you nuts? Finally I said give me a tablet and I quickly memorialized those worthy of such action.

Texas and Jack were first on the list, placed there without consultation. Robert for Robert E., Foy, Greta's last name—I wrote it down just to be polite. Lassiter and Chance for the same reason, this time for Mandy. Augustus. Lee, Tex's middle name but also Jessica's. There were a few others but nothing any of us wanted to go to war over. I had even backed off Texas Jack once it became clear that nobody else thought it had the same smashing panache that I did. Not even the boys were on my side.

After a few minutes of silence, I said, maybe we need a different approach. Maybe we use Mandy's last name. She is. In the long run, it might be easier for him. Mandy and I had always agreed that she would remain a Cassidy if we got married, originally just to maintain her own identity, not be absorbed into mine as so many women seemed to be, appendages to their husband's personality or career. Then more as homage to her father, although we rarely spoke of marriage again in the months after Jack's death.

Mandy got up from the table and trotted up the steps. In a second we could all hear her galloping decent. I was sure one day she was going to take a massive header the way she attacked a set of stairs but she survived once again, slipping back into her chair and sliding something across the table to me. A North Carolina driver's license with a pretty blond on the left side. It was Amanda or so the name said. Amanda Cassidy Barkley. I'm your wife, she said. And he's your son. We're Barkleys. Now can we pick some first name for him before he goes off to college?

So I guess I'm not the last Barkley, I laughed. No, she said. And neither is he. If you really like Texas Jack, I guess I'll get used to it. Well, I responded, you're the one who's going to have to. Plus him of course. So if you hate it, I'll concede it might be a bit hard to grow up with. But Junior is out too. We settled on Jack Cassidy Tex Barkley and decided to let everybody call him whatever the hell they wanted to. I chose Tex. The girls immediately started calling him Junior and I nearly started the whole process over again. But it was a good compromise. Still a little long and a little weird but Jack Barkley had a solid, masculine ring to it, a name a boy could be proud of and if they called him Tex, so much the better. We celebrated for an hour and then I got some help getting back to bed.

Chapter Thirty

By May first they were eating garden lettuce, fresh peas, scallions and broccoli and the tomatoes were close behind. My diet was almost all liquid by then and mostly brought to me on a tray. I could barely sit up most of the time and I was officially a burden, something that needed constant care and contributed nothing. On my best days, I could swing my withered legs over the side of the bed and get to my feet with the aid of a walker. Then, if I was really feeling strong, I could get to the bathroom and lower myself onto the handicap height toilet and listen to the rank fluids drain out of me. And wipe my own ass. Twenty minutes later I'd be back beside my bed, struggling to pull my bony carcass all the way up and in. On my worst days, I just pissed in my diaper and waited to be rescued from the humiliation. I don't know what Dianna had done to avoid this part of death and I sure wasn't going to call Josh to find out but when he'd said I probably won't be incontinent, he'd been way off base. Poor Greta took the brunt of it, refusing to allow Mandy or the girls to close the shop or miss their classes. Eugenia was our day care provider when she wasn't in school and she did some soup and dirty diaper duty for me as well. But she was enrolled in the summer program at UNCW so something was going to have to give. Greta couldn't watch a three-year-old and care for two infants simultaneously. I decided it was time to go. That was the last best contribution I could make toward the well being of my family.

That night I told Amanda. I'd been telling her to sleep downstairs or get a day bed for me, anything to avoid having to curl up next to a leaky corpse each night but she was adamant—she wasn't leaving me. So I'd leave her. It took me forever to tell her how much I loved her, how sorry I was to have put her through this and how happy I was that she would be here for the kids. I'm sure it wasn't the most eloquent farewell, repetitious and meandering, my voice an airy rasp when I could talk at all through my tears, and I'd been telling her right along most of my message but it seemed like a summation was in order. But it was hard, physically and emotionally. I was glad I had written down my thoughts, back when I could, anticipating this depletion and not wanting her to think that my final thoughts were this disjointed monologue. I pressed my Last Notebook into her hands and whispered to her as we wept. I love you so much, Sunshine. You are my beautiful, perfect Baby. I need you to be happy. We all do. You have to keep the family together, you and Greta. It's all in here, what I want done, what you should do with me. Tell everybody I love them. And thank them for doing this for me. You guys are going to be fine, if you stick together.

I fell asleep at some point I guess. Or stopped being conscious. I remember dreaming or being in a dream-like state, the faces of my family above me individually and then together. I distinctly remember Greta, inside my head, a soothing presence flowing through my mind. Then nothing at all. But I guess I wasn't quite dead because I have one more memory of that room, morning, the rising sun filtered through the gauze draperies, Mandy and Mom on one side of that huge walnut bed, Greta on the other, Billie at the foot with Tex nestled up to a teat. But I wasn't looking up at them, I was looking *down* and I remember thinking, this is such a cliché, can it really be true? Call it a dream fixed in my mind from so many months contemplating this exact moment and all the ones to follow. Or accept it as myth based on fact but there I was, part of me anyway, floating above myself, gazing at the Earth-bound remains of Last Chance Barkley. And I wasn't pretty, the worst looking I'd ever been, sunken everywhere, a uniform gray, head, arms and hands.

Then I was levitating even more or my vision was telescoping upward because my family and my body, the monster bed, all got slowly smaller and I thought, I'm going but at least I'm going up! Then a last flash, a white blankness and a wrenching loss of equilibrium like I'd been tossed up from a blanket without warning. Then warmth, completely enveloped in heat and comfort, and a feeling of total contentment. I opened my eyes and with near the surface yet still under water murky vision, saw a mountain of smooth tan flesh in front of me, a cascade of thick brown hair and the smiling face of my eldest daughter gazing down at me. Then I was gone.

Epilogue

Amanda tried to go into a black funk after Last's death. She really tried. After the arrangements were made, after the memorial service in the near ruptured Presbyterian church, after the three day wake, as the last battalions of infantry and horse marched slowly past, after taps was played for the final time, as the band was packing and the tents were coming down, she went up to her room and sobbed. They let her cry, gave her twenty-four uninterrupted hours of it. But then there were questions to answer, decisions to be made about work and school, classes to attend, children to care for.

Greta toted Jack up the stairs the next day and walked into the walnut room, now cleared of all the accoutrements of a wasting disease but still holding the lingering hospital aromas. She lay the child down next to her mother, Amanda's eyes open but vacant, then she pulled back the curtains. This place stinks, she said and opened all the windows, the ocean breeze blowing out the other smells in seconds.

Much better, she said. Don't you agree little Tex? The baby grinned at her and bucked his hands and feet. Now mom, you and I need to have a little quality time. Mandy rolled her eyes up to the old woman. After several minutes, she said, you aren't going to leave me alone are you. Not for one more damn second, girl. So you decide—you and me in this bed or you downstairs with the rest of your family. It took Amanda another couple of minutes before she began to stir. Okay, she said, let's do it.

Amanda and Jessica graduated in the same class year, Jessica with a BA in accounting and Mandy with a masters in history. Eugenia and Mandy finished a semester apart with a BS in Economics and a Ph.D. respectively. Mandy's thesis was published that summer and surprised everyone by reaching number two on the New York Times best seller list for nonfiction and staying in the top ten for a year and a half. There was talk of a movie, the rights having been sold to a production group headed by Sharon Stone. Greta did the talk show circuit, she and Opra becoming close friends, Amanda declining repeated requests to appear along side the central character in her book, *Inside Enemy Minds: the Colonel Greta Ann Foy Story*. Greta took Jack along as often as the television producers would allow, the two of them raising hell all over New York. It was enough that the limo drivers that picked them up at the Barkley homestead were ordered to immediately phone ahead if the randy old woman boarded with the blond haired, green eyed, devil boy.

Billie, Bubba and Gus ran the antique business with help from Eugenia and two of her sisters. The three of them traveled all over the country in the motor home, pulling a trailer, restocking the shop at dealer shows. Tax deductible vacations.

Celina was in the advanced program at a private school in Wilmington. Hippie Academy Mandy called it. She spent as much of her free time as they would allow in her play area building ever more complex sand and scrap structures, accompanied always by a hundred and twenty pound dog, usually by Greta and often by an assortment of friends and relatives.

By the time Jessica graduated, Randy and Otis were well on their way to becoming food service entrepreneurs. Their catering business employed a dozen part time college kids and local teens and the restaurant did a couple hundred meals a night in the beamed ceiling dining room below their home. They had an architect working on the plans for a gut rehab to an historic building on the Cape Fear waterfront that they had a lease-purchase on, the concept a mid-priced eatery with a high coefficient of fun. They were going to call it the Last Chance Saloon.

Mandy accepted tenure at UNCW despite offers from Texas Tech, the University of Houston and Penn State. Family comes first she politely explained to the deans of the history departments that tried to lure her away.

Robert E. kept his promise to Last, one year to the day arriving at the house with a dozen red roses and reservations for two at the just opened Barkley Room at Clyde's Famous. They had an excellent time together but she wasn't ready, the conversation inexorably curving back to Last despite both their attempts to steer it away. It was nearly another year before he tried again and two years after that before they married. Celina was the maid of honor and Jack the best man. They both took their duties very seriously and Jack's reception toast, quoted verbatim with accompanying picture of a child standing on a linen covered table with a champagne flute clutched in his hand, made the front page of the Wilmington paper and got play as far north as Philadelphia and New York.

Mandy pulled into the gravel lot before the shop was closed but after the lunch crowd at Clyde's Famous was gone. She was home early, a rare event. It was May second, hot and still, too early for summer, she thought. But just right for a swim. In fifteen minutes she was trotting across the back yard in a bikini top and gym shorts, beach towel around her neck. At the end of the mowed yard, in the tree line before the dunes, she stopped and looked down at the block of limestone resting beneath one of the monster oaks. Squatting beside it, she placed her hand on the cool rock and for the thousandth time read the words carved therein. Lassiter 'Last' Chance Barkley it read with the appropriate dates below. And below that in smaller script, Builder of Family. I'll always love you, Last, she said quietly, then kissed the chiseled letters, got to her feet and ran toward the ocean, hair flying, arms extended like a bird in flight and laughing aloud as she crashed into the waves.